Second Chances in Lavender Bay

Lavender Bay Chronicles Book 3

Michele Brouder

This is a work of fiction. Names, characters, places and incidents are either a product of the author's imagination or are used fictitiously, and any resemblance to actual persons, living or dead, events, or locales is entirely coincidental.

Editing by Jessica Peirce

Book Cover Design by Rebecca Ruger

Second Chances in Lavender Bay

Copyright © 2024 Michele Brouder

All Rights Reserved. No part of this book may be reproduced or transmitted in any form or by any means, electronic or mechanical, including photocopying, recording, or by any information storage and retrieval system, without permission in writing from the author.

PART ONE

ANGIE

Chapter One

Evangeline "Angie" Cook threw back a quick drink of water and laid the glass upside down on the drainboard. It was the same glass she used every morning before heading off to her café, Coffee Girl. On occasion when she had to turn the dishwasher on, she'd throw the glass in. But as that was as rare an occurrence as a white peacock, she usually washed it by hand every couple of days.

Angie lived in a small craftsman-style cottage on Cherry Tree Lane in the small beachside town of Lavender Bay. She'd like to say her home was her refuge, but she was so rarely in it she couldn't put her hand up and claim that one. She gave a quick look around her kitchen to make sure everything was in its place. Her gaze rested on the house's only other living thing: a variegated ivy in a red clay pot. Of course, the word "living" might be an overstatement. The houseplant was a gift from Debbie, her best friend since the second grade, who assured her this was one plant you couldn't kill. However, the heart-shaped leaves, once a marbled green and cream, were now brown, shriveled, and curled. Apparently it *was* a plant that could be killed.

She sighed. How had she forgotten to water that? She tried to think back to the last time she looked after it and came up blank. Not one to spend too much time ruminating, she quickly forgot about it, grabbed her keys, and headed off to work.

Angie was more wired than usual that day. The previous evening, as she scanned *The Lavender Bay Chronicles,* she came upon a notice placed by the town clerk. They were accepting applications for food trucks for the beach beginning the following spring. The deadline for filing the application was in two weeks' time. She'd make her way over there later today. The thought of branching out her successful business caused her an excitement she hadn't felt since the opening days of Coffee Girl. She'd been awake most of the night, ideas swirling in her head about all the possibilities. Opening day for the five food trucks chosen would be the following June fourth, Jacques Aubert Day, a local holiday named for the town's founding father.

It was a four a.m. start that morning. The early October sky was the color of a plum, and along the horizon ran a thin strip of dawn. Angie could easily walk the distance from her house to her café but as that would waste time, she always drove the straightforward route up Pearl, right on Cedar, and on toward the corner of Cedar and Main, where her café was located.

There was no one on the roads at this time of the morning. Behind the shops on Main Street, at the corner of Pine, was a small parking lot that was all but deserted, except for one car that had been there for months and most likely had been abandoned. She made a mental note, like she did every day, to call the highway department to get the car towed, knowing she'd forget about it as soon as she stepped through the café door.

She parked as close as possible to the back of her building and locked the car, scanning the environment around her, not wanting any surprises. As she arrived at the back door, a loud meow startled her, causing her to jump. To her right, in the shadows, stood a large black cat with a white chest. He meowed again and looked at her expectantly.

Putting thoughts of the cat aside, she keyed in the code on the alarm until the light flashed green. The cat stepped out of the shadows and into the swathe of light from a fixture that hung above the door. Able to get a better look, she noticed his prominent ribs.

"All right, hold on, let me see what I can find," she huffed. She didn't have time to be feeding stray cats. After dropping her purse and keys into the desk drawer in her office, she scrounged around in the employees' refrigerator in the break room and pulled out some lunch meat she kept on hand for sandwiches. The turkey had been there longer than the ham, so she opened the deli bag, gave it a quick sniff, and decided it was semi-okay. She took it back outside, where the cat walked around in a small circle, voicing his interest. She pulled out the last three slices of turkey and threw them on the ground, balling up the deli bag in her hand. The cat pounced on the meat, hunching over and eating quickly.

In a firm voice, she said, "Don't expect this every morning." The cat ignored her and continued to eat.

Locking the door behind her, she glanced at her Fitbit and saw that she was already running five minutes behind. She hoofed it to the kitchen, flipping on all the lights. The stainless-steel counters, refrigerator, sinks, and appliances gleamed in the overbright fluorescent lighting. Everything had been wiped down, cleaned, and put away the previous night at the end of the shift, like always.

With her hands on her hips, she looked around, surveying her kingdom, feeling that tug of satisfaction she always felt at the start of a new day.

This was home.

Some days she had to pinch herself; how lucky was she to make a living doing this work she loved? Right out of high school, she'd taken a job driving a coffee truck, going from job site to job site to sell coffee, pastries, and sandwiches. People were always so happy to see her. A great cup of coffee brought people joy. She knew of people who hated what they did, saw it on a daily basis, those workers whose lunch hour was up five minutes ago, but they stayed, dragging their feet going back to a job they didn't like. Not her. She hoped to be baking when she was ninety years old.

She allowed herself one minute to muse on that satisfied feeling before she got to work. These early starts were required to get ahead of the day's baking needs. She rolled out the industrial-size mixer from the corner. The first order of business were those pastries that required a yeast dough, like her cinnamon rolls and almond rings. She glanced at the list at the end of the table. There were muffins and donuts and cupcakes and pastry hearts to be made. Donning her apron and humming to herself, she gathered her ingredients and got down to business.

By six thirty, she was icing the last of the pastry hearts. When she finished, she cleaned up and began to take trays of baked goods out to the front and slide them into the bakery case. She flipped on all the interior lights, smiling at the empty café. It was so rare to see it like this as during the day, it was bustling.

Once her baking was done—her staff would continue baking until eleven as she prided herself on offering fresh-baked goods daily—she headed back to her office to do some paperwork, her least favorite part of being self-employed. But she liked to stay on top of it.

A glance at the clock told her she didn't have a lot of time before the café opened. She turned her attention to the sandwich board, where she would list the donut flavors and specials of the day. Because how would people know what wonderful creations the café held for them if she didn't tell them?

As she dragged the sandwich board out from behind the counter, she heard her assistant manager come in through the back door and call out a greeting.

"Hey, Melissa," Angie replied. She selected a piece of colored chalk from beneath the counter.

Melissa came down the narrow hall that led to the restrooms and the back door.

The girl wasn't even thirty and had worked at the café since the beginning, ten years ago. At the time, she'd completed one year at the Culinary Institute of America but had to drop out because her mother had become ill. Like a dutiful daughter, Melissa had returned home. She knew the café inside and out, almost as well as Angie, who considered Melissa her right hand.

Melissa approached the table, wearing a jean jacket over her uniform shirt, which had "Coffee Girl" emblazoned over the breast pocket, and a pair of jeans. Her dark hair was cut short, and her eyes were of the palest blue. Earrings lined both ears from the lobe to the top of the ear. Angie had once thought herself adventurous with her two piercings in each ear.

She pulled out a chair, leaned over, and began to write on the sandwich board.

"Can I talk to you for a minute, Ang?" Melissa asked.

"Of course." With a nod to the other chair at the table, she added, "have a seat."

Melissa pulled out the chair and plopped down.

"What's up?" Angie asked without taking her eyes off the sandwich board.

"I wanted to talk to you about my role here at the café," Melissa started.

Please don't quit was Angie's first thought.

"I've been here for a long time, and I'd say I'm a good employee," Melissa said with confidence.

Angie wondered if she was angling for a raise. "You're a great employee," she said.

Melissa's nod was almost imperceptible. "I'd like more responsibility. I think I've earned it—but you tend to micromanage everything, to the point where you're doing almost all the work." The younger woman's voice was laced with frustration. "It's like you're territorial, especially with the baking."

Ouch.

"What did you have in mind?" Angie asked weakly.

"I would love to do more experimenting. The whole reason I went to culinary school was I love to bake, but I'm not really doing that here."

Angie cut her off. "You're baking here. Aren't you coming in three mornings a week to do the pastries and the donuts for the day?"

Melissa's shoulders sagged. She shook her head. "You don't understand."

"Enlighten me." Angie reminded herself not to get frustrated and to listen to what her best employee was trying to tell her.

"I'd like to try coming up with new items for you to sell. I don't mind doing all the other stuff: opening up the shop, closing it, working weekends, doing inventory and ordering, but I feel like I'm not being used to my full potential."

Angie's first instinct was to protest and say that wasn't true, but being honest with herself, she acknowledged she'd allowed Melissa no creative duties. Weakly, she said, "We've got a pretty full assortment of baked goods here. Pastries and donuts that our customers clamor for." Had she just used the word *clamor*? Besides, Coffee Girl was all about Angie's baking. It was Angie's signature pastries and desserts that drew people in. She'd personally created and selected everything for her café. It was her brand. Admittedly, she'd been happy to pass off many of the things that didn't involve baking to Melissa. Maybe she *was* territorial.

"You do quite a bit as it is, Melissa," Angie said. "You're already opening and closing, managing the schedule, hiring, doing the payroll and handling the bank deposits."

Melissa was quick to speak. "And I don't mind doing all that. But I was hoping to have more creative input."

Chalk still in her hand, Angie thought for a moment. As much as she was loath to cede any of the baking to anyone other than herself, Melissa's background was pastries, and it wasn't fair to assume she'd be content with administrative tasks. And if she was successful in obtaining a food truck license, she wouldn't be able to do it all. There were only so many hours in the day.

Although she was hesitant, she also didn't want Melissa leaving and looking for work elsewhere.

"Okay, let's continue this conversation," Angie finally said. "I'm open to some suggestions as to what you might want to add to our pastry case." She refrained from saying she thought they had enough variety on hand, choosing instead to kick the ball down the road and deal with this in the future.

Melissa smiled, her eyes bright. She hopped up from her chair and pushed it in. "Thanks, Ang. Maybe next week, we can talk about some of my ideas?"

Not ready to be pinned down to a specific date, Angie stammered out a response. "Um, sure. Of course."

She stared at the retreating figure of her employee and tried to figure out how to keep Melissa happy without giving up too much control.

She finished the sandwich board and dragged it to the front door, which she unlocked. Across the street, Java Joe's had their Halloween decorations up, even though it was only early October, reminding her that pretty soon, she'd have to start baking her apple cider cake, which she only made in the fall.

As she was setting up the sandwich board near the curb, Tom Sloane, the owner of Java Joe's, pulled his own board outside. Once it was set up, he walked over to his newer-model pickup truck parked by the curb. Angie lived to give him a hard time for opening up his own café directly across the street from hers. But recently, as he'd given her nephew Everett a job, she'd had to back off. Just a little bit. No sense in letting him get complacent.

He spotted her and threw his hand up in a wave. "Good morning, Evangeline."

Begrudgingly, she replied, "Morning, Tom."

There was a pile of broken glass near the building, and she went inside to get the broom and the dustpan. When she returned, she was aware of Tom whistling to himself as he stood at the back of his truck, the tailgate open. It sounded like someone was in a good mood, and that irritated her. He was wearing some ridiculous getup that included a wide-brimmed hat, a fishing vest over his long-sleeved T-shirt, and a pair of sunglasses hooked to the neckline of his shirt. It was not his usual uniform of jeans and a short-sleeved T-shirt, usually black. Still whistling, he set a fishing pole against the truck and pulled a tackle box from the bed, opening it.

Angie swept the broken glass onto the dustpan and used the broom to brush all the debris in front of the café into the street, for the street sweeper to collect on its daily nine a.m. pass.

Curiosity got the better of her, and she leaned the broom against the front of the café and walked across the street. Tom stopped whistling and regarded her with a wide grin.

She got right to the point. With a nod toward all his gear, she asked, "What's up?"

"Going fishing." He looked up to the clear blue sky. It was a crisp fall day. "It's a beautiful day for it." He leveled a gaze at her. "Care to join me?"

She snorted in response. "I'm working, in case you hadn't noticed. I run a café."

He was still grinning as he returned his attention to his tackle box. "It's all about balance, Evangeline."

"Can you leave your business unattended all day?"

He turned back to her. "First, it's not unattended. I have employees I trust to keep things running smooth until I get back. And I won't be gone all day. I'll be back by lunch."

"Still." She sniffed in disapproval.

Tom closed up the box. "Evangeline, let me ask you a question. What do you do to relax?"

"I bake," she said.

"Other than baking."

"I still bake."

"My point exactly." He rubbed his beard and regarded her.

Man, he was maddening.

"You're wound up tighter than a drum," he said. "You need some hobbies. You need some balance in your life."

Reddening, she lifted her chin ever so slightly and said, "I have plenty of balance in my life." Even as the words were falling off her tongue, she knew them not to be true. And by the look in his eyes, she knew that he knew too.

Huffily, she said, "I do not need you as a life coach."

He threw back his head in a bark of laughter. "That's my girl."

"I am *not* your girl," she declared before turning on her heel. As she turned, something caught her eye on the sandwich board he'd set up outside his café.

Before you stop at Coffee Girl, try a mouthwatering sandwich at Java Joe's.

Angie saw red and she sputtered, "What is this!"

Tom shrugged with that maddening grin of his. "People should eat their sandwiches first before dessert."

Gritting her teeth, she spun around, marched back to her café, and went inside. With a damp rag in hand, she went back out and wiped her sandwich board clean, erasing all of the day's specials. In big, bold letters, she wrote: *Life is short. Eat dessert first.*

As she went back inside, she could hear Tom's laughter from across the street.

Chapter Two

Angie circled the occupied tables in the café. There were six people in line at the counter and only two vacant tables. A couple stood from their seats and waved goodbye to her. She waved back and said, "See you soon." As soon as they were out the door, she grabbed the bottle of disinfectant, a cloth, and a bus box and headed for it. She cleared the dirty dishes and sprayed the table, wiping it down.

Erica manned the cash register. She was a dark-haired, ponytailed, middle-aged mom of six who looked perpetually tired. Another table emptied and Angie repeated her actions: clear it of the dirty dishes and wipe it down.

She carried the bus box through the butler door and back to the room behind the kitchen where all the ware was washed. Jordan Bilewski, her most recent hire, was a college student who picked up shifts on the days he didn't have class. He nodded when he saw her and unburdened her of the box. She returned to the main area; there was no longer a line at the counter, and everything was under control. Melissa was in the kitchen, making the next round of baked goods with Iris.

She retreated to her small office at the back of the café, although she preferred to be out in the kitchen or behind the counter or walking around the tables, chatting with the customers. Usually by the end of the day, she was ready to crash into bed feeling a good tired, the kind that comes from doing hard work. At her desk, she leaned forward and glanced at the schedule to see who was working what shifts for the rest of the week. Her phone beeped with an incoming text. She glanced at it and frowned. A reminder from the radiology center about her mammogram appointment the following day. The joys of turning forty. She made a note to cancel before the day was out. She didn't have time for that. She returned her attention to a few invoices piled on her desk, deciding she'd pay them off before she did anything else.

Her work was interrupted by the arrival of her cousin Esther.

"Knock, knock," Esther said, rapping on the doorframe. Before Angie could even say hello, Esther parked herself in the chair across from Angie's desk.

"Wow, you've cut your hair really short," Angie said.

"Yeah." Esther brushed her hand through her new pixie cut. Her dark hair was now liberally streaked with blond. It was a different look altogether for her, but it was becoming.

"I like it," Angie said. Her own strawberry blonde hair fell just below her shoulders, but she always wore it in a sensible ponytail.

"It's so much easier. Wash and wear and all that. I can't be bothered with styling or drying. It takes up too much time."

The thought was slightly tempting to Angie. It would definitely make life easier. She dreaded hair wash day. Her hair was thick, and it took forever to saturate it with water and then rinse all the shampoo and conditioner out of it. She looked at her cousin's stylish pixie again. It was worth a thought. She tucked it away for future consideration.

Without preamble, Esther said, "Before I get to the point of my visit, did you know they're going to allow food trucks down at the beach?"

Angie nodded. "I saw it. I'm on my way down there later this afternoon to fill out an application."

"Good. With that out of the way, I'll get to the reason for my visit. I'm in a jam, and I need a huge favor."

"Sure, anything."

"I'm short a bowler for Saturday night."

Angie cringed. "Anything but that." Her sisters Maureen and Nadine had been roped in to joining Esther's team. Her cousin, now in her mid-forties, was the oldest of all of them and had been telling everyone what to do since they were kids.

"Do you know I even tried DeeDee?" Esther said with a laugh, referring to Angie's younger sister who lived in Florida. "Offered to fly her round trip if she'd bowl with us on Saturday night."

Angie's mouth opened slightly. Esther was off the wall. "What did she say?"

"I don't know. She hung up on me." Esther laughed so hard her shoulders shook.

"What is it with you and bowling?"

"I love it!" Her enthusiasm for the sport was unmatched. Esther turned serious. "You know, your sisters seem to be enjoying themselves. And Nadine's bowling has improved."

"In only a few weeks?" Angie shook her head. "I've heard the stories that she was a terrible bowler in school."

"True," Esther agreed. "But she has improved: she's gone from terrible to bad."

Angie laughed. "You're so bad."

Esther held out her hands, grinning as if to say *What can I do?*

"Is there anything I can do to change your mind?" Esther asked.

Angie shook her head. She wished she could help her cousin out, but not by bowling. "Even if I were inclined to bowl—and I'm not—I'm too busy."

"I know. It's your anthem."

Angie tilted her head and narrowed her eyes at her cousin.

Esther kept talking. "Work is your life."

Angie was quick to counter that. "But it's not work if you love it."

Esther opened up her mouth and then abruptly closed it, finally saying, "I got nothing."

Without even realizing she was going to say it, Angie blurted, "Melissa wants to do more creative things around here, bake her own desserts."

Esther frowned. "And the problem is?"

"I do the baking," Angie said, realizing as she said it that she sounded like an eight-year-old.

"Come on," Esther said. "Let her do some of it. Make your employee happy."

When Angie didn't say anything, Esther said, "It's no secret that she did some training as a pastry chef. To be honest, I'm surprised she hasn't gone off and either worked for someone else or opened up her own business."

Angie felt herself pale. She hadn't thought about that. Melissa would be well able to open and run her own café.

Esther continued, ignoring Angie's rising ire. "She has talents that are not being employed here."

Angie pressed her lips together to avoid venting her spleen.

"I'm certainly not one to give managerial advice," Esther said, "but wouldn't it be best if you maximized your employees' potential?"

Angie had thought she was a good boss, but maybe not.

As an aside, Esther added, "I could never be a boss. I'd make it mandatory that my employees join my bowling team."

"Can I ask you a question?" Angie asked.

"Are you going to ask if you can join my bowling team?" Esther quipped.

"No, I'm not," Angie said firmly. It was time to get her cousin off that particular subject. Esther was a remote worker, and Angie didn't know how she did it. Out of curiosity, she asked, "Do you like working from home?"

Eyes bright, Esther said, "I love it!"

"Why?"

"Because all my stuff is there. Speaking of which, I've got to get back to work." Esther hopped out of the chair, said goodbye, and was gone.

Angie stared after her cousin, shaking her head.

Chapter Three

After lunch, when the crowd had thinned out and the café had quieted down, Angie drove over to the town hall, where she stood in line at the clerk's office for an application for a food truck license. The fact that it would only be operational for the warm summer months appealed to her. It wouldn't be too much more to take on, and she'd have all winter to plan for it. There was plenty of time.

Three people stood ahead of her in line. Hopefully they weren't all there for the food truck application. The person at the counter stepped away and the clerk called, "Next!"

She hoped this wouldn't take too long. She needed to get back to work. As she stood there, she checked her phone repeatedly, scanning for any messages from her staff. There were none.

"Evangeline," said an unmistakable voice behind her.

Angie closed her eyes, choosing to ignore the way the sound of his voice made the hairs stand up on the back of her neck. She turned and came face to face with Tom.

"Tom."

Why did he always seem to turn up? Were the Fates conspiring against her? Granted, he wasn't too shabby to look at. His hair was close-cropped and his beard neatly trimmed. His solid, muscular biceps suggested he never missed arm day at the gym. One of the tattoos on his arm was the official seal of the United States Army, a nod to his military service. She tried to avoid meeting his gaze. Up close, she had a front-row seat to those magnificent eyes of his: hazel, an interesting mixture of green with striations of amber. If she stared long enough, she feared she'd get lost in them. Annoyed with herself, she tried to dismiss those thoughts from her head. And the best way to do that was to show irritation.

"Are you here for the permit for the food truck?" he asked.

"I am. You?"

"Yes. It's a great idea. Figured I'd better get down here and apply." He regarded her. "I guess you had the same idea."

"Yes, Sherlock."

He grinned.

"It'll be pretty crowded if everyone and their brother shows up at the beach with a food truck next summer," she said.

"That's why there'll be a limit. Five."

She was about to blurt, *That's it?* but reined it in, not wanting him to know she was unaware of this stipulation. No sense in giving him any kind of advantage.

"I've got my one hundred words ready. 'Why I think I should be granted a truck license.'" He patted his front pocket.

"Me too," she said quickly. One hundred words? How had she missed that? Here she was with only one person ahead of her in line, and she now had to come up with a reason for why she thought she was the best person to operate a food truck on the beach? Her annoyance rose.

"Are you perpetually ticked off, or is it a day-to-day thing with you?" he asked, grinning.

She would not oblige him with a reply. Curtly, she said, "May the best man win."

He lifted an eyebrow. "Or woman."

With a heavy sigh, she turned and faced forward, waiting for her turn. He chuckled behind her. Had he been placed on this earth to irritate the hell out of her? To be the stone in her shoe? Sometimes, it seemed that way. He was a charmer, of that there was no doubt. But she was not the type to fall prey to those kinds of charms. She'd learned the hard way. One terrible marriage at nineteen to a bad boy, all because he had a motorcycle, had cured her of that.

When it was her turn, she was handed an application and told to fill it out and bring it back with the fee. There was no way she was leaving the building without handing it in, so she took it to one of the wooden counters that lined the back wall. The two pens on the counter were dry.

She walked back to the clerk, who was now shooting the breeze with Tom. She scooted up next to Tom until their arms were touching, and a tingle went through her, causing her eyes to widen. She cut them off mid-conversation and said, "I need a pen."

"I'm sorry, you'll have to get back in line, Angie," the clerk said sternly.

She looked up at Tom, who regarded her with amusement, and said, "Tom doesn't mind."

"I don't," Tom agreed.

"Thanks."

The clerk pulled a pen from a box on his side of the counter, muttering something about rules, and handed it to her.

With as sweet a smile as she could muster, Angie said, "Thank you."

She filled out the application quickly. The usual questions of name, address, et cetera, she filled out as if on automatic. But the last page asked for a hundred-word essay about why she thought her food truck would add value to the Lavender Bay beach community. She'd hated having to write essays back in high school, and nothing had changed since then.

Whistling interrupted her thoughts as Tom parked himself about three feet away from her. As she'd done, he filled in the form quickly, and when it came to the last part, he pulled a piece of lined paper out of his pocket, unfolded it, and laid it down on the counter in front of him, copying it onto the application form.

She was still gathering her thoughts, still having not written one of the one hundred words required, when Tom, still whistling, picked up his things, looked at her, and winked. "Good luck, Evangeline."

"Yeah, you too, Tom."

Once he was gone, she found it much easier to concentrate on what needed to be written, trying not to think about how his presence left her feeling slightly undone. She returned her attention to the essay and pushed Tom far out of her mind.

"What are you doing here?" Louise Cook asked the following morning, when Angie stopped by her mother's house on Heather Lane.

"Good to see you too, Mom," Angie said good-naturedly. "I had to take the morning off, thought I'd stop by." The previous day, she'd forgotten to cancel the mammogram and was now committed. She wasn't in her mother's house five minutes when perspiration began to line her brow. "Mom, what do you have your thermostat set at? Cremate? It's roasting in here."

"I'd rather be hungry than cold," Louise said.

"Maybe you could turn it down a degree or two? I feel like I should put on my bathing suit," Angie said.

Her mother arched an eyebrow. "Do you own a bathing suit, Evangeline?"

"Actually, no I do not."

The conversation pivoted.

"Why did you need to take the morning off?" Louise asked.

Angie rolled her eyes. "A stupid mammogram. I meant to cancel it yesterday but now it's too late," she said with a huff. "As I'm forty, Dr. Acker suggested I go for one."

"It's a good idea," Louise said seriously. "You'll have a baseline they can use to compare all your future mammograms."

"Oh goodie," Angie said. This was one of those things she filed under "time suck." If it had nothing to do with baking or running the café, she wasn't interested.

"Don't be like that. These things are important. And what did I always tell you when you were kids: Sometimes, we have to do things we don't want to do. Or like to do. There's coffee there, by the way," Louise added.

"Yeah, sure, I'll have a cup." Angie walked over to the coffeemaker, took a mug off the stand, and poured herself a cup. She joined her mother at the table.

"As I was saying," Louise continued, "these tests aren't for the fun of it. Early detection is the best weapon against cancer."

"I suppose," Angie conceded. Theoretically, she understood the importance of mammograms but reality-wise, it was a major hassle. "Does it hurt?"

"More of a discomfort."

Changing the subject, she said, "What's new around here?"

"If you joined us once in a while for Sunday morning coffee, you'd know," Louise said.

Every Sunday, a gathering was held at her mother's house: Maureen, Nadine, sometimes Maureen's husband Allan and all the grandchildren. Nadine's only child, Emma, was home from college as well as Maureen's youngest, Ashley. Aunt Gail would be there, along with Esther and Suzanne and her kids.

"I don't have the time." Angie said remembering Esther's comment about this phrase being her anthem.

Her mother tilted her head slightly and smirked. "Really? Come on. No one is *that* busy."

Angie bristled. "Well, I am. Owning your own business means eighty-hour work weeks."

Her mother sighed. "We never see you. You're missing out on so much." When Angie didn't reply to that, Louise continued, "Family and relationships are the most important thing."

"I must have been home sick from school the day they taught that," Angie joked.

"I hope someday you realize it before it's too late."

Chapter Four

As Angie made her way back to Coffee Girl after her mammogram, she tried to calm down. She'd been made to wait thirty minutes in the reception area before being called in. During the wait, she constantly checked her phone. Finally, she texted Melissa to see how things were going. Melissa had texted back one word: *fine*. But now Angie reminded herself that she wouldn't have to have another mammogram for a whole year, and she began to settle. She couldn't wait to get back to work.

She parked her car out back and as the lot was almost full, she ended up at the far end, against the wooded field. The day was dull and damp and a light drizzle coated everything. As she neared the back door of the café, she spotted the black cat with the white chest. He looked as if he were wearing a tuxedo.

He took one step toward her and meowed.

"You again?" she asked. "I think you're making a habit of this."

The cat followed her to the door, and as she unlocked it, she looked down at him and smirked. "All right, hang on, I'll see what I can find."

She scrounged around in the break room refrigerator, but there was nothing. She'd eaten the last of the ham yesterday for her lunch and hadn't yet replaced it. She went to the kitchen, announced to everyone that she was back, and quickly fried up an egg and added some cheese to it. After it cooled down, she walked down the narrow hallway to the back door, carrying the egg in one saucer and a little water in another. When she opened the door, the cat was nowhere in sight, but then to her left, she heard a meow.

She half turned, spotted him, and lifted up the two saucers. "Come on," she beckoned.

The cat regarded her but didn't move.

She approached him, not wanting to put the saucers down directly in front of the door as they were in and out of it all day. The cat took a step back.

She set the food and water down within reach of the cat and retreated. It stepped up to the dish and began eating. Satisfied, she went back inside. She gave her hands a good wash before she went out to the front.

She had just stepped behind the counter when she spotted Everett, who was paying for something at the register. In his hand he held one of the café's signature white pastry boxes with the Coffee Girl logo emblazoned on the lid.

"Hi, Everett." She smiled, happy to see him. He was recently out of residential rehab for drug addiction, and by all accounts doing well at his job over at Java Joe's. She was grateful to Tom for giving him a chance, even if she didn't always show it.

Everett smiled in response. "Hi, Aunt Angie." She noticed he wore the St. Anthony medal around his neck that had once belonged to Angie's grandmother. This pleased her to no end. Strangely, her sister Maureen, Everett's mother, had found it on the beach decades after it was lost.

"How are you doing?" she asked. He should smile more often, she thought. It lit up his face.

"Good. Taking it one day at a time," he said.

"That's the way," she said encouragingly. "What brings you here?"

"Pastries," he replied, lifting the box slightly.

"Enjoy. How's your mom doing?" she inquired.

"She's fine. Busy with work and all that."

"Sure."

"I better get back."

"Okay, honey, it's good to see you."

He walked away, crossing the street and walking directly into Java Joe's. Why was he bringing a box of pastries into the competing café? she wondered.

Over the course of the next few days, she noticed one employee after another from Java Joe's coming over for a box of pastries. Everyone, that is, except Tom. As she watched the latest one walk back across the street, she sidled up to one of her employees, Joel, who manned the till.

"Hey, Angie, what's up?" Joel asked.

"Why are all these employees from Java Joe's coming in and buying pastries?"

"Probably because they like them," Joel said sensibly.

"Do they come in every day?" she asked.

"Like clockwork."

"What do they order?"

He rattled off a list. It came to almost a dozen pastries and donuts.

Angie nodded, turned on her heel, went outside, and marched across the street to Java Joe's.

Curiosity propelled her into Tom's café. The aroma that greeted her when she stepped inside was slightly different from the one at Coffee Girl. There was the common scent of brewed coffee, but whereas her place smelled of baked goods, his smelled of grilled foods. Her mouth watered.

What was he up to with her pastries?

She quickly scanned the counter and the glass case, checking out the baked goods on display. It was the usual suspects: cakes and muffins. Approaching the counter, ignoring the line and trying not to be offended by his full café and obviously brisk business, she said to one of his counter staff, "Where's Tom?"

"Back in his office."

With a nod, she pushed through the doorway marked "Employees Only." She'd never been back there before. The first door on the left was an employee restroom. Across from it, on the right, was a small room crammed with shelving and all the paper supplies. She was slightly offended at how organized and tidy it was. *Does this guy have any faults at all?* Yeesh. She tried the handle on the third room, but it was locked. The room directly across from that was a break room. One female employee sat there, legs stretched out in front of her, crossed at the ankles, eyes glued to her phone. She didn't even notice Angie passing.

The door to the last room on the right side of the corridor was open, and despite the sign that read "Gone fishing," Tom Sloane sat there in his desk chair, feet up on his desk, eating one of her pastries and scrolling through his phone. On the desk was a small plate with a second pastry heart. Next to it stood a tall cup of coffee.

Spotting her, he smiled. "Evangeline, this is a surprise!"

I bet.

He swung his feet off the desk, wiped flaky pastry from his hands, did a quick sweep over his beard for any runaway flakes, and set his phone down on the desk.

Now appearing all businesslike, he leaned forward, picked up a pen, and tapped it against the desk blotter. "To what do I owe the pleasure?"

"Well—"

"Sit down."

"No thanks. I won't be here that long."

He shrugged and said, "Suit yourself."

"I'll get to the point."

"Thanks."

"Every day, someone from your staff walks over to my café and purchases a box of pastries."

"I know. We love your pastries. I can't get enough of these pastry hearts."

Oh boy. They purchased the pastries for themselves. There was no nefarious intent on his part. No attempt to copy her creations and pass them off as his own. In her stupidity, which she had in spades, she'd almost gone and made a fool of herself. It was time to beat a hasty retreat.

But there was an expression of dawning realization on Tom's face, which resulted in him jumping out of his chair and closing the distance between them. With a grin, he stood right in front of her, placing one large arm up on the doorframe, forcing her to take a step back into the hall to put more space between them.

"I get it," he said. "You thought I was up to no good with your baked goods? Possibly trying to pass them off as my own?" His smirk was maddening.

"I, uh . . ." she stuttered.

"You always think the worst of me, don't you?" he asked. "Always ascribe the worst possible motive to me, isn't that right? Why is that?"

The back door opened, interrupting them, and they both looked over at a delivery man, who wheeled in boxes of supplies on a dolly.

"What's up, Tom."

"Hey, Mac, I'll be with you in a minute."

Angie couldn't say anything; she was too embarrassed. Mortified was more like it.

Once the delivery man disappeared down the hall, Tom turned his attention back to Angie. The grin was gone, and his voice was low and serious. "Do you always look for the worst in people? Or is it just me? Maybe if you took the time to get to know me, you might find that I'm not your worst enemy." A muscle ticked along the edge of his jaw. "Can I do anything else for you, Evangeline?"

She knew she should apologize, but the words would not come out. "No, thanks," she said curtly.

"Then let me get back to my pastry heart."

She turned and made her exit.

By the time she arrived back at her own café, she was feeling pretty low. Why did she insist on giving him a hard time, all the time? Was it really because he'd opened up a café directly across the street from hers? There were thoughts coming up from the bottom of her mind that had nothing to do with his café, thoughts she didn't want to examine too closely. But deep down, she knew the real reason. It wasn't only Tom; it was any man that showed or expressed any interest in her. Her policy had always been to shut it down immediately. A failed marriage would do that to a person.

The best thing was to throw herself into her work; it was what she'd always done when she didn't want to think about difficult things.

Chapter Five

Angie hung up the phone, her hands shaking. Her doctor, Beverly Acker, had called to let her know something suspicious had shown up on her mammogram.

"Like a tumor? Like cancer?" Angie asked.

"That needs to be determined. The report is inconclusive. I'm going to book you in for a biopsy as soon as possible." Dr. Acker paused. "As difficult as this is, I'll ask you to try and relax and not stress out about it too much until we have the biopsy results."

Easier said than done.

After that phone call, things happened rapidly. The breast biopsy was scheduled and a few days before, the nurse called her to touch base. As the nurse went over the instructions on the phone, Angie wondered whether she could return straight to work afterward. But something the nurse said caught her off guard.

"I'm sorry, what did you say?" Angie asked.

"I said that due to the anesthetic, you're not allowed to drive for twenty-four hours. Whoever is picking you up will need to come into the clinic and sign you out."

Angie protested. "I should be fine to drive."

"I'm sorry, but that's the policy. No driver, no biopsy."

All sorts of swear words floated across Angie's mind. "All right, I'll get someone to pick me up."

"Great, we'll see you Monday morning."

Once she hung up, she bit her lip, mentally going through her list of people who could provide a ride back and forth, of whom there were plenty. But she hadn't told anyone about her impending biopsy. Not even her sisters or her cousins, and especially not her mother. She couldn't. They'd only worry and if it turned out to be nothing, then they'd have been anxious for nothing. She didn't want her employees to know either. There was only one person she could call: her best friend, Debbie Melvin. Her call went to voicemail and Angie left a message, stating she needed a favor.

Twenty minutes later, Debbie appeared at her office door, wearing a chocolate-brown long-sleeved thermal top, jeans, and big gold hoop earrings. Before she said anything, she opened the back door wide, and then focused her attention on Angie.

"I was at the drugstore picking up my meds when I got your message, so I thought I'd pop by," Debbie said.

She remained in the doorway. Angie did not invite her to sit down. Her friend had a thing about rooms with no windows, one of her many quirks.

Debbie Melvin was unlike any person Angie had ever met or would ever meet.

Their first encounter was in the second-grade lunchroom. Debbie had been a transfer student, arriving in February. She was freckled with carrot-colored hair and missing her front teeth. She'd been alone at the lunch table, Angie had sat with her, and they'd been together ever since. Debbie had always been the kind of person Angie could depend on.

She was still freckled, and almost always wore her carrot-orange hair piled into a messy bun on top of her head. Her teeth had come in straight and perfect, one of the few things that had gone right in her life.

Angie had a lot of acquaintances and not many close friends. There were her sisters and her cousins and Debbie, and that was enough for her.

Debbie spotted the bag of cat food on the floor next to the door. "What's this?"

As if on cue, there was a meow from the open back door.

Debbie leaned her head back and must have spotted the stray cat because she said, "Aw, poor kitty." Angie's friend had a large soft spot for animals, especially strays, and had provided a home over the years to a few. It was as if the word was out among the stray cat community: there was a house over on Peach Street that would house and feed you and your soul.

"He started coming around and, well, I was roped in to feeding him," Angie said.

Debbie smiled. "Bless your heart, Angie."

"How've you been?"

"Good. Nothing new. You rang?"

Angie lowered her voice so as not to be overheard and told her friend about the dodgy mammogram and the need for a biopsy. She finished with, "So I need a ride. And most importantly, I don't want anyone to know, especially my mother and sisters. There's no sense in getting them all worked up."

Her friend nodded. "Remit understood and accepted," Debbie said solemnly.

Angie had to suppress a grin at her friend's funny choice of words.

"When and what time?" Debbie asked.

Angie gave her the details, and Debbie nodded. She had a memory like a steel trap. They spoke of general things for a few more minutes before Debbie left.

The following Sunday—the day before her scheduled biopsy—Angie took a few hours off in the morning to go to her mother's house for brunch. Louise had invited everyone to discuss the holiday plans for the year, which included Thanksgiving and Christmas. This year, Thanksgiving would be held at Louise's house and Christmas at her sister Gail's. As Angie hadn't seen anyone in her family for a while, she figured she'd go, promising to bring pastries and donuts. She had no business taking time off, especially when weekends were so busy at the café. But if she didn't, she'd be assigned to bring or do something she didn't like.

The house on Heather Lane was full of happy memories. They'd all grown up there, and there'd been a time when her grandparents had also lived with them. Just thinking about her grandparents always brought a smile to her face. But now her mother lived there by herself as Angie's father had died years ago. That was a pain that never went away. She wondered how her mother had felt about the transition, going from a house full of three generations and a total of eight people under one roof, to living alone. But her mother never complained, always made the best of it. Sometimes, Angie wondered where she came from.

It was a damp, rainy day, and Angie had bundled up in jeans and a heavy oversized sweater. The house was full by the time she arrived with two boxes of baked goods in her hand. There was the commingled smell of freshly brewed coffee and the pumpkin-scented candle burning on the counter. Her sisters Maureen and Nadine were there, moving around the kitchen, setting dishes on the table. Aunt Gail was there with her daughters Esther and Suzanne. The holidays were a big deal to Louise and

Gail. They'd always planned the two dinners by the end of October.

"Well, well, look who's here!" Louise said, wearing oven mitts and carrying a pan of bacon, egg, and cheese strata over to the old farmhouse table that had been bought when DeeDee was born and the family had grown to eight.

"Hi, Mom," Angie said, leaning in to kiss her on the cheek. Louise shifted the hot pan away from Angie to accept her kiss.

Nadine stood at the coffeemaker, spooning coffee into the paper filter. Maureen removed bacon from a frying pan and placed it on a paper-towel covered plate. Esther used a slotted spoon to stir a compote of fruit salad as her sister, Suzanne, walked around the table with a carton of orange juice, filling all the small glasses on the table.

Hugs went all around and then all at once, everything that was needed for Sunday brunch was on the table. Everyone sat, with Gail next to Louise at the head of the table.

They began to help themselves. Nadine asked Angie, "What's new? I haven't talked to you in a while."

"Nothing," Angie lied.

"How are things going with Melissa?" her mother asked, dishing out the strata as plates were passed down to her end of the table. She then passed the plate to Gail, who dished out a helping of her blueberry French toast bake. When the plate was passed back to Angie, she helped herself to two pieces of extra-crispy bacon. She looked at her plate for a moment, thinking there'd be no need to eat for the rest of the day.

In an earlier phone conversation, she'd relayed Melissa's request to her mother, whose immediate response had been, "Let her do what she wants!"

"I'm still thinking about it."

"What's there to think about?" her mother asked, forking off a piece of French toast bake and popping it into her mouth.

"Mmm," Gail said thoughtfully. "She's an invaluable employee, I wouldn't want to lose her." Obviously, Louise had discussed the situation with her sister.

"Exactly," Maureen said, biting off a piece of bacon. Apparently, the whole family had been briefed.

"We forgot the cream for the coffee," Nadine said. She stood and retrieved a carton of half and half from the refrigerator.

Angie's cousin Suzanne spoke up, her voice soft. "It's hard to give up control." She cast a sympathetic smile in Angie's direction.

Angie would not concede. "Possibly."

"Did you apply for the food truck permit?" Esther asked.

"I did." Angie said.

Her mother's lips pressed into a thin line. "When are you going to find time to run a food truck?"

"It's only for the summer months," Angie replied, sipping from her juice glass.

"And there are only so many hours in the day," her mother said. "You can't do it all, honey."

Angie laughed. "I'm going to try." She pulled out her phone and dashed off a text to Melissa to make sure everything was all right at the café, ignoring her mother's scowl. The rule on Heather Lane was no phones at the table. Hurriedly, she shoved it back into her pocket. She looked up and everyone had gone quiet. Unusually so. Her gaze traveled around the table. Seven women and no one had anything to say. Rare.

"What?" she asked. It was as if they all knew a secret and were withholding it from her.

Finally, her mother spoke up. "Do you want the truth, or do you want us to tell you what you want to hear?"

Angie blinked. *What does that mean?* "The truth, of course."

Louise exchanged a glance with her sister.

Gail piped in. "You need to delegate more. You're doing too much, and you micromanage everything, including your employees. If they're good employees, you need to trust them to do their job without you looking over their shoulders."

"Let Melissa explore her creative side," Maureen chimed in.

Angie felt her cheeks burn. Her aunt had no employees at her antique shop other than a retired sniffer bloodhound, but she refrained from pointing that out. And Maureen, an interior designer, had no one working for her either, for that matter. Everyone else had their heads down, staring at the brunch items on their plates. Even the usually outspoken Esther did not look at her. Angie sat back, folding her arms across her chest.

"All right. What else?" Angie asked.

"I'd like to say something," Nadine said, raising her hand. Angie rolled her eyes; it wasn't a classroom.

"Go for it." It looked like it was going to be a no-holds-barred session.

"I realize I haven't been back in Lavender Bay a long time but from what I've seen, Melissa seems more than capable of running the whole café if she needed to. Maybe you could start out small. Have her make one or two things."

"Give her a sense of purpose," said someone else.

"That isn't the problem," Angie said. "The problem is we've got a great variety of products already."

"You can't let her come up with one new item?" Maureen asked.

"*I* make all the pastries at Coffee Girl."

Everyone went quiet again. The only sound was the scrape of cutlery against plates, and spoons stirring inside of coffee mugs.

"Angie," her mother asked with a pointed look. Why did Angie feel like she was eight years old and being scolded for something she'd done?

Esther leaned forward past Suzanne, who was sitting next to her. "Can you sit down and talk to her and listen to her ideas? And maybe offer her a pay raise." She sat back and announced, "But then that's just my two cents."

"I'm not a bad boss," Angie said defensively.

There was a chorus of "No, no, of course not" and "We know that." But Angie wasn't convinced.

"I think you should back off the café and have a life," Suzanne said bravely.

Angie protested, "But I love the café, it's my baby."

"No one is saying you have to work part time, but my darling girl, you have no personal life," Louise said.

"I don't need one." Angie realized as she said this how lame it sounded. Everyone stared at her before returning to their brunch. Sighing, she said, "I'll take everything said here under consideration."

Gail's smile was broad as she lifted a bejeweled hand and waved her fork around. "That's all we ask, honey. Just think about things."

Angie nodded. "Will do."

Louise took her spoon and tapped it against her mug. "All right, who's bringing what for Thanksgiving?"

Despite the change of conversation, Angie remained unsettled.

Chapter Six

Debbie arrived ten minutes early on the morning of Angie's scheduled biopsy. Angie was almost relieved, as she was ready and eager to get going. Her staff knew she wouldn't be in that day, and she'd been bombarded with texts from everyone asking if she was all right. She sent a text to Melissa asking her to feed the cat out back. It was a cold morning, and she didn't want him going hungry.

Debbie had a purple knit hat pulled over her hair. She looked sympathetically at her friend. "Are you nervous?"

"Not really. I just want it over with," Angie admitted.

"All righty then, let's get this show on the road," Debbie said with a reassuring smile.

After grabbing her purse, house keys, and phone, Angie followed her out the door.

She opened the passenger-side door and slipped in, buckling up. She waited patiently for Debbie to go through her routine. Her friend pulled the seatbelt over three times, back and forth, counting under her breath before locking it in. Then she put her hand on the rearview mirror as if she were going to adjust it, even though it wasn't needed as she was the only one who drove her car. She picked up her phone and set it in the well in the center console, face up. She looked in her side-view mirrors and then her rearview mirror before pressing the keyless ignition button. Debbie had a routine for everything, and she'd had a routine for driving since she got her license at sixteen. It was Angie's father who had given Debbie lessons, as her own parents weren't wont to.

"Did you have to take time off from work this morning?" Angie asked, worried.

Debbie, who'd excelled in math all through school and helped Angie earn a passing grade in high school geometry—to this day, Angie still didn't get the whole proof thing—was a numbers cruncher. She loved numbers more than anything else.

"I have all that personal time saved up in my bank, so I took the day off," Debbie told her. "While you're getting your biopsy, I'm going to take Bella and Sam to the vet for their vaccinations," she said, referring to two of her cats, both rescues.

"At least it won't be a total waste," Angie said.

Debbie looked over at her. "Even if I had nothing else to do today, driving you to your biopsy is not a waste of time." She was dead serious.

"Okay."

As they pulled up to the front doors of the medical center, Debbie asked, "Are you sure you don't want me to come in with you?"

Angie shook her head. "No thanks, I appreciate it. Go take care of your kitties."

"I'll give you a full report later."

Angie laughed and said, "I know you will."

As she stepped out of the car, she said, "I'll text you when I'm ready to leave. You'll have to come inside and sign me out."

"Consider it done," Debbie replied.

Angie reported in for her breast biopsy at the outpatient department. Now that it was happening, her anxiety rose. She sat in the room, taking some deep breaths. A nurse soon arrived, took her medical history which, other than having her appendix removed at nineteen, was unremarkable. The nurse laid a brand-new paper gown on the exam table, explained the procedure to Angie, and had her sign the consent form, but not before disclosing everything that could possibly go wrong. Angie chose to ignore those bits; she was anxious enough.

The procedure didn't take long at all, and when she was told she could go home, she rang Debbie, who picked up on the first ring. She told her she was ready and gave her directions to where she was in the medical center.

She'd been advised to take it easy for the rest of the day, but she had no intention of sitting around her house, fretting. The biopsy results would take two to three days, so it was best to keep busy.

Debbie arrived so quickly that Angie wondered if she'd been waiting outside the medical center.. Her friend hesitated in the doorway, noted the big, wide window, and stepped inside.

"I'm waiting for the nurse to come back and remove this." Angie lifted up her hand to show the canula for the IV still taped to it. "I told her you were on your way."

"How did it go?"

Angie shrugged. "Fine."

The nurse arrived, a pleasant middle-aged woman who wore scrubs the color of purple grapes and a pair of sneakers on her feet. Around her neck hung a lanyard with her identification badge dangling from it. She smiled when she saw Debbie.

"Are you Miss Cook's ride home?"

"Yes," Debbie said.

"Great. Evangeline has her discharge paperwork, and I'll need your signature here to confirm you're driving her home. She's not to drive for twenty-four hours." She eyed Angie as she said, "And she's not to return to work until tomorrow."

Angie hadn't planned on mentioning that part to Debbie, was going to gloss right over it and head back to the café and hang out in her office.

"Got it." Debbie looked at Angie and narrowed her eyes. Her friend knew her too well.

Once she signed the paperwork, they made their way out of the building.

"Wait out front, I'll bring the car around," Debbie suggested.

Angie shook her head. "My legs are fine. I can walk."

Once Debbie pulled out of the parking lot, she asked, "Home?"

Angie frowned. "I think I can hang out in the office at Coffee Girl."

Debbie shook her head. "No way. You were told not to return to work today. You were told to take it easy."

Angie sighed. She didn't particularly look forward to spending the day at home. There was nothing to do.

As if sensing her reluctance, Debbie said, "Here are some options: we can go to my house, and I can make you something to eat and we can hang out. Or, I was going to go to the beach for my walk. You can wait in the car, roll the window down, and breathe in the fresh air. No walking though. Let's not push it."

Those options sounded better than going home. She knew Debbie walked every day along the shore no matter what the weather. She loved it best in the winter when she tended to be the solitary walker on the beach.

Angie was agreeable. "The beach."

"Good. Do you want me to pick up coffee or something?"

"Yeah. Stop at the café and we'll get some coffee to go."

"I'll only stop at the café if you promise to stay in the car," Debbie said firmly.

"All right," Angie grumbled.

CHAPTER SEVEN

As if taking no chances, Debbie parked her car in a vacant spot a block away from the café.

"Be back soon," she said, and she slammed the door and walked briskly in the direction of Coffee Girl.

In ten minutes, she reappeared in Angie's line of sight, carrying a takeout cup in each hand. Her bright red hair spilled out from beneath her purple knit hat. Debbie was such a caring and kind individual it surprised Angie that she was single. But like herself, she'd had an early, disastrous marriage, and she didn't seem to mind her singleness.

As she neared the car, Angie reached over and opened the driver's-side door.

"Thanks," Debbie said, handing her the coffees so she could get in.

Angie set the two cups in the cupholders between the front seats.

Debbie went through her routine and then looked over her shoulder before pulling out into traffic.

At the end of town was a gravel parking lot behind a low concrete wall overlooking the beach. You had to sport an annual resident sticker that was obtained from the town hall to park there. Debbie's bumper was littered with previous years' stickers. She pulled into the lot and parked right up against the wall.

Once the car was turned off, Debbie turned to her. "Are you sure you don't mind?"

"Not at all," Angie said honestly. She knew how important the walk was to her friend. She'd once said it cleared the cobwebs from her mind.

"What will you do? Besides text your employees with instructions?"

Angie glanced at the low wall. "I might sit outside for a bit and think."

"Very good, then I'll leave you to it." Debbie jumped out of the car and opened the back door, pulling out a scarf and gloves. As she wrapped the scarf around her neck, she said, "You know, if your neck is warm, that's half the battle."

Angie smiled.

"Do you have a scarf, Ang? The wind is kind of bracing today."

"No, I didn't think to bring one."

"No matter, I've got an extra one." Debbie tossed a knit scarf over the front seat, and Angie caught it.

"Thanks."

"I won't be long."

"Take your time."

Debbie headed off, hands shoved into the pockets of her winter jacket. Angie dashed off a quick text to Melissa to let her know she wouldn't be returning for the day. And to prevent a round of texts, she added that she was fine and taking the day off. It almost felt like back in high school, when she and Debbie played hooky. After she sent the first text, she followed it with a second, asking Melissa to feed the cat out back before she left for the night.

Angie wrapped the scarf around her neck and stepped out of the car, coffee in hand. She had no gloves, but the coffee was hot and warmed her hand. Carefully, she swung a leg over the low concrete wall and settled in.

For October, the air was unseasonably cold. Almost like winter. She shivered and took a sip of her coffee.

The lake was turbulent. All gray and green, rushing into the surf with speed and large foamy whitecaps that suggested it had somewhere to be. The roar was thunderous, nearly drowning out the cries of several seagulls who circled overhead. The wind was bracing. Angie looked in the direction Debbie had gone, her friend's form diminishing as she walked farther away.

Angie looked back to the lake, and her thoughts shifted to the food truck. She could so easily picture it there, parked in the parking lot, the side open, the day sunny and bright. The more she thought about it, the more excited she got about this potential new side venture. And even though they were only awarding five licenses, not only was she hopeful, she was confident. She kept visualizing it, the colors she'd use and what she'd offer. Some people drank coffee no matter how hot it was, and of course there'd be a menu of iced coffees. The thought brought a smile to her face. It was like it was back in the beginning, when she first opened up Coffee

Girl. Her coffee cooled down quickly in the cold air, and she downed the rest of it in one gulp. She swung her legs over the wall and walked to the nearest trash can to dump her empty cup.

Shivering, she got back into the car and pulled a notebook and pen out of her purse and started scribbling down ideas about the food truck. She was so engrossed in her task that when Debbie opened the car door, Angie jumped.

Debbie laughed. "I didn't mean to startle you." She unwound her scarf and tossed it in the back seat with her gloves. She pulled off her knit hat and tucked it between her seat and the console. Her hair was matted, her cheeks were red, and she was slightly breathless. "Come on, let's go to my house and we'll have something to eat," she suggested.

Debbie lived over on Peach Street. The cluster of streets between Orchard and Vine was known as the fruit belt of Lavender Bay: Apple Court, Berry Street, Grape Avenue, Lemon Lane, Peach Street, and Plum Corner.

She'd lived in this house for fifteen years. What had appealed to her was the larger-than-normal backyard, which was currently ringed with white vinyl fencing. The house had started out as a summer cottage, but rooms and additions had been added over the years, giving it a hodgepodge appearance. But Debbie didn't care about that, as long as there was enough room for her dogs and cats. She pulled into her driveway. In the front window sat two cats, one a ginger, the other all white.

As they got out of the car, Angie could hear the excited barking of Debbie's dogs, even though all the doors and windows were closed.

Debbie looked over at her, concerned. "I'll go in first and let them out back so they don't knock you over."

"Sure."

As Angie waited outside, she heard the back door open and the dogs bound out to the backyard. She was thinking how weird it was not to be at the café, when Debbie opened the door and said, "Okay, the coast is clear."

She stepped inside Debbie's house and ended up in the kitchen. Debbie began pulling items out of the refrigerator.

"Toasted bagel with cream cheese okay?" Debbie asked.

"It's perfect."

The house was decorated in various shades of gray. There was a faint but pleasant smell of lemon-scented cleaner.

In the living room, old bedsheets covered the sofa and two chairs. Dog beds and cat beds were lined up against one wall.

"I've got sesame seed bagels or plain."

"Sesame seed," Angie said.

Angie pulled off her jacket and winced, aware of a soreness in her breast. She chose to ignore it and sat down.

As she did, a ginormous cat wearing a diaper walked through the kitchen. Or waddled. Angie blinked and her mouth fell open. "What *is* that?"

Debbie turned around and smiled. "That's Po."

"Po?"

"Mm-hmm," Debbie said, popping a sliced bagel into the toaster. "Short for Potato."

"When did you get him?"

"About two weeks ago. He's a foster. He's got a few issues."

"You don't say," Angie remarked.

"As you can see, he has a little bit of a weight problem."

"Yes, that's obvious."

"There's no fat-shaming here, right, Po?" Debbie called after him. The cat meowed once and made his way to one of the empty pet beds in the living room.

"Why the diaper? Is he incontinent?"

"No, he's not litter-trained."

"And you willingly took this on?" Angie asked in disbelief.

"Sure. Cyril from Lavender Bay Rescue called me and said no one wanted him." Angie's assessment of that was that Cyril knew Debbie had a big, soft heart. "I've got to get his weight down, litter train him, and help him socialize with the other animals."

"Is that all?"

"Yes. And then hopefully, he'll be able to be put up for adoption. The fact that he isn't litter-trained is holding him back."

"I can imagine."

Debbie carried two plates over to the table and set them down. "Did you want coffee or tea?"

"A glass of water is fine, thanks."

The dogs were at the sliding door at the back of the house, barking and whining to come in.

Debbie opened the door and the two dogs, Oscar and Bogie, charged inside, their sights firmly fixed on Angie. Angie was used to this.

"Come on, guys, calm down," Debbie said.

They ignored her. Angie knew if she paid them a little attention and petted them, they'd settle down. They only wanted to be acknowledged. Within a few minutes, they calmed and lay on the floor near the two women. Oscar, who'd been a rescue, snored loudly at Debbie's feet.

They ate their bagels companionably, talking about nothing and everything. When they were finished, Debbie apologized for not having any sweets in the house.

"I thought if Po has to cut back, it wouldn't be fair to have a pack of Oreos here."

"Is Po partial to Oreos?"

"No, but I didn't want to eat them in front of him."

Angie had nothing to say to that.

"Did you want to watch a movie? Hang out?" Debbie asked, her expression expectant.

Angie dreaded going home, and watching a movie might be just the thing.

"I've had an itching to watch *The Maltese Falcon* again," Debbie said, moving on to the living room and popping a DVD into the player, her dogs following her.

"How many times have you seen it?" Angie asked.

Debbie laughed. "Too many to count. It was your grandmother that got me hooked on old black-and-white movies."

"I know."

Debbie pulled a sheet off the recliner so Angie could sit down. She folded it up and put it aside. She pulled the living room drapes shut, throwing the room into darkness.

"How's your family? Your mother?" Angie asked. Even though it was a sore subject, she felt compelled to inquire.

Debbie shrugged. "You know. The same." Her friend had often said that the only thing she had in common with her family was the last name and that was it.

As soon as Debbie settled on the couch, lying on her side, the dogs jumped up and curled themselves at her feet. Three cats came out of nowhere and jumped up as well, two settling on the back of the sofa and one snuggling up in the crook of Debbie's knees. Po waddled over and looked at them. He tried to jump up but was too heavy. In one fell swoop, Debbie reached down, lifted him, and placed him in front of her.

In the semi-darkness, Angie glanced over at them. "I'm surprised there's any room for you over there."

With all seriousness, Debbie asked, "Did you want one?"

"I'm good. Besides, I don't want to upset anyone." The image of the stray cat behind the café came to mind, and she hoped they remembered to feed him.

Debbie pressed the play button on the remote, and the television came to life with orchestral music, shades of black and white, and the opening credits of the movie. As they watched, Angie sent off various texts to her employees until Debbie spoke up.

"If you don't put your phone down, I'm going to take it away."

She sounded so stern, which was unlike her, that Angie had to suppress a chuckle.

They ended up watching two movies back-to-back, and it was late afternoon when they finished. Debbie popped up, her hair flattened against the side of her face, and all the dogs and cats stood from their positions. She popped out the second DVD, *Leave Her to Heaven*, and placed it on the shelf with the hundreds of others.

She peeked out the window and said, "Hmm. It's already dark outside."

"Winter's coming."

Angie stood from the recliner and stretched. Oscar watched her, wagging his tail. She picked up the folded sheet, shook it out, and placed it over the recliner.

"Did you want to grab some dinner?" Debbie asked.

Angie shook her head. "I'm not hungry, and I think I'll go home."

"You must be exhausted."

"I am, actually," Angie said. She was surprised at this. She'd relaxed all day as instructed, and she still felt as if she were ready for bed.

"Come on, I'll let the dogs out before we go, then I'll drive you home."

"Take your time."

Oscar and Bogie ran to the back door, their paws scrabbling furiously on the kitchen floor. The cats on the couch stared at Angie, decided she wasn't worth any scrutiny, and moved on to other parts of the house.

As Debbie pulled into Angie's driveway, she asked, "Do you want me to drive you to work tomorrow?"

Angie shook her head. "Not necessary. I'll be fine. I am fine."

"When do you find out the biopsy results?"

"In a few days."

Debbie leaned over and pulled her into a hug. "Okay, I'll be praying for you. Let me know."

"Thank you. I need it. And I'll talk to you later."

She got out of the car, her housekeys in her hand, and waved her friend off. Although she'd enjoyed her day with Debbie, she was anxious to get back to work in the morning.

Chapter Eight

The following morning, Angie was eager to return to work. Other than some soreness at the incision site, she felt good. After spending the day with Debbie at her house with her menagerie of pets and watching old black-and-white movies, she'd had a good night's sleep.

As she approached the rear of the building, her gaze bounced around, searching for the cat. Eventually, she spotted him curled up behind the dumpster. "Hello?" she called softly. At the sound of her voice, the cat lifted his head and looked over his shoulder at her, then emerged from his sleeping spot, stretching his front legs and then his back ones.

"Oh goodness, someone is tired today," Angie said. "Busy night?"

She went inside, scooped some kibble into his dish, and set it out back. The cat ran toward it. Folding her arms across her chest, she said, "I suppose we'll have to give you a name."

Satisfied that he was fed, she slipped back inside and went about the business of running her café. It would have been too easy to let Melissa deal with everything. But she hadn't been in yesterday, and she couldn't pass off her duties to other people. Not two days in a row. Deciding she needed a strong cup of coffee, she headed to the kitchen, where Melissa had finished the morning baking and Angie's two oldest employees, Joel and Iris, were getting ready for opening.

Joel had retired from an administrative job two years ago at the age of sixty-two, only to find out he was bored at home and his wife didn't want him there. He was efficient and a good worker and had a penchant for plaid shirts and bow ties.

Like Melissa, Iris Hunnicutt had worked at the café since the beginning. She'd taken the job to supplement her social security. Her permed hair was steel gray in color, and she wore thick-framed eyeglasses.

"Good morning, everyone," Angie said brightly.

They all looked up at her.

"Enjoy your day off, boss?" Joel asked. She wished he wouldn't call her that. He was old enough to be her father. In the beginning, she'd reminded him several times, but gave up after a while.

"Actually, I did," she said honestly. She turned to Melissa. "How was everything here yesterday?"

Melissa hesitated. "It was fine."

"But?" When Melissa didn't say anything and shot a look at Iris, Angie looked over to Iris and said, "But what?"

"Edna Knickerbocker and Edith Bermingham were in the café at the same time."

Angie closed her eyes and groaned. That was a recipe for disaster. The two sisters hadn't spoken in decades. There had been close calls in the past, when one was going into the café and the other was coming out.

"Was it ugly?" she asked.

Melissa winced.

"That bad?"

"All we needed was a boxing ring and a referee," Joel said, trying to inject some humor into the situation.

"There were some harsh words traded loudly," Iris explained. "But Melissa came to the rescue and told them if there was any fighting, they'd be banned from the café."

Angie looked at Melissa, whose cheeks pinkened. "I didn't want it to escalate," Melissa said. "And it worked. They settled down."

"Sounds like a good decision," Angie said. There couldn't be fighting in the café. It was unacceptable; she didn't care that the two women were in their eighties. "We're all set for today?"

They all nodded.

"Good, I'll go open the front doors. Sandwich board ready?" she asked.

Iris nodded. She had the best handwriting of all of them, and she liked to do the boards on her shifts using all the different colors of chalk.

Angie headed out to the main part of the café, where she slipped behind the counter and made herself a double-shot Americano. She skipped the sugar and the cream, needing the perk-up. After she took a couple of tentative sips, she set it down on the counter and went to unlock the front door. Already, a couple waited outside for the café to open. They were regulars, a retired couple who walked the beach in the early morning and ended up at Coffee Girl for breakfast.

"Good morning!" she said with a smile.

"Hey, Angie, we missed you yesterday," said the husband.

"I took the day off."

The couple exchanged a glance.

"It's a miracle!" the wife declared, laughing.

"Come on in for your breakfast," Angie said, holding the door open for them.

Once they were inside, she pulled the sandwich board out front. The air was sharp with damp and the sky began to lighten. Across the street, Java Joe had placed his sandwich board at the curb.

Angie gave it a quick glance and her eyes widened.

Java Joe's, the #1 café in Lavender Bay.

"We'll see about that," Angie said through gritted teeth. She hurried inside, grabbed a piece of chalk, and marched across the street. Quickly, she rewrote part of the sign. She stood back, looked at it, and nodded in satisfaction. *Java Joe's, the #2 café in Lavender Bay.* She glanced toward the windows, wondering if anyone had spied her.

Smirking, she returned to the number one café in Lavender Bay.

The following day, she sat down in her office with Melissa as soon as there was a lull in the lunch crowd.

The other woman took the chair across from Angie's desk. Angie leaned back and said, "Melissa, I've given a lot of thought to what we talked about last week." That was only partially true. She hadn't thought about it until the previous night, when she couldn't sleep despite being tired. And she hoped she'd come up with a solution.

"I'm so glad to hear that," Melissa said.

"First, why don't you tell me some of your ideas regarding baked goods," Angie prompted. She leaned back in her chair and clasped her hands over her abdomen. Her stomach felt queasy, and she wasn't sure if it was because of the biopsy or the fact that she might be ceding some control of her business.

Melissa appeared to be caught off guard. "I've got a ton of them."

Okay, not too many. Stay in your lane, Angie thought.

For the next forty-five minutes, Melissa laid out her ideas, mentioning items Angie had never thought of and some she'd never even heard of. As she spoke, her pale blue eyes were bright with excitement. Angie couldn't help but remember how she'd been the same when she first opened the café. It would be cruel not to let Melissa explore her creative side.

Not everything she mentioned had to do with baked goods; she had other ideas for the café as well. Angie began to feel apprehensive, like her business was being taken out from under her. She forced herself to remain open-minded, but it was proving to be difficult. If Melissa implemented every one of her ideas, would it still be Coffee Girl? Would she recognize the place? The uneasiness grew, but she tamped it down.

Her family's advice came back to her. Maybe they were right. Maybe she tried to micromanage everything too much. Maybe it was time to trust Melissa. She'd certainly been a valued employee. And hadn't she herself needed encouragement when she'd first started out?

When Melissa finished, she smiled and said, "What do you think?"

"You've given me a lot to unpack," Angie started. "And some of your ideas sound interesting."

Melissa waited, but her smile faltered.

At that moment, a genius thought occurred to Angie, and even she became excited.

"Your list is certainly exhaustive, and I'm curious about some of these things. I've got a couple of ideas myself."

Melissa leaned forward on her seat, her many earrings lining her ears in a perfect silver crescent.

"First, I'd like you to start baking some of these things," Angie said, and then clarified, "one at a time. The staff and I will be your tasters. If it passes muster, we'll use it as a 'dessert of the day' and see how the customers like it."

Melissa nodded excitedly.

"From there, we could rotate them using some sort of roster—except for the bestsellers, like the cinnamon rolls with cream cheese frosting and the pastry hearts. Those sell out every day, so they're permanent."

"And what if one of my desserts becomes a bestseller?"

Angie was gracious. "Then that would become part of the permanent collection."

"Thanks, Angie, you have no idea how much I appreciate it."

Handing over a piece of her café didn't feel as awful as Angie had thought it would, and she gave Melissa a genuine smile.

Melissa stood and said, "I'll make something for you tomorrow."

"Whenever you can. It doesn't have to be tomorrow," Angie said.

"I don't mind."

Once she left, Angie closed her eyes and sighed, glad that the conversation was behind her and that Melissa was happy with her suggestions.

By the end of the week, the weather had turned colder, and Lavender Bay experienced the year's first snowfall: light, gentle flakes that melted as soon as they hit the ground. It was a reminder of the holidays coming up.

Thursday afternoon, Angie was in the kitchen, teaching Erica how to make the dough for the cinnamon rolls. On the other side of the room, Melissa was using a kitchen blowtorch to finish browning the tops of the mini lemon meringue pies she'd made. Angie had tasted one and begrudgingly admitted that they were very good, causing Melissa to beam with pride.

Angie's cell phone rang, and she pulled it out of her back pocket and saw Dr. Acker's name on her screen.

She excused herself and stepped out of the noisy kitchen into the back hall, glancing around to make sure no one was in earshot. "Hello?"

"Angie Cook?"

"Yes, that's me."

"I'm calling from Dr. Acker's office. She'd like you to come in tomorrow morning at nine so she can discuss your biopsy results."

Angie swallowed hard. "Sure. I'll be there." When she ended the call, she stared at the blank phone screen, her hands shaking.

She'd hardly be called into the doctor's office to be told everything was fine. That kind of information was usually imparted over the phone.

This was not going to be good news.

Chapter Nine

Angie arrived fifteen minutes early for her appointment with Dr. Acker the following morning. She took a seat in the waiting room after checking in at reception but didn't bother with the magazines on the table. There was no way she'd be able to focus. She hunched forward in her seat, her arms crossed against her belly, bouncing her knee up and down, like she had a restless leg.

The office had already been open an hour, and the waiting room was packed. She hoped it wouldn't be too long; she didn't think her nerves could handle it. She'd been awake most of the night after spending the evening googling everything to do with breast cancer and treatment. She'd gone over every possible scenario in her head. If it was cancer—and to her that seemed a foregone conclusion—what would that entail? Surgery? A lumpectomy? A mastectomy? Chemotherapy and radiation? When would she have time for any of that? Especially the surgery part. That would require hospitalization, which would mean she wouldn't be there to run the café. She'd already taken a day off for the biopsy; she was at her quota for the year.

"Evangeline Cook."

Deep in thought, Angie startled but jumped out of her chair, anxious to get the visit over with and hear the bad news. She followed the nurse and was led to an exam room and asked to take a seat.

With a smile, the nurse said, "Dr. Acker will be with you shortly." And she slipped out of the room, closing the door softly behind her.

It was fifteen minutes before the door burst open and Dr. Acker appeared. She was a middle-aged woman who had about ten years on Angie, and she was slightly breathless. Her dark hair was liberally streaked with gray. Her cheekbones were prominent, and her eyes were dark, and it could be said that she was more handsome than pretty.

"Angie!" her voice reverberated throughout the room, seeming unnaturally loud. She gave her a quick smile and rolled the wheeled stool out from under the counter and sat, pulling a pair of readers from the pocket of her white lab coat and putting them on.

"Okay, I've got the biopsy results." She paused, which irritated Angie. She wished she would get on with it. Dr. Acker clicked a few buttons on the laptop and said, "The lump has come back positive for malignancy."

Angie slumped in the chair, sagging.

Cancer?

How could that be? That was something that happened to other people.

Dr. Acker continued to read the radiologist's impression from the report, but Angie did not hear any of it. Cancer was a big word. Any words coming after it were too small to get around the biggest one of them all.

"What happens now?" Angie asked.

"I'm referring you to an oncologist, and he'll discuss your treatment options."

"Will I have to have a mastectomy?" she asked. She'd only recently turned forty; how could this be?

"The oncologist will go over a treatment plan with you. I won't say what that will be, because I don't want to give you the wrong information."

"Will I have to wait long for an appointment?"

"No, not at all. I'm here if you need me," Dr. Acker said, standing up.

Angie nodded. She was pretty sure that as soon as the doctor left, she'd have all sorts of questions. But at present, her mind was blank.

She followed the doctor out of the room, paid her copay at the desk, and informed the receptionist that she did not need a follow-up appointment.

In a daze, she walked out of the Lavender Bay Medical Center and walked right past the lot where she'd parked her car, not even thinking about it. She kept walking, not seeing anything, and if she had to recall her route later, she would not be able to do so. She headed in the direction of Coffee Girl, but it didn't seem to register with her. All she kept thinking was, "I have cancer." But it wasn't sinking in.

Tom stood out front of Java Joe's with Everett, arms folded over his chest, having a laugh. Everett was smiling. Tom threw his hand up in a wave and said, "Hey, Evangeline."

"Hi, Aunt Angie," Everett called out.

She lifted her hand halfway and said flatly, "Hi, Tom. Hi, Everett."

She walked right past Coffee Girl, unaware of Tom staring after her. She continued walking, ignoring the nippy air and the soft snowflakes that fell in slow motion. Not seeing all the Halloween decorations that adorned the shop fronts. She did not notice Rufus the bloodhound sitting in the front window of her aunt's antique shop, Prime Vintage, or the crunch of leaves beneath her feet. Did not realize she'd left her fleece jacket hanging up in the medical center waiting room.

She came to a stop in front of her mother's house on Heather Lane and stood on the sidewalk, feeling comforted by the familiar. The house was painted the same shade it had always been, for as long as she could remember, and the small front porch was decorated the same way it had been every October in recent years: A tall, rectangular black slate "Welcome" sign leaned against the corner. An autumn wreath in browns, maroons, and oranges hung on the door. And on each step leading up to the porch sat a small orange pumpkin.

The need to see her mother was strong. She supposed no matter how old you got, there were always times when you wanted your mother. Despite her spiky personality, Angie Cook was no exception to this rule. Crossing her arms over her chest and shivering, she walked up the steps to the porch and pushed through the front door.

From the kitchen came the sound of voices. Did her mother have friends over? She hoped not. But someone laughed and instantly, she recognized the voice as belonging to her sister Nadine.

She reached the kitchen doorway and froze in place, unsure how to proceed. Her mother sat at the table with Maureen and Nadine. They couldn't hide the surprise on their faces at seeing her.

"Angie, what are you doing here?" Louise asked, smiling.

"Where's your coat? It's freezing outside." This from Maureen, who would forever be the bossy older sister.

Nadine's oversized dog, Herman, stood from underneath the table, bumping his back on the underside of it as he lumbered out and approached her, tail wagging.

"Hello, handsome," Angie said, lavishing him with affection. His tail wagged harder.

They were all staring at her and finally, Nadine asked softly, "What's wrong?"

Angie started shaking, opened her mouth but no words came out. She didn't know what to say or how she could tell them.

Her mother and her sisters jumped up from the table and circled around her. Even Herman nudged his nose between Nadine and Maureen to get closer to her, sensing her distress.

"What's happened?"

"Are you hurt?"

"Were you in an accident?"

"You're shivering. Let me get you a sweater," Louise said, heading to the front hall closet. She returned with a heavy cardigan and held it out for Angie to slip into. They led her to the table, where Maureen handed her a tissue so she could wipe her nose, which was cold and runny. As she sat, Nadine poured her a cup of coffee and set it down in front of her.

Once they were all seated around the table, Louise said, "Now, tell us what's going on. You're as white as a ghost."

Angie looked around at the concerned faces of her mother and her sisters. "I just found out I have breast cancer," she said.

Her mother blinked and gasped. Nadine threw her hand to her mouth, and Maureen sat there with her mouth hanging open. Then came the volley of questions.

"When?

"How do you know?"

"Are you sure?"

"When did this happen?"

"Have you been to the doctor?"

She nodded, cradling the warm coffee cup in her hands, and slowly poured out the story of her first mammogram, the suspicious mass, and the follow-up biopsy. She concluded with an account of her earlier appointment with Dr. Acker.

"Why didn't you tell us?" Louise asked, her face full of worry.

Angie had anticipated this question. "Because I didn't want you to worry about it until I knew for sure. What if it had turned out to be nothing?"

Nadine began to weep. Maureen reached over and placed a gentle hand on her arm and gave her a reassuring rub.

Although Angie wasn't a crier, she certainly felt like it. Her chin quivered, but she reined it in.

"What happens now?" Maureen asked.

"I'm waiting for an appointment with an oncologist, who'll go over my treatment options."

"Don't wait for it. Call them and see if you can get in as soon as possible," Louise suggested. "In fact, insist on it."

Angie didn't want to be *that* patient.

"Will you have to do chemotherapy and radiation?" Nadine asked, wiping her eyes with a tissue.

Angie shrugged and sipped her coffee. Between the hot coffee and the heavy sweater, she was beginning to warm up. "I won't know anything until I see the oncologist."

"I'm going with you," her mother said.

Before she could protest, Maureen and Nadine chimed in. "Me too."

She held up her hand and said, "Not necessary."

"It's good to have someone with you. At least one person, because you won't remember everything the doctor tells you," Louise said knowingly.

Angie supposed that was true. After all, she couldn't recall anything Dr. Acker had read from the biopsy report earlier that morning.

"It isn't necessary for all of you to go," she said.

But they ignored her.

"I'll drive," Maureen said.

"As soon as you find out the date and time, let us know," Nadine said.

Angie sighed. It was a losing battle. They weren't listening. But she lacked her usual energy to fight with them.

Her mother stood. "I've got some nice salami," she said. "I'll make you a sandwich."

"Mom, you don't have to do that," Angie said. She hadn't eaten her breakfast yet, and salami was her favorite, but she didn't want to see her mother going to any trouble.

But Louise was already pulling a deli bag out of the refrigerator along with a jar of Weber's mustard. It didn't take her long to make a sandwich, and she did a half turn and asked Maureen and Nadine, "Would you like one, girls?"

"Yeah, okay."

"Sure."

In the end Louise made four, one for each of them. Nadine brewed another pot of coffee.

As she finished the last bite of her sandwich, Angie said, "I really have to get back to work."

"Work?" Maureen repeated.

"You can't go back to work," Louise protested.

"Why not?" Angie asked. What was she supposed to do, climb into bed and wait? That wasn't how she operated.

"You should go home and take it easy," Nadine said.

"But I don't feel sick," Angie said. "And I don't know what kind of treatment I'll need, and I'll probably have to take some time off then."

"Did you get things straightened out with Melissa?" Maureen asked.

"I did. We've come to an agreement," Angie said, deciding to keep it vague. But at the same time, in light of her recent news, it was a big relief to think she'd be able to rely on her assistant manager.

"Will you let her utilize her skills?" her mother asked. So much for keeping it vague.

"Yes."

"Good girl," Louise said.

Finally, Angie stood. If she didn't get going soon, she'd never get to Coffee Girl. She was sure her employees were wondering what had become of her.

"I really have to go," she said.

"Okay, but I'll talk to you later," Louise said.

Angie scratched her head. "Can someone drive me back to the doctor's office? I left my car and my jacket there."

Both Maureen and Nadine jumped up.

"I'll do it," Nadine said to Maureen. "You have a work appointment."

Maureen waved her off. "I can be late."

Angie made the final call, or they'd be debating about it all day. "Okay, Maureen, go to work. Nadine, thanks for the ride. Mom, I'll return your sweater later."

"You can keep it," Louise said.

They all walked to the front door.

"Come on, group hug," Louise said with outstretched arms.

Angie rolled her eyes but stepped forward into her mother's warm embrace. Her sisters joined in. They broke away laughing.

Her mother placed her hands on either side of Angie's face and smiled, just like she used to do when she was a kid. "Everything is going to be all right, you'll see."

More than anything, Angie wanted to believe her.

Chapter Ten

"Are you afraid?" Nadine asked when they were alone in the car.

A heavy sigh escaped Angie. "I don't know. I know I should be, but it doesn't seem real. I don't think it's sunk in yet." She looked over at her sister. "Do you know what I mean?" It felt like a bunch of words with the requisite reaction, but she didn't feel sick, and that's what was throwing her off. If she didn't feel ill, how could her body be occupied by something so deadly?

"I do," Nadine said quietly. She turned off Heather Lane, heading for the medical center. "At least you don't have to go through it alone. We'll all be here for you."

But she did have to go through it alone. She knew Nadine meant well, and she was grateful for her family's support. But only she had a foreign invader in her body.

Only she could go through treatment and deal with any unpleasant side effects. It was her future that hung in the balance, no one else's.

"Are you sure you don't want to go home? Let the news settle in?"

Angie shook her head. "That's the last thing I want to do. I don't want to dwell on it. I want to continue living as I have. And work will take my mind off things."

"All right, if you're sure," Nadine said in a tone that suggested she wasn't wholly convinced. She pulled into the parking lot of the medical center a short time later and stopped behind Angie's parked car.

Before she got out, Angie reached over and hugged Nadine, surprising her. Thank goodness for sisters. Aware that she was at risk of getting all teary-eyed, she said in a gruff voice, "I'd like to keep this under my hat for a while."

"Of course."

Angie waved her sister off and went inside to retrieve her jacket, switching it out for her mother's sweater, which she folded and placed on the front seat of her car.

On arriving at Coffee Girl, she glanced around. The lunch rush would begin soon. Melissa was clearing tables and wiping them down. Iris was cashing someone out at the register. Erica was loading fresh trays of pastries and other baked goods into the case.

"Are you all right? We were worried about you," Melissa said, straightening up, spray bottle and damp rag in hand.

At the counter, Iris added, "We've been texting you, but you didn't answer."

"I'm sorry, time got away from me," Angie said glibly. "And I shut my phone off. I'll switch it back on now."

They looked at her but said nothing. Angie never turned off her phone.

Before they could ask any questions, she said, "Any news here?"

Melissa shook her head. "Nope. All is well."

"Busy as usual," Erica said, sticking in another tray of pastry hearts.

"Did anyone feed the cat?" Angie asked.

"I did," Melissa said.

Iris looked at Melissa and lifted her eyebrows. "I fed him, too."

"I fed him when I went on my break," Erica piped in.

Angie laughed. "Okay, he's all set then."

"Ang? I want to show you something," Melissa said. She pulled a piece of paper from her apron pocket and unfolded it. It was a color photo of the cat out back.

The first thing Angie asked was, "How did you get him to sit still for this?"

Melissa laughed. "He had just finished eating."

"That explains it," Angie said with a wry smile.

"Anyway, I was thinking of having a contest to name him, with the customers?"

Angie mulled it over for less than half a second. "That's great. Do what you want, Melissa. Set it up."

Melissa nodded.

"Anything else?" Angie asked.

"Yes, I left a cherry almond cupcake on your desk for you to try."

"They're delicious, I've already had two," Iris said.

"Great, I'll be in my office for a while." Before they could respond, Angie headed to the back.

With a sigh, she sank into her desk chair, leaned back, and stared up at the ceiling. From where she sat, the muted sounds of the café floated around her: cutlery clinking, conversations, and the background music. On a small plate on her desk was a cupcake with pink frosting, topped with a maraschino cherry. Unable to resist, she took a bite. It was delicious, a nice balance of cherry and almond. She finished it and threw the paper wrapper into the bin.

Now what?

Remembering her phone, she pulled it out of her purse and powered it up. She gave Debbie a quick ring and when it went to voicemail, she left a message asking her to give her a call when she got the chance. She needed to call her mother and Maureen and remind them that she didn't want anyone to know yet. But her phone started ringing before she could make those calls. Aunt Gail's name flashed across the screen. Her heart sank. She could probably forget about calling her mother.

"That was fast," she muttered before answering the call with a "Hello?"

"Honey, it's Aunt Gail. I just spoke to your mother. She told me your news. I can't believe it. I'm so sorry. Is there anything I can do?"

"No. I'll know more when I see the oncologist."

"Your mother could have knocked me over with a feather."

"You and me both," Angie said, and relayed all that had happened so far.

"This is awful." Her aunt made some *tsk-tsk* noises and asked again, "What can I do?"

"Nothing. I'm sure Mom will keep you informed." Louise and Gail spoke every day, sometimes multiple times.

"You know she will. Okay, call me if you need anything. I'll be praying for you."

"Thanks, Aunt Gail, I appreciate it."

She had no sooner hung up than her phone started ringing again. Her younger sister, DeeDee, was calling now. Angie grumbled; her mother must be telling everyone they knew.

"Hi, DeeDee."

DeeDee, always one for dramatics, was loud, and Angie had to hold the phone away from her ear.

"Mom called me. She said you have breast cancer! Oh my God! How did this happen? I'll be home on the next flight—"

Angie cut her off. "Whoa, whoa! You do not need to come home."

"That's what Mom said. But I think I should."

"Please don't do that, DeeDee," Angie said firmly.

"But you're sick. I want to see you."

Angie sighed. DeeDee hadn't been home in a while, and Angie didn't want this to be the reason she finally decided to make the trip. "No, stay put. I don't feel sick. I'm still working."

"You are? Shouldn't you be home in bed?"

"No, that's the last place I need to be."

"What happened?"

Again, Angie relayed the story, thinking if she had to tell it one more time that day she was going to lose her temper. But she remembered how sensitive her younger sister could be. There was less than two years between them, but they were as different as night and day.

"That's awful. I wish there was something I could do," DeeDee lamented. "I feel so helpless."

"I know what you mean," Angie said honestly. Already tired of the subject of her health, she asked, "How are you?"

They texted from time to time, but they led very different lives, and she didn't think any of her sisters spoke with DeeDee regularly.

"Fine."

"Are you at work?" Angie asked.

"I usually don't go into rehearsals until the afternoon, but the latest play I was in was canceled due to poor ticket sales." DeeDee's voice was hard to read.

"I'm sorry to hear that."

"That's how it goes."

They spoke for a few more minutes until Angie spotted Melissa standing in the doorway and said she had to go.

"All right, Ang, take care of yourself," DeeDee said before she hung up.

Angie looked up to Melissa, who wore a worried expression. "Everything all right?"

"I just spoke to your mom," Melissa said.

Mom! Angie leaned forward, putting her head in her hands and brushing her hair back. Before Melissa could say anything else, she said, "I'm fine. I feel fine. And I don't know yet what the next steps are going to be."

"Is there anything I can do?"

"Not at the moment," Angie said, softening her tone. Her frustration with her mother couldn't be taken out on Melissa. "You're already doing enough."

"Okay. But you know—"

"Yes, I do know, if I need anything, I only have to ask. I appreciate it." With a nod toward the front of the café, Angie asked, "Does everyone else know?"

Melissa grimaced. "Yes, I'm afraid so."

Defeated, Angie said, "That's all right. They were bound to find out sooner or later."

"I've got everything under control out front if you want to hang out here a little longer."

"Thanks. What time are you here until?"

"Four, but I can stay late," Melissa said.

"Nope, I'll be fine." The café served coffee, breakfast, and lunch. No dinner. By that time, things would be winding down and she'd be able to handle it.

"Are you sure?"

"I am, thanks." Again, Angie thought how grateful she was for Melissa. "That cupcake was delicious, by the way."

"Thanks, Ang."

Melissa disappeared when Angie's phone started ringing again with a call from Debbie.

"Have you heard about your biopsy?" was the first question Debbie asked.

Angie filled her in, and her friend's response was, "Oh, poop."

Esther poked her head around Angie's office door.

"Deb, I'll call you tonight," Angie said. "Esther's here." She hung up and set her phone down on the desk.

"Hey, I just spoke to my mom," Esther started, stepping into the office and plopping down in the chair.

Angie rattled off a list of preemptive answers: "I'm fine. I don't need anything. I don't feel sick. I don't know what my treatment plan is going to be. I haven't seen the oncologist, and I don't have an appointment yet."

Esther snorted, her grin wide. Then she put her hands up as if to say *what can you do?* "You know how Mom and Aunt Louise are. The two of them are together right now—my mom even closed her shop—so they can put together a roster of rides for you."

"A roster of rides?"

"Yep. You know, if you need rides to chemotherapy or radiation."

Angie blinked in surprise. "I don't even know if I'm doing those things yet."

Esther laughed. "As I said, you know how they are. They're like two battle generals, getting ready for the invasion of Germany."

"I think they're getting ahead of themselves."

"Of course they are, but they have to feel like they're doing something. Or helping."

"I wish they wouldn't help me so much," Angie griped.

Esther laughed and stood. "Anyway, I just wanted to drop in. Call me if you need anything. Any time, day or night."

"I know, Esther, and I appreciate it," Angie said.

Esther said her goodbyes and disappeared. For a full five minutes Angie's phone didn't ring, and no one showed up in her office. She reveled in the peace and quiet.

She turned her phone off to avoid any further calls and decided to stay behind the scenes in the kitchen for the rest of the day, getting things ready for tomorrow's baking.

A few minutes after six, after all her employees had gone home, she turned the lock on the door, savoring the end-of-day stillness of the restaurant. She was glad to be alone. All afternoon, Erica and Iris had treated her as if she were an invalid, cutting her off with variations on "I'll do that. You sit down." Finally, she'd had to call an impromptu meeting where she advised them that she was perfectly fine to continue as is and that if she needed help, she would ask. Their looks were unsure, but her tone convinced them to back off.

Erica had mopped the floor before she left, and now that it was mostly dry, Angie began unloading the chairs from the tables. There was a knock on the front window, and she looked up to see Tom on the other side.

"Watch the floor, it's wet in some places," she said as she let him in.

"Gotcha."

Despite the frosty late-October air, he wore only a long-sleeved thermal top. Black, of course.

"Two questions," she said. "First, do you not own a coat?"

He squinted as if giving it serious thought and finally said, "Yes, I have a coat at home."

She rolled her eyes. "Second question: do you ever wear anything other than black?"

"Black's my favorite color."

She shook her head. "Figures. The absence of light. The Dark Lord of Lavender Bay."

Laughter erupted from him and rumbled through the empty café.

Angie resumed pulling the chairs down off the tables. Tom joined her, careful to avoid the odd wet spot on the floor.

"I have a question of my own," he said as he took down the last chair.

She looked everywhere but at Tom. She didn't think she could bear it if she saw pity in his eyes.

"Evangeline," he said.

Finally, she met his gaze. There was no pity there, only concern. She could deal with that. After all, she'd been dealing with it all day.

"There's a rumor going around that you've got breast cancer," he said.

There. He'd said it. It was out in the open.

"That is not a rumor," she said.

"I'm very sorry to hear that." He took a step closer to her. "How are you holding up?"

"I'm all right," she admitted. "It's come as a shock."

"I can imagine. What's the plan?"

"I don't know yet. Waiting now for an appointment with the oncologist."

"If anyone can beat this, it's you," he said.

"I appreciate that."

"If you need a ride to your appointment, I'd be happy to take you and go with you," he said.

"It's covered, Tom, but thanks anyway. Most of my family are insisting on going with me and to be honest, I don't think there'll be room in the car."

He let out a bark of laughter. That brought a smile to her face. The first real one of the day.

"But I promise, if I need anything, I will call you," she said.

"Good," he said softly. He pulled out his phone. "Give me your number."

She rattled it off, and he inputted it into his phone. "I'll send you a text so you'll have mine," he said.

She tilted her head to one side. "Does that make us friends then?"

With a smile, he said, "We've always been friends, Evangeline."

As she locked up, she watched him walk across the street to Java Joe's, thinking she was glad to have a friend like him.

Chapter Eleven

When she first woke the following morning, all was right with the world as far as Angie was concerned. But within seconds of opening her eyes, the harsh reality that had become her life came to the forefront.

Cancer.

She still couldn't believe it. She felt removed from the idea and truth of it, as if she were on the outside of her body, looking in, a mere spectator of what was happening to her.

She went about getting ready for work, her mind sluggish and unable to keep straight what she had to do first when she got to the café. It was as if her brain was at full capacity and could not take on one more thing to think about.

Melissa had the four a.m. start that day, and Angie was glad as she'd tossed and turned for a while last night before finally falling into a deep sleep. Once dressed, she didn't linger, and headed to work.

The café was half full when she arrived. She peered out through the window in the stainless-steel butler door that separated the kitchen from the restaurant, spotting some of her regulars along with a few unfamiliar faces. A shoebox wrapped in tissue paper stood on the counter next to an eight-by-ten framed photo of the cat. As Angie watched, a customer approached the counter, filled out a slip of paper, and shoved it into the wide slot cut into the top of the box.

Angie had a quick chat with Melissa and the rest of her staff, making sure they were all apprised of her diagnosis. Joel seemed to be at a loss for words. His bow tie was crooked, but she said nothing. Before she retreated to her office, she double-checked the glass case and did a quick walk through the floor, greeting her customers and stopping at tables to say hello.

The quiet sanctuary of her office was soon interrupted by the appearance of Edna Knickerbocker, who strode in and sat in one of the chairs before Angie could even say hello. For as long as anyone could remember, Edna had been known as "Mrs." Knickerbocker, despite never having been married. Angie didn't know the genesis of that and decided it was information not important enough for her to pursue.

"Angie, I heard your terrible news, and I had to come back and say something," Edna started. She set a brown paper bag at her feet and clutched her boxy navy handbag in her lap. "Now, don't despair. Did you know my mother had breast cancer when she was sixty-three? She had her breast lopped off"—here Angie arched an eyebrow at Edna's stark delivery—"and the chemo made her sicker than a dog, but she lived twenty years after all that. And it wasn't cancer that got her in the end. It was pneumonia."

Somewhere in that revelation, Angie was sure there was a nugget of encouragement, but she'd have to sift through to find it.

"Anyway," Edna said, "Mother did well, and that was more than fifty years ago, when they didn't have the treatments and the advances they have today."

"That's true."

"And look, if you have to have your boob removed, I think I may still have some of my mother's mastectomy bras up in the attic." Edna glanced at Angie's chest. "What are you, a double-D?"

This had morphed into one bizarre conversation. Why had Edna kept her mother's custom-made bras? "I'm a C, actually."

Edna frowned. "Are you sure? You look bigger than a C." She peered again at Angie. "Which side?"

"Left side."

"Drat! Those bras won't work for you. Mother's right breast was the one that had cancer."

"It just wasn't meant to be," Angie said smoothly.

Edna pulled something out of a brown paper bag and chuckled. "Take a look at this. It's my neighbor Hal's birthday today and I got him a little gift."

Angie took the small plastic packet that housed two Q-tips. The label read *Beginner Weights*. She burst out laughing. "Oh, that's good."

"You'll need a sense of humor, dear. We all do," Edna said sagely.

Angie sighed. "That's for sure."

Edna stood. "Anyway, what I'm trying to say is, chin up. You got this."

"I appreciate that, Mrs. Knickerbocker," Angie said honestly, thinking it was kind of Edna to make the time to stop in.

Edna looped the short handle of her handbag over her forearm. "Ta-ta," she said, and made her exit.

Chin up. Was that all it took to beat cancer? Angie wondered.

God, she hoped so.

Chapter Twelve

The oncologist, Dr. Meskal, was a tall, slender man with gray hair and gray eyes. He did not mince words but took time to answer all their questions. Angie's mother and sisters had accompanied her to the appointment, insisting on going in with her to see the doctor. One of the nurses had to bring extra chairs into the exam room. Maureen brought a small steno notepad and took copious notes. It was just as well, as Angie would only remember half of what he told her. Luckily, between her mother and Maureen and Nadine, they asked all the questions, even ones Angie hadn't thought of. Maybe they were right; it wouldn't have been a good idea to go in there alone.

First there would be a lumpectomy, along with a sentinel biopsy of local lymph nodes to see if the cancer had spread. The results of that sentinel biopsy would determine the course of treatment and whether or not she'd need both chemotherapy and radiation.

The visit had been sobering. Somehow the discussion of surgery, chemotherapy, and radiation had brought it all home. That period between her appointment with Dr. Acker and her appointment with Dr. Meskal had been a time of limbo, but now that she had a date for surgery—a lumpectomy—suddenly, things felt very real.

Her mother and sisters had only dropped her off at home in the last half hour, and as she went over the details of the oncologist visit in her mind, she acknowledged something she'd refused to think about since she'd received her diagnosis: She might die from this. Only forty, this might be the end of the road for her. Coffee Girl, everything she'd worked for, might have been for nothing if she wasn't around to see it.

What else did she have to show for her life, other than a successful business? Coffee Girl was now a staple in Lavender Bay, but it had come at the cost of any kind of personal life. Nearing forty, children did not seem to be in the cards, more so now with her recent diagnosis.

She didn't travel, and other than her sisters, cousins, and Debbie, she didn't really see that many people. She hadn't taken a vacation where she actually left Lavender Bay since before she opened the café.

Had she missed out? In being so consumed by her business, had life passed her by? Should she have had more balance? She honestly didn't know. There was no regret about the time she'd spent building up her business. But did she regret not doing other things? She wasn't sure.

Her thoughts were interrupted by the doorbell ringing. She frowned. Because she was so rarely home, visitors hardly ever graced her doorstep.

Tom stood on the porch, holding a Dutch oven in his hands and a box of Premium saltine crackers beneath his arm. Before she could say anything, he said, "Melissa told me you were home."

She stepped back to let him in.

"I brought you some of my world-famous chicken noodle soup," he said.

"World-famous?"

"Yes, in the world of Lavender Bay."

"I'm glad you clarified that." She led him toward the kitchen. "But you didn't have to bring anything."

"Yes I did. Besides, you won't get soup that tastes better than this."

"Actually, your timing is perfect. I was just thinking about what I wanted for lunch."

"Good." He set the pot on the stove and turned on the burner.

"Can I get you something to drink?" she asked. "Tea, coffee?"

"Nah, I'm good, I'm drinking that stuff all day long at work."

Angie laughed. "Yeah, me too."

He leaned against the counter, folded his arms across his chest, and crossed his ankles, a pose that was becoming familiar to her. She sat at the kitchen table and crossed her legs.

"I wanted to see how you made out today with the oncologist," he said. "I'm sorry, I didn't want to wait."

"It's all right. I planned to call you anyway, I was only sitting here gathering my thoughts." She filled him in on what Dr. Meskal had told her.

He nodded. "Has the surgery been scheduled?"

"Yes. Ten days."

"Are you scared?"

"I don't know what I am," she admitted.

"Understandable. It's a lot to take in all at once."

"Yes."

She looked over toward the pot on the stove. The soup bubbled and steam rose from it, filling her kitchen with a rich herby aroma "Chicken noodle, huh?"

"Smells great, doesn't it," he said. His self-assuredness was attractive.

"Let's see if it's as good as you say it is. Will you join me?" she asked, standing from the table.

"Sure," he said.

Angie pulled down two bowls and set them on the counter next to the stove. From a drawer, she grabbed a ladle and handed it to Tom, who used it to dish out the soup. She pulled a sleeve of crackers out of the box and set it in the middle of the table with the butter dish, then gathered spoons and knives. Tom carried over two steaming bowls and joined her at the table. Angie's stomach growled in anticipation.

She spooned up some soup, noting the celery, carrots, noodles, and generous pieces of tender chicken. She blew on the spoon to cool it down before slipping it into her mouth.

The soup was delicious. She took a second spoonful, then a third, trying to figure out that mystery spice.

"This is probably the best soup I've ever had," she said.

Tom grinned. "I told you."

"What's your secret ingredient?"

"Now if I tell you, it won't be secret anymore," he said.

"If you told me, you'd have to kill me? Ha-ha."

"Nah, you're too pretty to kill."

Her spoon froze halfway to her mouth. Had he just said she was pretty? He must have, because he coughed to cover up that slip.

This was interesting.

Glossing over it, she asked, "Do you serve this at Java Joe's?" She should really go across the street and try some of the items on his menu if the soup was anything to go by.

"No, it's a family recipe from my grandmother, who was Polish. She was a great cook. She used to watch my brother and me after school until my parents got home from work. We helped her with a lot of her cooking."

They drifted onto the pleasant subject of grandparents, and over a second bowl of soup, she shared with him how her grandparents had lived with them. After he left, she thought it had been a pleasant way to pass the time: eating good soup and remembering important people.

Chapter Thirteen

It was still dark outside when Angie's alarm went off. Not that she'd needed it; she'd been awake all night, thinking about the lumpectomy scheduled for that morning. Tired and cold, she got out of bed and padded to the bathroom, where she took a shower. As she scrubbed, she took one last look at her breast, sucking in a deep breath, wondering how different it would look afterward.

Despite these worrisome thoughts, the café came to mind. Her staff were aware of her procedure this morning. They did not expect her to make an appearance today, and they'd reassured her several times that they would look after the cat. Debbie had offered to take him home with her, but Angie had refused, thinking it would be too much of a change for him.

There was no need to make breakfast or even a cup of coffee because she'd been instructed to fast since the night before. And now that she couldn't have anything, she craved a meal. *Oh well*, she thought, *I'll be able to eat something later.*

Maureen knocked on the side door and walked in. Angie pulled her coat from the hall closet.

"Ready?" Maureen asked softly. She was similarly bundled up. They'd had frost overnight.

"As ready as I'm going to be."

"Is that your bag for the hospital?" Maureen asked, indicating the floral bag parked by the door.

Angie nodded and Maureen picked it up. "Come on, Ang. Mom and Nadine are in the car."

Her mother and her sisters had all decided to go with her, and she had protested and told them she could manage on her own. They'd been horrified at the suggestion. They made such a stink that she kept her mouth shut and didn't say another word about it. But now that the day had arrived, she was relieved that she wasn't alone.

She got into the passenger seat in the front, as her mother and Nadine were in the back. A blast of hot air from the heater greeted her. She shivered in her seat, her hunger adding to the feeling of being cold.

In the back seat, Louise leaned forward, the comforting scent of her perfume, Amazing Grace, wafting into the front. "All set?" she asked softly.

"I am." Angie was ready. She wanted it over with.

The night sky had morphed into a dark gray. As Maureen reversed out of the driveway, Angie's phone pinged. The screen illuminated her side of the car. It was an incoming text from Tom.

Best of luck today.

Smiling, Angie texted back: *Tx*.

Behind her, Nadine had leaned forward and peered over her shoulder. "How romantic!" she said.

"Nadine!" Angie scolded, hiding her phone screen against her chest.

But her older sister proceeded to tell Louise and Maureen about the text from Tom.

"That *is* romantic," Maureen said.

"He seems like a nice man," Louise added.

Angie kept her feelings on that to herself, unsure of what they were.

The remainder of the drive to the hospital was quiet. Occasionally, the silence was punctuated by a comment about the frost, the lack of traffic, how they'd slept, what kind of candy they were passing out at Halloween, and what was new at their homes: innocuous, everyday conversation that circled around, without ever touching, the purpose of them all being together that morning.

The closer they got to the hospital, the more Angie's heart rate accelerated. She was practically shaking by the time Maureen pulled into the parking lot.

The four of them walked silently through the main entrance, Louise's arm linked through Angie's. First stop was the admissions department. Despite the early hour, the hospital was bustling and well lit, the overhead fluorescent lighting harsh. Angie filled out the forms and then signed all the paperwork that had been pushed toward her. The admissions officer gave her directions for where to proceed. They took the elevator to the third floor, where the surgical suites were. Angie checked in at the desk, and the nurse stationed there smiled and led her to a small room, telling her to remove her clothing and put on the hospital gown.

Having done as instructed, she poked her head out into the hallway, where her mother and sisters were waiting. "All clear," she said.

Her mother and sisters filed in.

"Let me tie that in the back for you," Maureen said. Angie turned around, and her sister tied the straps. Shivering, she pulled on her fleece bathrobe over the hospital gown.

She hopped up onto the bed. Maureen directed their mother to a chair. She and Nadine stood on the other side of the bed. The conversation was hushed and solemn. Angie couldn't focus, and her attention jumped back and forth between the conversation around her and the multitude of thoughts swirling around in her mind. *Am I making a mistake? Maybe I should get up and go home.*

To distract herself, she turned her thoughts to work.

Melissa would be at the café by now, and she sent her a text reminding her, yet again, to feed the cat. The box on the counter asking patrons to suggest a name for him was getting pretty full. At the end of the week, she'd go through all of them and pick the one that best suited the stray. The winner would receive a twenty-five-dollar gift card to the café.

Two nurses walked in, one carrying a chart. Both wore scrubs, one set bearing a holiday motif of pumpkins and autumn leaves, the other the standard-issue medical blue.

The younger nurse with the swinging ponytail and the holiday scrubs asked, "Evangeline Cook?"

"That's me."

The nurse with the chart stood on one side, and the other nurse raised Angie's wrist and read off the patient number from her hospital band.

"That's correct. All right, we're going to take you over to the surgical suite. The surgeon will speak to you before the procedure."

Angie nodded, not sure a response was required.

To her mother and sisters, the nurse said, "I'll show you where you can wait."

"How long will it take?" Louise asked.

"About one to two hours," the nurse replied. "Once Evangeline's out of recovery and her vital signs are stable, she can go home."

Home. Angie focused on that.

Her sisters crowded around the head of the bed. Maureen and Nadine hugged her first, while her mother held her hand.

"We'll be praying for you," Nadine whispered.

"Thanks, I need all the help I can get," Angie said.

When her sisters pulled away, her mother placed a hand on the side of Angie's face. She bent and pressed her cheek against Angie's and whispered, "Oh, my sweet girl, I wish you didn't have to go through this." Angie felt wetness on her face, and she realized her mother was crying.

"Me too, Mom," she whispered with a wobble in her voice.

The gurney she was on was rolled out of the room, and she held on to her mother's hand as long as she could, afraid to let go.

Chapter Fourteen

Ten days later, her mother and her sisters accompanied Angie to her follow-up appointment with the oncologist. Again, the nurse had to bring in two extra chairs. Angie and her mother sat directly across from the doctor's desk, and Maureen and Nadine sat behind them. The arrangement reminded Angie of theater seating.

Dr. Meskal walked in and said, "Good morning."

They all murmured "Good morning" in response. Angie tried to read his expression, but it was neutral. He seemed his usual self. It was maddening.

At his request, she hopped up on the examination table so he could take a look at her lumpectomy incision. Her sisters and mother made to leave, but she waved them off.

"Any redness or drainage?" he asked.

She shook her head, and he declared, "It's healing nicely."

The bruising had faded, but she'd been left with a dent along the side of her breast. It was uncomfortable to look at the disfigurement. When looking in the mirror, she kept her gaze planted firmly on her face. Hopefully, as time went on, she'd get used to the new landscape of her body.

"Take a seat, Angie," the doctor said.

Quickly, she rehooked the front closure of her bra and pulled her turtleneck over her head, ignoring the resulting static in her hair. She returned to her seat next to her mother.

Louise reached over and held out her hand. Angie took hold of it, likening it to an anchor that moored a boat.

Dr. Meskal sat down, pulled his chair close to his desk, and opened her chart. There was no preamble. "As you might remember, we did a sentinel biopsy in conjunction with the lumpectomy."

Louise gave Angie's hand a gentle squeeze.

The doctor continued. "Unfortunately, one lymph node tested positive for malignancy."

Angie drew in a sharp breath. Her mother looked straight ahead. Behind her, Nadine whispered, "Oh no." Dr. Meskal continued to speak, but Angie felt as if she were at the other end of a long tunnel. She heard words like chemotherapy and radiation, but all the other words fell away. She hoped her mother and sisters were paying attention.

Upon leaving, she was given a folder of pertinent information. She didn't bother opening it. Dazed, she let herself be led like a child to the parking lot, her mother's arm linked through her own. Her mother and sisters remained subdued as they all returned to Louise's house. They ordered Chinese takeout for dinner, but Angie had no appetite.

Maureen leafed through the folder from the oncologist's office as she ate. "You should go through this, Ang. There's a lot of information in here. What to expect during radiation and chemotherapy. Some things you can do for yourself. Also, there's a support group that meets every Wednesday evening at the hospital."

"That might be a good idea," Louise said. "Meet with other people who are going through the same thing."

Angie couldn't think of anything more depressing. Sitting around with a bunch of cancer patients. No thanks. She said instead, "Did anyone pay any attention to when I'm supposed to start treatment? Because I didn't get that part." Overwhelming anxiety caused her voice to rise in pitch and volume. "I should have paid more attention."

Louise, Maureen and Nadine were immediately at her side, reassuring her.

"I took notes," Maureen said. "Arrangements are being made and you'll be notified. Probably in the next week or two."

"That soon? I'm not ready . . ." Angie's voice trailed off. There were a million and one things to be done at the café.

"You have no choice, honey," Louise said solemnly.

"It's a lot to take on," Nadine added. "You're feeling overwhelmed right now, which is understandable."

"It's going to be all right," Louise said.

Was it? It didn't feel like it was. Everything felt far from all right. Angie's gaze bounced around the room, taking in everything that was familiar, trying to focus on one thing but unable to settle.

She voiced the question that had filled her mind on the drive home. "How am I going to work and do treatment?"

Her mother and her sisters exchanged a glance.

The food they'd ordered was left half eaten, plates half full.

"Honey," Louise said, "your health and this treatment have to come first, above everything else. Melissa can run the café."

Angie groaned.

"Mom's right," Maureen added. "Nothing in your life is more important right now than beating this."

"Angie, I know it's dire," Nadine said, "but you're tough."

"Am I?" This wasn't a business setback or a failed marriage, this was a death threat. Suddenly, Angie stood up from her chair, her napkin falling to the floor.

"Where are you going?" Maureen asked.

"I want to go home," Angie replied.

"Why don't you stay here overnight?" her mother said. Angie looked at her. Her poor mother. She was pale. She'd aged considerably in the last few weeks.

Angie shook her head. "Mom, there will be plenty of times in the future when I'll need to stay over." Tears pooled in her eyes. "I'd like to be alone."

Maureen put an arm around her. "All right, Ang. I'll drive you home."

"Thanks." She hugged her mother and Nadine, and her mother held her for a few extra seconds.

Maureen pulled into Angie's driveway. "Do you want me to come in with you?" she asked. "We could watch a movie or something or hang out."

Angie shook her head. "I appreciate it, but I need to be alone for a while."

Her sister nodded. "I understand."

As Angie got out of the car, Maureen said, "Call me any time, for anything you need."

"Thanks, Maureen."

"Hold on, Angie. You forgot this." Maureen held out the folder to her.

"Thanks."

Angie reached the side door of her house and waved to her sister, who returned the wave before driving off. She went inside and locked up for the night, dropping the folder on the kitchen table and making her way to her bedroom, flipping on lights as she went.

She changed into her pajamas and heavy robe and padded to the living room, where she sat down on the sofa in darkness. After a while, she picked up her phone and called Tom to fill him in. He'd stopped in the café earlier that day and asked her to call him after her follow-up meeting with the doctor. When she told him that she'd need both chemotherapy and radiation, he said, "Best to throw everything at it."

"I guess."

"Where are you?"

"I'm home."

"Are you alone?"

"Yes," she said.

"Want company?"

She smiled. "I appreciate it but no. I need some time alone."

"Understood."

They made small talk for a few more minutes before hanging up.

Her life; her work; the café, which she loved more than anything; everything was going to change. Nothing would ever be the same. And she had no control over this. She was livid. The world she'd carefully constructed over the last decade was under threat. And her own life hung in the balance.

She clenched her fists and ground her teeth to stifle a scream.

Chapter Fifteen

The following morning, Angie returned to work, eager to get started. Before she did anything, she went out back and checked on the cat. He stepped out from behind the dumpster and meowed.

"Good morning," she said to him. "Soon, you'll have a name other than 'Cat.'" She fed him and went back inside, giving her hands a good wash.

As was now the habit, she checked Java Joe's sandwich board parked outside his café. It read: *Great minds drink coffee.*

Seeing that her own sandwich board was not curbside yet, she went inside, grabbed a piece of colored chalk, and scribbled on her board before dragging it outside. *Greater minds drink their coffee at Coffee Girl.*

Satisfied, she marched back inside. First, she met with Melissa privately back in her office. Then she had an impromptu meeting with her employees before the morning rush and told them of her need to go for treatment soon. Her plan, she told them, was to be at the café as much as she could and for as long as she could, but for the most part, Melissa would be in charge, and any issues should be addressed to her.

She parked herself behind the counter with Joel, wanting her customers to see her front and center, as she was pretty sure everyone in town was now aware of her cancer diagnosis. Making coffee and serving her customers put her in her element and improved her mood. She noticed the shoebox was beginning to fill with ballots. The cat-naming contest would run until a few days before Christmas. Going through those suggestions would be fun, and she was looking forward to it. Until then, the stray would be known as "Cat."

Grace Gibson, the town's oldest resident and heiress to the Gibson's Grape Jelly fortune, approached the counter and ordered a pear tea and a scone. The woman was still able to get around town despite being almost one hundred years old. With her was her companion,

Ada, who ordered a mocha and a triple-threat chocolate muffin. Ada, a woman in her seventies with dyed auburn hair and dark eyes, had been with Grace for as long as anyone could remember. Her mother had worked alongside Grace when they were Red Cross workers during World War II. Grace was a sight to behold in her fuchsia-colored winter jacket, her jaunty pale pink knit cap, and her red slacks.

"How are you doing, Angie?" Grace asked, her facial features contorted with concern.

"I'm okay," Angie said truthfully.

"Have you started treatment yet?"

"Soon. Chemo and radiation," she told her.

"Well, you're a strong person, and that will serve you well," Grace said.

"Thanks."

Grace looked at Ada. "Don't you agree?"

"I do," Ada said.

Angie hoped if she made it to Grace's age, she'd look as good. Grace would be one hundred next year, and plans were afoot to have a big birthday bash. And because the people of Lavender Bay couldn't keep a secret to save their lives, she was pretty sure that Grace had already gotten wind of it. Knowing her, she'd go along with it and act surprised all the same.

Grace and Ada stepped away from the counter and the next customer stepped up. With a smile, Angie said, "Can I help you?"

There was no place she'd rather be than here.

Chapter Sixteen

Six cycles of chemotherapy at three-week intervals was scheduled, to be followed by thirty radiation treatments. Angie had no idea what to expect but wanted it started and over with. It was a shame that she'd be going through this during the holidays, but there was nothing that could be done about that. Cancer did not defer to Thanksgiving and Christmas.

And true to form, her mother, with Aunt Gail's help, had arranged Angie's transportation for the first week and promised to set her up for the rest of the sessions as well.

Debbie was her first driver on Monday morning. She was all bundled up and had a car blanket waiting on the passenger seat.

"In case you're cold," she explained when Angie got into the car.

"Thanks."

For the first week of November, it was colder than usual, and there was a pretty dusting of snow on the ground. Angie was quiet on her side of the car.

"Are you nervous?" Debbie asked.

"A little bit. I just want to get the first session over with. And I'm worried about the cat." Once she started chemo, she'd have to keep her distance from him. Apparently, chemo wreaked havoc on your immune system.

"Angie, where'd you go?" Debbie asked. "You just zoned out on me."

"Sorry, just thinking," she said, glancing out her window. Some houses already had their Christmas decorations up and they hadn't even had their Thanksgiving dinner yet.

"About what?"

Angie explained the dilemma about the cat.

"I can understand your concern. You don't want to get too near him. You don't know what he might have,"

Debbie said. "But Melissa and Iris will make sure he gets fed."

As they pulled into the hospital parking lot, Debbie said, "Maureen is picking you up, so make sure you text her when you're finished." Apparently, everyone and their brother had a copy of the roster.

She pulled up to the main entrance. "All right, good luck, Ang."

"Thanks, Deb. I'll talk to you later."

"Send me a text. I know you'll have a lot of people to call."

Angie laughed. "That's for sure. Thanks."

She waved her friend off and headed into the hospital. She took a deep breath, then wandered through the lobby to the bank of elevators.

The chemotherapy infusion lab was in a large room. Recliners were placed in a line against the wall with infusion stands behind them. The chairs were upholstered in a hospital-grade vinyl material that could easily be wiped down.

She was directed to a seat by a friendly nurse. A few days ago, a mediport had been implanted just below her collarbone for the chemotherapy. There was some apprehension when the infusion started. She took some deep breaths and closed her eyes.

This is it.

It was an all-day affair, like putting in a shift. She'd brought some magazines to read and had downloaded some music on her phone. Although she did text her staff occasionally, she tried to back off and not bother them too much.

When the infusion was complete, Angie was surprised that she felt okay. Slightly queasy but other than that, she didn't feel as bad as she thought she would. Of course, she'd had no idea what to expect, but she'd known it wouldn't be pleasant. The nurse told her that the next day might be the worst day of it: nausea or fatigue or weakness. Or all three.

"How are you feeling?" was Maureen's first question when Angie slid into her passenger seat. Angie hoped that wouldn't be the script every time she climbed into someone's car.

"I wish it was next year," she said.

"I'll give you a piece of advice that Everett's counselors have given him," Maureen said as she pulled away from the curb. "Take it one day at a time. Don't look too far ahead."

"I know."

"Just get through the day in front of you," Maureen reiterated.

"Easier said than done."

"I know. But we're all here for you."

"And I appreciate it," Angie said truthfully. She could not begin to imagine going through something as epic as this alone, without any support. She shuddered at the thought.

As they pulled out onto the main highway, Maureen said, "Home?"

Angie shook her head. "No, I'll go to the café."

"Do you think that's a good idea?" Maureen asked, worry etched along her forehead. It made Angie feel like she was five years old again and her sister was leading her by the hand to the kindergarten classroom.

Angie tried brushing her off with a laugh. "I won't know until I get there."

"Why don't you go to Mom's if you don't want to go home."

Angie sighed. She didn't want to argue with her sister. "I want to go into work while I still feel able for it. For a little while, while I feel okay."

"That's understandable," Maureen said. She offered no more protests and headed in the direction of Coffee Girl. "But if you start feeling unwell, you'll go home?"

"I will. I promise."

As Maureen turned the corner onto Main Street, she said, "Mom wants you to move in with her for the time being."

"That's good of her, but I prefer to be in my own home," Angie said.

"I get that, but you know how she is. She wants to feel like she's doing something."

"She's already doing a lot for me," Angie said. "And I'm grateful."

Her mother had stopped over on the weekend and done two loads of laundry, the ensuing ironing, and a little cleaning, despite Angie's protests. The woman was almost seventy years old; Angie didn't expect her to clean up after her or take on any extra work just because of this cancer diagnosis.

"It must be hard for her," Maureen said. "As a mother, it's hard to watch your children suffer." Angie knew her sister spoke from personal experience after everything she'd been through with Everett and his drug addiction.

"Luckily, I'm not suffering," Angie said. *Yet.* Although the scar on her breast brought home to her how serious her diagnosis was, she was no longer in that surreal phase of disbelief. Since the surgery, she felt like she had cancer. Like she had a serious health problem.

As they pulled up behind Coffee Girl, Maureen said, "What I mean is that you should let Mom help you as much as she can. It will take her mind off it and make her feel useful."

"Noted," Angie said, opening the car door. "Thanks again, Maureen."

Maureen leaned over the console between the two seats. "Did Mom give you a copy of the driving roster?"

"She did," Angie said, trying not to think about the grueling half year ahead of her.

"Good. You're all set then."

"I am. Thanks, Maureen."

She waved her sister off and approached the back door, looking for the stray cat, but he was nowhere to be seen.

It wasn't yet time for dinner, so he might be off gallivanting. She went inside, thinking he'd be back later. He never missed a meal.

She made her way to the kitchen, feeling relief in being back in her own café. This was home. Melissa and Joel and Erica were surprised to see her. But she reassured them that she felt all right and promised she would go home if that changed. By the looks on their faces, they didn't seem convinced. But she jumped right into work, and they had no choice but to carry on.

Angie popped outside to see if there was anything inflammatory written on Java Joe's sandwich board.

Home of real coffee lovers.

"We'll see about that," she muttered. She wiped off her board, grabbed the chalk, and wrote:

Home of Java Joe's ex-customers.

With a smirk, she returned to work.

She went out back later to give the cat his dinner, but he didn't turn up. Her heart sank. She hoped nothing had happened to him.

It was too cold to be standing around outside, and her teeth were beginning to chatter. As soon as she stepped into her office, her phone started ringing. Debbie's name flashed across the screen.

"Hey, Deb, I thought you told me to text you tonight," Angie said. She'd already been on the phone that day with her mother, Nadine, DeeDee, Aunt Gail, Esther, and Suzanne.

"I wanted to let you know that I have your cat," Deb said.

"What? Why?"

"I thought about what you said, about not being able to get too close to him. So I took him to the vet this morning. He's had his vaccinations, he's been dewormed, and he's had a flea dip. Tomorrow morning, he's being neutered."

"I can't ask you to do all that. It's too much," Angie said.

"You didn't ask. I went ahead and did it on my own. It's important to neuter these strays. Too much inbreeding and it wouldn't be long before the town was overrun with stray cats with three eyes."

Angie stifled a snort and remembered her manners. "Thanks, Debbie, I appreciate all the trouble you've gone to."

"It's not a problem. You know I love to do stuff like this."

Angie did know this about her friend. "How did you manage to catch him?"

Debbie laughed. "A little tin of wet cat food in the carrier. It works every time."

"I'll remember that."

"Anyway, after he's neutered, I'll keep him here at my house for a night or two. He'll be fine."

"I suppose it would be better than sleeping outside," Angie said.

"Yes. It's too cold. And when I bring him back to you, I'll bring something for him to sleep in outside."

"It sounds like you've thought of everything."

"I'm trying," Debbie said with a laugh.

Chapter Seventeen

Angie managed the first round of chemotherapy, as well as the accompanying medications: steroids and nausea meds. She did as much as she could at work, washing her hands constantly and not spending too much time among the public, anxious not to catch anything. And when she did have to mix with crowds, she wore a mask. Despite all the support—and she knew how lucky she was to have that—no one close to her truly knew what she was going through. It was as if a thin wall had been thrown up separating her from the rest of the world. Cancer made her feel singled out, which made her feel alone, despite always being around other people.

Fed up with feeling depressed and needing to deal with it somehow, she finally opened the folder she'd received at the oncologist's office. It had sat untouched on her kitchen table since she dropped it there the day she learned she had cancer. She leafed through it, reading all the information provided, until she found the page that listed the support group. It gave the day (Wednesdays), the time (six p.m.), and the location (a room on the second floor of the hospital).

She stared at it and sighed. Finally, she decided she'd give it a try. If she didn't like it, if it was too depressing or made her feel worse, she wouldn't go back. She'd try this first before asking Dr. Acker for antidepressants.

She arrived at the hospital fifteen minutes early, having not told anyone of her plans as she didn't want them making a big fuss. And they were a family that loved to fuss over people and things. She loved them, but she needed to do this for herself, by herself.

The room was not far from the cafeteria. Her goal was to find a seat at the back where she could observe. As she stepped inside, she winced, disappointed to see the chairs were arranged in a circle. That formation suggested sharing and intimacy. She almost backed out of the room but a voice behind her said, "Are you coming or going?"

"Sorry, I didn't see you there," Angie said, stepping out of the way.

The person behind her was a middle-aged Black woman who wore a headscarf in bright shades of gold, red, and orange. She leaned heavily on a leopard-print cane and as she passed Angie, she said, "You're new. Come on, you can sit next to me. I don't bite."

Dutifully, Angie followed her and took the seat next to her.

Once the woman settled in her chair, she turned to Angie and held out her hand. Her fingernails were acrylic and bright pink. "I'm Nena. Liver cancer."

Angie shook her hand. "Angie. Breast cancer."

"Welcome."

Angie looked around. By the looks of it, it was an education room. Posters were tacked up on the wall, showcasing various diseases: heart disease, diabetes, chronic obstructive pulmonary disease, and others. There was a table against the wall with a practice defibrillator and the CPR mannequin, Annie.

People began to file into the room, about ten or twelve in total. It was obvious to Angie that they were all at different stages of their disease. Some wore a head covering or a wig. And some had a full head of hair. She'd learned from Nena that she'd been doing well for three years but her cancer had returned. Angie didn't know what to say to that. She hadn't even thought about the possibility of cancer returning. But then she remembered Grammie's oft-repeated advice about worry: *Don't borrow trouble.*

An elderly man jauntily walked in and smiled when he spotted Nena. She patted the empty chair on the other side of her and he made his way to it. Once seated, he leaned past Nena and said to Angie, "A newcomer? First time here?" His voice was hoarse.

"It is," she replied, swallowing hard.

"This is a lot of fun," he said.

Angie thought the support group would be a lot of things, but fun wasn't one of them.

Nena gestured toward the man and said, "This guy here with a head like an egg is Floyd."

Floyd laughed, his shoulders shaking. He rubbed his hand over his bare head. "I lost all my hair one month into my treatment."

Angie was about to murmur a sympathetic response when Nena let out a loud round of laughter, startling her. "Well, Floyd, you only had seven strands to begin with. So it wasn't much of a loss, now, was it?"

Floyd laughed, scratching his head. "I suppose you're right, Nena."

"I'll tell you what I tell my husband, Frank. I'm always right," Nena said.

"You two are pretty cheery for cancer patients," Angie blurted, immediately regretting her choice of words.

The smiles disappeared from their faces, but they appeared not to be offended.

"We're farther into our journey than you are," Nena explained.

"Colon cancer," Floyd said, raising his hand.

"Why are you raising your hand, you old fool," Nena said with a laugh. "This isn't a classroom."

"Old habits die hard," he joked.

A smile emerged on Angie's face.

"Ah, there it is, she can smile," Nena said.

"I knew it! We haven't scared her off yet." Floyd chuckled.

Nena looked at Angie and said, "The two of us can be overwhelming to the newcomers."

A woman stood up from one of the chairs. She had long blond hair and wore a figure-hugging black dress with black boots and a bright orange cardigan.

"For those of you who are new, I'm Katharine, and I'm the moderator of the support group." She sat and crossed one leg over the other, setting a clipboard on her lap. "Why don't we go around the room and introduce ourselves. I encourage everyone to contribute, but if you're not yet ready to share, that's okay too." She looked at Angie and smiled.

It was like being called on in class and not knowing the answer.

Angie took a good look at the people that sat around the circle. They were of varying ages, and there was a woman who sat across from her, looking thin and pale, who Angie clocked as being younger than herself.

They did a quick round, telling everyone their names and adding anything they wanted to about themselves. More than half were retired and spoke about grandchildren. The young woman across from Angie was called Lisa, and she had two young children.

When her turn came, Angie simply said, "My name is Angie, and I own Coffee Girl."

There came a chorus of "I knew you looked familiar," "I love your pastry hearts," and her favorite, "I love your dueling sandwich boards with Java Joe's."

One of the women in the group nodded to Angie and said, "I see you're sitting with the troublemakers." Everyone laughed.

"Maybe we'll go around the circle again," Katharine said, "and you can tell me what you think about your own personal journey with cancer."

When it came time for Angie to speak, she said simply, "To be honest, in the beginning, I was more angry than scared. Angry at how it was going to interfere with my life and the job I love. But now I feel isolated. No one else in my orbit really understands what I'm going through."

There was a round of understanding nods and sympathetic smiles.

Next to her, Nena spoke up. "Well then, it's great that you're here. Because we *do* understand what you're going through."

When it was Floyd's turn, he leaned forward, hands on his knees, and in total seriousness said, "Well, to be honest, from the beginning, I've always thought if I could survive my wife's cooking, I could beat cancer."

Some snorted, others guffawed. Angie covered her face with her hand and shook with laughter.

As the meeting was winding down, Katharine reminded everyone that there'd be no meeting the following week due to Thanksgiving. The hour flew by as they spoke openly about their anger and frustration as well as their hopes, and as Angie walked out the door, she knew she'd return.

It was the first time since she was diagnosed that she didn't feel so alone.

Chapter Eighteen

Thanksgiving that year was held at Louise's house. Angie wasn't due for her second cycle of chemo until the Monday after Thanksgiving, and thank goodness for small favors. She managed to make three pies: the traditional pumpkin that no one would eat unless served with mounds of Cool Whip; a lemon meringue; and a chocolate cream. In the past, she would have placed all three in a long, narrow cardboard box and carried the whole thing out to her trunk at once. But being extra careful, she placed the box in her trunk first and carried the pies out one by one.

It was still early, but she thought she might as well go over to her mother's and hang out there and see if she needed any help. For the first time since she launched the café, she'd closed it for the holiday, thinking her employees would like the day off to spend with their families.

In the past, she'd thought of every family gathering as something to get through, time she could not get back. Now, she was ashamed for feeling that way.

The Halloween decorations that had adorned her mother's porch had been replaced by Thanksgiving-appropriate ones. A wreath with a male and female pilgrim leaning together for a chaste kiss hung over the front door. A wooden sign reading "Happy Thanksgiving" and ringed with engraved acorns had been attached to the siding.

Aunt Gail's Cadillac sat parked in the driveway behind Louise's car. In the front window sat Gail's dog, Rufus. He regarded her with curious disinterest. Rufus always reminded Angie of a seasoned British general. All he needed was a monocle.

She went inside, carrying one of the pies. The smell of roast turkey emanated from the kitchen, as did Louise and Gail's voices, punctuated by laughter. Louise appeared wearing a pair of oven mitts and holding a baster.

"Hi, honey, come on in," she said.

Angie carried in the lemon meringue pie and put it on a shelf in the refrigerator, moving things around to make room.

"Lemon meringue, my favorite," Gail said.

Her mother pushed the oven rack back in, closed the door, laid the baster on the counter, and removed the mitts.

"I've got two more pies in the trunk."

"I'll walk out with you and help you carry them in," Gail offered.

"I got it."

"Why make two trips when you can make only one?"

Rather than stand there debating about it, Angie nodded, and the two of them went out to her car.

"I see you made pumpkin," Gail said with a frown.

"Someone will eat it," Angie said with a laugh. "Is it even Thanksgiving if we don't have pumpkin pie?"

"Let me check and see if your mom has any whipped cream or Cool Whip."

Angie slammed the trunk shut and Gail asked, "How are you doing, honey?"

She nodded. "This is a good week. Round two next week."

"I know, your mother told me. Hang in there, kiddo."

They carried the pies inside, and Angie had to make more room in the refrigerator.

She looked around; her mother seemed to have everything in order. There were pots on every burner of the stove with all the staples: potatoes, turnip, carrots, and green beans. The Thanksgiving menu hadn't changed in more than thirty-five years.

"I hope you brought your appetite," Louise said.

Angie didn't want anyone worrying about her today. "My appetite isn't what it used to be, but I'm looking forward to dinner."

"That's all right. Don't overeat, you don't want to get sick," Louise advised.

Her plan was to enjoy herself and indulge in her favorites, but not too much.

"Is there anything I can do?" she asked.

"Would you like to set the table?"

"Yes," Angie said, grateful that her mother hadn't suggested she go sit down or worse, go lie down on the bed upstairs.

The kitchen table had been extended to accommodate everyone.

"Mom, you didn't carry all these chairs down from the attic by yourself, I hope," Angie said.

"No, not at all. Everett and Lance came over last night and brought them down for me," Louise answered, referring to Maureen's boys.

"Good. How are they doing?"

"Fine, Lance is in the middle of his electrician's course and seems to like it. And Everett's put some weight on and looks so much better. Healthy. Did you know he asked me to be one of his support people?"

"Aw, that's great, Mom." Louise Cook lived for her grandchildren. "Is that a thing? Having support partners?"

"It is. He's asked Lance, too, and Java Joe."

"His real name is Tom," Angie reminded her.

"I know, but I think of him as Java Joe."

Tom was very upfront about being a recovering alcoholic, and she thought that had been a wise choice on Everett's part.

"Is Suzanne coming?"

Gail shook her head and said sourly, "No, she's going to his side for Thanksgiving."

Suzanne's husband was not a popular figure in the family.

"Probably to keep the peace."

"Probably."

Louise laid silverware on the table as well as wine and water glasses. Angie counted out the knives and forks, recounted, and then mentally added all the family members. "Mom, you've got two extra place settings here."

"Because we have two guests coming today," Louise said brightly.

"We do? Who?"

"Funny thing, I ran into Java . . . into *Tom* the other day—"

"And?"

"And I thanked him for helping Everett, and he was so gracious about it, and then I thanked him for being so nice to you, especially when you've always given him such a hard time—"

Angie protested. "I don't give him a hard time."

Louise scowled. "Yes, you do. When it comes to Java Joe, you're difficult."

With a huff, Angie said, "Anyway, you were talking to him and . . . ?"

"I asked him what he was doing for Thanksgiving, and he said he was cooking a turkey for himself and his brother."

Angie frowned. How had she not known Tom had a brother?

Louise continued. "And I thought to myself, well, that sounds lonely, and I invited the both of them to join us."

"And he said yes?"

"Not without some arm-twisting," Louise said. "But it's all settled. They're both coming."

Angie wasn't sure how she felt about Tom joining them. Six months ago, she would have blown a fuse. But now, there had been a shift in her perspective, and more than anything, she was confused. She tried to look at it from the angle that her mother had done the charitable thing and the right thing by insisting they come here.

"Do you have a seating arrangement," she asked, "or doesn't it matter?"

"The girls have done a seating chart," Louise replied. The two granddaughters, Emma and Ashley, were both home from college for the short break. "When they get here, they can set the place cards around the table."

"So that's thirteen for dinner," Angie confirmed.

"That's correct."

Gail opened one of the bottles of wine she'd brought. "Anyone for a glass?"

Angie shook her head, but her mother said, "Will you pour me a half glass?"

"Will do." Gail filled half a glass and handed it to Louise. "Happy Thanksgiving."

"And to you too!"

At one o'clock, Louise turned on the potatoes and the turnip, as dinner would be served at two. And it wasn't long after that that everyone else began to trickle in. Maureen and Allan arrived first with Everett and Lance, carrying in trays and pans of food: cornflake potatoes and platters of Christmas cookies. Every Thanksgiving, Maureen brought two batches of holiday cookies to kick off the holiday season. This year was no different, and there were two trays of Hershey's peanut butter blossoms and a plate of frosted cutouts.

Allan approached Louise, laid a hand on her shoulder, and kissed her on the cheek. "Louise, it smells great, and I brought my appetite."

"That's all I ask," Louise said with a laugh. "How are you?"

"I'm fine. Fighting tooth decay in Lavender Bay one patient at a time." That was Allan's tagline that he used frequently.

Louise chortled. "Someone has to take the hit for the team."

He turned to Angie and leaned in and kissed her on the cheek. "And how are you doing?"

"I'm fine."

"I'm glad to hear that."

Esther came through the door next with her arms full. She had picked up dinner rolls and brought a chocolate cake. Following her, Nadine arrived with Emma, Ashley, and Herman, who hesitated on the porch before turning himself around and walking in backward, a particular quirk of his. Angie rolled her eyes. Nadine and the girls carried two pans of bread stuffing and two apple pies. No matter how many pies they had, it never proved to be enough.

Ashley and Emma made themselves busy setting up the place cards for the seating, and Angie was just about to interfere and make sure they didn't seat her next to Tom—that would be too obvious—but the doorbell rang, and her mouth went dry. It could only be him, and she didn't know why she was so nervous.

"Angie, would you get the door?" her mother asked sweetly.

Subtle.

"Sure, Mom."

The two dogs, Herman and Rufus, made their way to the front door. Herman practically knocked over Rufus in his excitement, scrabbling across the floor to greet the new arrivals. Rufus, vertically challenged, tried to increase his pace from a waddle to a shuffle but kept tripping over his ears.

"Herman!" Nadine hollered.

Angie followed the dogs to the front door and opened it to find Tom and his brother standing there, each holding a platter in their hands. Through the cling wrap, Angie could see an elaborate charcuterie board and a veggie tray. With a smile, she opened the door wide to allow them in.

The dogs barked, and Herman pranced around while Rufus stood there wagging his tail slowly.

Tom's brother strongly resembled him. But where Tom had dark hair, his brother's was blond. Like Tom, he was well-muscled and solid.

She smiled, genuinely glad to see Tom and grateful that her mother had invited him.

"Happy Thanksgiving!" she said warmly.

"Thanks, same to you," he said. "This is my younger brother, Jim."

Angie extended her hand. "Hi, Jim. Angie Cook."

His grip was warm and firm. "Nice to meet you, Coffee Girl."

Herman whined, and Rufus continued to wag his tail.

"Hey, buddy, how are you?" Jim said, leaning over to pet the bloodhound. Everyone in town knew who Rufus was.

Herman whined louder.

"That's Nadine's dog, Herman. If you don't acknowledge him, he'll probably explode."

Angie held the charcuterie tray for Tom while he got down on his haunches and rubbed the sides of Herman's face. "Hey, boy."

Herman settled down, and Tom stood.

"Come on in, I'll introduce you to everyone," Angie said.

The three of them made their way to the kitchen with Herman at their side and Rufus bringing up the rear. All conversation stopped as the family looked at the newcomers.

Angie made quick introductions, and Louise and Gail rushed the two guests.

"Oh look, you came bearing gifts, thank you," Gail said adroitly. She and her sister relieved them of the platters and set them down on the table, removing the cling wrap and inviting everyone to help themselves.

Allan was the first to step up to the charcuterie board, taking a small plate and filling it with olives, cheese, crackers, and prosciutto. "I never met a charcuterie board I didn't like."

Maureen took an olive off his plate and popped it into her mouth.

"How are you?" Tom asked Angie.

She gave him a reassuring smile. "I'm good."

"That's good to hear. How's it going with Melissa?"

"Great," she answered truthfully. "She's really stepped up to the plate." Angie now realized there was no way she would have been able to endure surgery and treatment and run her business full time. Thank goodness for Melissa and the rest of her staff.

"An employee like that is worth their weight in gold," Tom observed.

"Agreed."

She realized that some of her family members were watching them intently, and she felt herself redden.

Louise broke the spell. "Allan, would you mind taking the turkey out of the oven?"

It was a twenty-five-pounder that would be too heavy for Louise to lift.

"Not at all," Allan said, setting his half-finished plate of cheese and olives down on the counter. Louise handed him the oven mitts and he slipped them on, opening the oven door and waving the heat away with a mitt-covered hand. He lifted the pan out and stood there. "Where do you want it?"

Louise pointed to a space on the counter where she'd laid two potholders. Allan set the bird down.

"Do you want me to transfer it to a platter?" he asked.

"Yes, please, because we need to make the gravy."

Using a carving fork and knife, Allan carefully lifted the roasted turkey from the pan and set it on the platter.

"Let that rest for ten minutes before we carve it up," Gail advised. She said this every year. She went into the cupboard and pulled out a canister of flour, adding some to a jug along with some water and mixing it up with a fork to get all the lumps out. Louise drained the trimmings through a sieve into a pan on the stove.

Within ten minutes, everyone grabbed a dish to take over to the table and were told to take their seats. Allan carried the turkey over to his spot at the table and began carving once Gail said it was okay.

Angie looked for her seat and saw that she'd been placed right next to Tom, with his brother on the other side of him. She looked over to her nieces, who giggled when they saw the look on her face.

Tom grinned at her as he pulled the chair out for her to sit down.

"Thanks," she said.

Once everyone had their plates full, Allan asked, "Jim, you own the Ink Stain, correct?" Allan referred to the one tattoo parlor in Lavender Bay.

Tom's brother swallowed a mouthful of mashed potatoes and gravy before saying, "That's right."

Gail spoke up. "He's right across the street from me."

"You two know each other?" Angie asked, wondering if her aunt had a tattoo.

Jim spoke up. "Yep. I love her dog, Rufus. He's awesome."

"He is pretty awesome if I do say so myself. He's a retired tracker. Came up from the South," Gail said.

"That's amazing." Jim said, scooping more mashed potatoes into his mouth. "I never get tired of hearing that story."

"How long have you been doing tattoos?" Nadine asked.

"For as long as I can remember."

"He did the one on my back," Tom chimed in.

Although Angie had never seen it, she'd heard about it, and would definitely like to see it. It was rumored to be a bald eagle against the American flag, covering his whole back.

"Now this is what I call funny," Louise said. She gave a little laugh before continuing. "Gail and I were talking the other day about getting tattoos."

"Really, Grandma?" Lance asked, surprised and amused.

"Sure, why not?"

"I thought we weren't going to tell anyone," Gail said, her eyebrow arched.

"I guess the cat is out of the bag!" The two of them launched into a fit of laughing, which caused everyone either to roll their eyes or shake their head.

"Tattoos? You're a little old for that," Esther teased.

Jim, not knowing Esther's brand of humor, said, "I get a lot of people who are, um, elderly, coming in for a tattoo. The oldest was ninety-three."

"Really?" Louise said, surprised.

Jim nodded, trying to keep up with the three-way conversation.

"Esther, you could get a tattoo of a bowling ball on your arm, or your back or your bum or wherever," Gail joked.

"Thanks, Mom."

"That's a good idea!" Louise said.

Esther shook her head, but she was grinning.

When dinner was over, Angie stood up and began to help clear the plates.

"No you don't, Angie. You're on vacation from cleanup this year," Maureen announced.

Angie reddened, hating being the center of attention or getting special treatment just because she had cancer. "I can help. I've always pitched in with the cleanup."

"Not this year," Nadine said, siding with Maureen.

Louise quickly sensed that her third daughter was offended and suggested smoothly, "Why don't you let Maureen and Nadine do the dinner dishes and you can do the dessert cleanup with Esther."

"Fine," she said tightly.

Angie joined the rest of them in the living room. Allan turned the television on so they could watch the football game, and Lance and Everett carried chairs in from the kitchen so there'd be enough seats.

In the corner, Emma and Ashley huddled and giggled over their phones, showing each other their screens. Angie couldn't help but smile.

She looked around at her family, thinking how grateful she was to belong to this tribe. There was a strong sense of belonging with this crew. She'd recovered from her initial awkwardness at Tom being invited. Currently, he and his brother were deep in conversation with Allan and the boys about football.

Her diagnosis had certainly opened her eyes to what was truly important.

An hour after they'd eaten, Louise stood in the doorway of the kitchen and announced, "Time for dessert."

She, Gail, Maureen, and Nadine carried pots of coffee and tea out to the table, and all the pies, cakes, and cookies were brought out with a stack of dessert plates.

Most carried their desserts back to the living room to watch the game. As Tom helped himself to a variety of desserts, he said to Angie, "I'm glad your mother invited us. We weren't having anything as grand as this."

Angie smiled at him. "I'm glad she invited you too."

He winked at her and headed back to the living room.

Chapter Nineteen

It happened the second week of December as Angie was getting ready to go into work. A huge clump of hair fell out of her head. Startled, she stared at it on the bathroom floor. She groaned. As she picked it up, she felt around her scalp to see where it had come from. She picked up her makeup mirror and turned around so her back was to the mirror hanging over the bathroom sink.

There it was. A bald patch on the back of her head. Even though she'd expected this, she wasn't prepared for it. It still came as a shock. And she'd just started to feel marginally better after her second chemo treatment. The nausea and the general malaise had increased from the initial treatment but were beginning to subside.

The clump was a long lock, and she regretted not cutting her hair short before she started treatment. She couldn't go to work yet. What happened if another clump fell out in the café? The New York State Department of Health would love to hear that. She ran to the kitchen and rummaged around in the drawer for a pair of scissors. Back in the bathroom, she cut her hair as close to her scalp as she could, dropping long locks of strawberry-blond hair into the bathroom sink. When she was finished, she studied her reflection in the mirror.

Stick to the baking.

The small amount of hair left on her head was uneven and clumpy, making her look like a six-year-old who took the matter of school pictures into her own hands.

She couldn't go into work looking like this. She walked out of the bathroom, unable to look at her beautiful hair filling the sink. It hurt. She'd deal with it later.

She rummaged through her dresser looking for any kind of headscarf, berating herself for no forward planning as far as this was concerned. She *knew* at some point her hair was going to fall out. Or had it been a subconscious hope that it wouldn't?

Finally, she pulled out a red paisley bandanna from the back of a drawer. When she was in her twenties, she went through a country–western phase and used to wear this tied around her waist. She'd no longer be able to do that. Standing in front of the bedroom mirror, she did the best she could with the scarf. At least her head was covered.

Finished, she rushed off to work.

As was her new routine, she fed the cat first and then went out front to check Java Joe's sandwich board, not removing her winter coat just yet. As she made her way through the kitchen, Joel, Iris and Melissa took note of her headscarf, and all three cast her sympathetic looks.

Angie put her hands on her hips and decided direct was the best way. "We all knew my hair would fall out. I'm fine." And before they could reply or say anything, she sailed out of the kitchen and through the café until she pushed through the front door and stood on the sidewalk in the freezing cold of December.

Her eyes landed on Java Joe's sandwich board.

Our coffee's out of this world.

"We'll see about that," Angie muttered, heading back in. She pulled out the sandwich board, grabbed the chalk and scribbled, *Java Joe's on another planet. Our coffee's great.*

Satisfied, she dragged it outside and set it up on the curb. Across the street, Tom stood with his arms across his chest. With a grin, he gave her a two-finger salute.

She waved and returned inside.

The café was busy, and the day flew. Angie was happy to be at work. Not wanting to push her luck, she rested several times in her office. But at the day's end, she collapsed in her chair in her office. Joel appeared in the doorway.

"I can close up if you want to go home," he said.

"I appreciate that, Joel, and I think I might take you up on your offer."

"Good."

"I'll feed the cat and then I'll go."

"I've already fed him. See you tomorrow, boss," he said.

As she went out the back door, she saw the cat was in his new home. Debbie had bought a plastic storage box, lined it with straw, and cut a hole in the side of it so the cat could access it. His left ear had been tipped to indicate that he'd been neutered.

Before she left work, she rang Maureen and Nadine, asking them to meet her at her house.

Both sisters were already there, parked out front, when Angie arrived home. She pulled into her driveway, and they got out of Maureen's car and walked up to meet her at the side door. Maureen held up a black kit and said, "I found it."

"Good."

The three of them proceeded into the kitchen.

"Do you want coffee or tea?" Angie asked.

"No, I just had dinner," Maureen said. "And I'm stuffed. What about you, Nadine?"

She shook her head. "It's too late for me to drink either. I'd be awake all night."

Maureen set her kit on the table. "Sit down," she instructed.

Angie sat on the kitchen chair and pulled off the bandanna. As she did, another clump of hair fell off and landed on the floor.

Both her sisters looked at her cut hair, eyes wide.

"Can't leave you alone with scissors," Maureen teased. She opened the kit and said with a laugh, "Allan went through a phase where he wanted to save money by cutting the boys' hair at home."

"How'd that work out?" Nadine asked, throwing the clump of hair in the garbage.

"It didn't. The boys were teenagers at this point and wouldn't let their father near them." She pulled out the hair clippers. "These have been sitting in the utility closet ever since. Never used."

Angie sighed. "Let's get to it."

Maureen pulled out a black plastic apron from the kit and shook it out with a flourish before draping it around Angie's neck.

"Angie, what did you do with all the hair you cut off?" Nadine asked.

She'd forgotten about that. "I filed it under 'to be dealt with later' and left it in the bathroom sink."

"I'll clean it up."

"You don't have to, Nadine."

"I don't mind. Where are your garbage bags?" Nadine asked.

"Under the kitchen sink."

Nadine found one and headed to the bathroom.

Maureen selected a guide comb, attached it to the clippers, and turned them on. She looked at Angie and asked, "Are you ready?"

"Yeah, I am," she said. It was best to get it over with.

"It will grow back," Maureen reassured her.

"I know."

The low hum of the clippers was like white noise as Maureen began to roll it over her sister's head. Angie watched as the remainder of her hair fell to the floor. Nadine appeared holding the garbage bag at her side.

"I'll get a broom and a dustpan," she said.

"The closet in the hall," Angie instructed.

As Nadine swept up the hair from the floor, Maureen set the clippers down, removed a brush from the kit, and swept it over Angie's head and neck, brushing off any stray hair. She removed the black plastic apron, shook it out, and folded it up.

Angie stood, brushing off her T-shirt. "Well?"

Nadine leaned on the broom and her chin quivered.

"No crying, Nadine," Angie warned. She didn't want to start blubbering.

In a shaky voice, Nadine said, "It's just that you're our baby sister. This stuff isn't supposed to happen to you."

Maureen put her arm around Nadine and gave her a reassuring squeeze.

"I know, I'll be okay," Angie said, trying to convince herself as well.

Nadine nodded and pulled herself together.

But that was life. Things happened to people that shouldn't happen, and there was nothing that could be done about it.

Chapter Twenty

The loss of her hair bothered Angie more than she thought it would, and she looked forward to going to support group Wednesday night if only to be with other people who understood what it felt like. There was also the bonus of being entertained by Nena and Floyd.

Tuesday night, she was parked on her sofa sipping flat 7UP, hoping her stomach would settle. The draft on her bare scalp made her feel chilly, so she'd donned a knit cap. She heard her side door open.

"Angie?" her mother called out.

Angie stood and made her way to the kitchen. "Mom, what are you doing here?"

Her mother had carried in a cardboard box, which she set down on the kitchen table.

"Were you sleeping?" Louise asked.

"No, only watching television."

Louise pulled off her jacket and hat and laid them on a chair. She hugged her daughter and said, "Maureen called me last night and told me about your hair."

Angie nodded, unable to speak as the mention of her hair loss choked her up.

When they pulled apart, Angie told her mother, "I don't know why it bothers me so much, but it does. And then I think I must be vain and shallow."

Her mother waved her hand dismissively. "Don't think like that. You're entitled to how you feel. And women and their hair are a thing."

Angie tilted her head slightly and considered what her mother said.

"Our hair and how we wear it are a part of our identity," Louise continued. "And a woman's hair is part of her feminine aspect. Those are my thoughts on the subject. It's okay to grieve for your hair. But remember, it's temporary. It will grow back."

Impressed, Angie said, "Gee, Mom, that's pretty good."

Louise smiled. "I know, right? Not bad for a high school graduate. Women and their hair is something I've thought a lot about, with my mom losing hers in that accident before I was born." She looked around the place, hands on her hips. "Where are your Christmas decorations?"

"Still in the basement." She only had a few. As she was hardly ever home, her decorations would best be described as sparse.

"It's December!"

"I know what month it is," Angie said defensively.

"All right, never mind."

"Mom, do you want tea or coffee?"

"I'll make it, honey. Do you want anything?"

Angie shook her head. "No. I've got a glass of 7UP that I'm working on." Someone at the café had told her that if she boiled it, it would flatten faster, and she could sip it once it cooled down.

"Nausea?" Her mother's expression was one of concern.

"Not too bad today," she lied.

Louise filled the kettle from the tap and returned it to the stove and turned on the burner. While she waited for the kettle to whistle, she opened the flaps of the cardboard box.

"I took a look through my cedar chest today and look what I came across." She pulled out a pile of headscarves and turbans that had once belonged to her mother.

Angie smiled, picking one up. "I haven't seen these in years. I didn't know you'd kept Grammie's headgear."

Louise shrugged. "Of course. I'd never throw these out. You'll always want to save something that belonged to someone you love."

"I suppose so."

Angie went through them, smiling as memories came back to her. She lifted them to her nose to smell them to see if she could get the scent of her grandmother off them. But they smelled of laundry detergent.

"Sorry, I had to wash them, they smelled like cedar," Louise said.

Angie lifted one turban, which was a sapphire blue. "I remember this one. Grammie always wore it to weddings and events." She turned it around. The rhinestone brooch was still there, front and center. She used to think it made her grandmother look like an exotic princess. Laughing, she held up a pink scarf that had the characters from Disney's *Beauty and the Beast* on it. "Remember when DeeDee was obsessed with this movie? And Grammie made this for herself to wear while she watched it with DeeDee, and then DeeDee wanted her own?"

"I do. I don't know what happened to DeeDee's," her mother said.

"Grammie sure was accommodating."

"She loved you all very much."

"I know. She showed us every day."

"I sure do miss her," Louise said.

"We all do. I can't believe she's been gone this long."

"Sometimes it feels like yesterday and then other days, it feels like she's been gone a lifetime."

Angie's thoughts turned dark, wondering if she'd be seeing her grandmother sooner rather than later, and before everyone else. Although she missed Grammie, she was in no hurry to reunite with her.

The kettle's whistle was shrill, and Louise turned off the stove and made herself a cup of tea.

She carried her steaming mug over to the table as Angie sifted through the rest of the box. It was full of scarves of various fabrics and colors and prints. Digging a little further, she pulled out a small bag that contained more scarves, individually wrapped in tissue paper.

"How come these ones are wrapped so carefully?" Angie asked.

Louise blew across her mug of tea. "The loose ones were her everyday scarves, but these ones had special meaning."

Angie set the box aside for a moment and carefully unwrapped the tissue paper holding a navy-and-white floral silk scarf. She could see why it had been packaged with such care. It was beautiful. The print reminded her of a watercolor painting.

"That was the scarf Mom wore the day she married Dad," Louise said.

"It's beautiful," Angie said. She folded it up carefully and wrapped it back up in the tissue paper.

The next scarf she unwrapped was cream-colored with the word "Victory" printed all over it in blue and red.

"That's her scarf from before the accident. She used to wear that to the aviation plant where she worked during the war."

"How old was Grammie when she went to work at the plant?"

Louise thought for a moment. "Twenty, twenty-one. She was only there a year when the accident happened."

The next thing she unwrapped had Angie frowning. "What is this, a bathing cap?" It was a pink rubber cap with a chin strap. The design was made to look like flower petals.

"Mom loved the beach, and she took us every chance she had. Everyone used to wear swim caps back then, and that was her favorite. She wore it all the time until the chin strap broke."

After she went through all the scarves wrapped in tissue paper, Angie carefully tucked them away into the box, thinking about how Gram had marked the important events in her life with a headscarf. She liked it.

"I thought you'd like them. I mean, you don't have to wear them, but maybe they'll bring you some comfort," Louise said, sipping her tea.

"I am going to wear them." Angie rifled through the pile and found a Christmas one: a white headscarf with a pattern of holly, ivy, and berries. "And we'll start with this one."

She whipped off her knit hat, exposing her head. Immediately, her mother's eyes widened at seeing the state of her daughter's head for the first time: bald.

With deftness, Angie fixed the headscarf and tied it together. "Now, Mom, it's okay. It's only hair. It'll grow back. Isn't that what you just said?" Her mother nodded, her eyes wet. "How do I look?"

Louise's eyes welled up. "You look like Grammie."

Angie gave her mother a reassuring smile. "Perfect."

She stood and retrieved her glass from the living room and sat at the table with her mother, sipping the flat 7UP.

"How did Grammie cope with her hair loss?" Growing up, they'd been used to Grammie and her variety of headscarves.

There was a pained expression on Louise's face. "In the beginning, not well at all. Wouldn't get out of bed. Thought life wasn't worth living. Typical things you might see with someone who's suffered a major trauma."

"I didn't know that," Angie said. "Grammie always seemed so happy."

"With the help of her mother and her friends, she managed to get through the aftermath and create a life for herself," Louise said.

Angie continued to sift through the box. "It's amazing, really. I, mean, I know how I feel without my hair, but I remind myself every day that it's only temporary, whereas for Gram, it was permanent. Boy, that must have been tough."

"It was."

Angie realized she knew almost nothing about her grandmother's early life, especially those years right after the accident. "How did she do it?" she asked.

Louise had a faraway look in her eyes. "It wasn't always easy. But let me tell you what I know."

PART TWO

DIANA

Chapter Twenty-One

1942

Diana Quinn stood with her mother, Millie, at the end of the narrow gravel driveway of the small, modest home at 36 Peony Lane in the town of Lavender Bay. Born and bred in Pennsylvania, twenty-year-old Diana stared at their new house. Their *first* house. She squeezed her mother's hand. "Can you believe it?"

Her mother had inherited it from an aunt she'd always kept in touch with. Diana's father had died when she was six, and they'd been renting ever since. Until now.

It was a damp, gray March day, but neither one of them were bothered by the dismal weather.

"I can't," Millie Quinn said, beaming. "Our own home." Her voice shook as she said it.

Despite the glee, there was no camouflaging the fact that the house needed work. The roofline above the porch sagged, and the paint peeled in various places. The color was something close to butterscotch, or it had been at one time. But to Diana and her mother, it didn't matter. No more worrying about how they were going to make the rent payments or, worse, dealing with questionable landlords. Diana could scream at the top of her lungs inside this house if she wanted to. Not that she would.

Out front was a large sycamore tree, and at the side of the house was an oak with a wide trunk. Beyond the driveway, in the backyard, stood a weeping willow. Their one-story home was flanked on either side by two-story houses with wide porches that were in much better shape, making theirs look like a poor relation in comparison. But they didn't care.

Millie's cousin Herb had offered to drive them up to Lavender Bay in his pickup truck, which they packed with the few things they owned after selling most of their furniture and larger items. Herb owned a general hardware store back home and had to take a day off work for the three-hour drive from Pennsylvania. He was a man of few words. Diana had made a game of counting how many he spoke on the journey: twenty-two, to be exact.

"Ready?" "Need to stop for gas." "Does anyone need to use the restroom?" "There's the New York State line." "Here we are."

On arriving in Lavender Bay, Herb had carried their belongings into the house for them and dumped everything into the parlor. He then said goodbye, got back into his truck, and left immediately, refusing any offers of hospitality. There'd been no hugs or well wishes. Life got on with.

The inside of the house was in decent shape, needing only a good scrubbing and cleaning. It was apparent that Millie's elderly aunt had been on the decline and the housecleaning had suffered because of it.

It didn't matter. Millie and Diana were cheerful about it. The house was left as Aunt Lavinia had left it, furniture and all. There were even some old cleaning supplies in a back room. Both women left their belongings in the parlor, tied kerchiefs on their heads, and got down to the business of cleaning.

Being that the house was small, they were able to concentrate what was left of the first day on the kitchen and bathroom and one of the three bedrooms, so they could store their few boxes there. The following day, they tackled the remaining two bedrooms and the parlor.

As the sky darkened on that second day, Diana and her mother collapsed on the sofa, still wearing aprons over their dresses and scarves on their heads. Every muscle in Diana's back and legs ached. But the house had been spruced up and cleaned, and it was beginning to feel like home.

"Won't it be nice to take a hot bath?" her mother asked with a smile.

"No more worrying about someone else in the apartment block using up all the hot water. Or banging on the door, shouting that they need to use the toilet." Diana wouldn't miss that at all.

Her mother looked around with a smile. "I can't believe my aunt left this to us."

"To *you*," Diana corrected.

Her mother shook her head. "There's only the two of us, Diana. Someday when I'm gone, this house will be yours."

"Let's hope that day is a long way off," Diana said.

Chapter Twenty-Two

Diana studied her reflection in the mirror above her bureau. She brushed her hair again, loving the way it shone in the light. She'd washed it the previous night, and the faint scent of the shampoo she'd used filled the air. She pulled a brand-new dress on over her head, adjusting it over her slip. She'd made the dress herself. It was a lot cheaper to sew your own clothes rather than buy them from the dress shops. And she loved sewing. She could replicate all the new styles. She twirled around, trying to see as much of it as possible in the mirror. The red-and-white striped fabric suited her coloring, and she'd found the perfect shade of lipstick to match. In front of the mirror, she puckered up and applied it from a small gold tube, smacking her lips together and then double-checking to make sure there was none on her teeth. Satisfied, she slipped on a pair of shoes, grabbed her handbag, and headed out of her bedroom.

"Mother, I'm going out for a bit."

Once spring arrived and the weather warmed up, Diana had begun going out every day to investigate the town. And she liked what she saw. The charming tree-lined streets and the Victorian houses. The long stretch of sandy beach and the lake. And Main Street, with all the different shops and boutiques.

Her mother popped her head out from the kitchen. She was in the midst of drying a plate with a dishtowel. When she saw her daughter, she frowned. "You're all dressed up. Who are you going to lunch with, Eleanor Roosevelt?"

"Oh, Mother, you're so droll."

"Diana, be careful, you don't want to be seen as vain," her mother advised.

"I'm no such thing," Diana said, and she flounced out the front door.

She walked to the end of her narrow gravel driveway, careful with her heels among the stones.

As she continued along the sidewalk, she took everything in, not least the lovely single-family houses with their neat little lawns and wide porches. Lavender Bay was a wonderful place. The only thing missing was men. In the last few months, a lot of them had joined up and marched off. Her mother was probably right; it was useless to prance around town all dolled up when there was no one of the masculine persuasion to appreciate it. She hesitated, briefly contemplating returning home, but was distracted by a wolf whistle. It came from the other side of the street. She shielded her eyes with her hand, and in lifting her arm, slightly raised the hem of her dress to her knee. Across the street, a man her age dressed in a short-sleeved shirt and trousers smiled broadly and saluted her.

She laughed at the attention and turned on her heel. Apparently, not every male had run off to the war.

She heard him call out behind her, but she kept walking. She wasn't that type of girl. Although flattered by his appreciative whistle, to be seen talking to a strange man in the middle of the street simply because he whistled at you just wouldn't do. She walked over to Main Street and browsed the shop windows, especially the dress shops, not in the mind to purchase anything but to see what was on display and get ideas. She was deep in thought, studying necklines, sleeves, hems, and the cuts of these dresses, making mental notes, when a masculine voice said behind her, "Hey, beautiful, didn't you hear me calling you?"

Without turning her body, she glanced over her shoulder and recognized the whistler from earlier. He was tall, with sandy brown hair and deep brown eyes.

"So, if you whistle, I'm supposed to come running like I'm some kind of dog?" she asked, managing to keep a straight face.

The guy looked horrified, his mouth opening slightly before closing without any sounds coming out. Then it opened again, and his words came tumbling out over one another. "Gosh, miss, no, I didn't mean that at all." He lowered his voice. "I thought you hadn't heard me. Or maybe you were . . . ignoring me?"

She flashed him a brilliant smile. "Maybe." She pulled at her bottom lip with her top teeth. His gaze fixed on her lips.

Suddenly, breaking the spell, she thrust out her hand and said, "Diana Quinn."

"Oh, yeah. Preston McGee," he said, and shook her hand heartily like she was one of the guys.

"As in Fibber?" she asked.

He frowned. "Huh?"

"Never mind." Where had he come from? Still, she was amused.

They spoke for a few more moments and then she said, "I really must be going."

She turned to walk away, but he sidestepped her and stood in front of her. "Wait, wait a moment."

She stopped and looked up at him.

"Look, can I take you out dancing?" he asked. She hesitated, and before she could say anything, he went on. "I've joined the Navy, and I'm heading out next week."

"Oh." She was genuinely sorry about that. It made the flirting seem superficial. Because behind all of it, the men were gone so that they could fight a terrible enemy on the other side of the world. The thought was sobering.

"How about tomorrow night?" he pressed.

"All right," she said, thinking she'd like to go dancing. She knew there were dances in town at the Pavilion, but she hadn't made any friends yet, and she certainly wouldn't go to a dance by herself. Besides, the neighbor had told her mother that the few men that attended were outnumbered by the women, three to one.

"Gee, that's swell, Diana. May I call you Diana?" he asked.

"Well, you wouldn't call me Janet, would you?" she teased.

He laughed. "You sure are a hoot. Can you give me your number?"

"No, but I'll give you my address." Then, changing her tone to stern, she said, "You'll have to meet my mother first if you want to take me dancing, Preston."

"Oh yes, of course," he said hurriedly. He repeated her address three times, committing it to memory.

"Now, I must go," she said with a smile. "I'll see you tomorrow night at seven at my house."

"I'll be there," he said eagerly.

Smiling, she turned and walked away, thinking the trip to town hadn't been a waste at all.

"Oh, Ma, you should have seen him," Diana recounted later over their supper with a laugh. "He was falling all over himself."

"Diana," her mother said in a mock scold. "You shouldn't tease people like that." Beneath the admonition, her mother was smiling, amused.

"Aw, it was just a good laugh," Diana said, spooning up the broth her mother had put in front of her. "Anyway, he's taking me dancing tomorrow night."

Her mother frowned, her soup spoon halfway to her mouth. "Is that a good idea? You only met him today."

"There'll be other people there for sure. I saw the notice for the dance in *The Lavender Bay Chronicles*.

"If you think it's all right."

"He's coming here to the house. I insisted he meet you first."

"That's better," her mother said, the anxiety easing from her face.

"He's joined the Navy and heads off next week."

"That poor boy," Millie said with a shake of her head. It's what she said about all the men serving.

Chapter Twenty-Three

Diana wore one of her favorite dresses to go dancing. It was a dark emerald green. She copied the hairstyle of Veronica Lake that she'd seen in a magazine at the beauty parlor. There was a knock at the front door. She applied some red lipstick, capped the tube, and set it down.

Her mother had been waiting for Preston's arrival, and by the time Diana stepped into the parlor, he and her mother were seated at opposite ends of the sofa, making small talk. As soon as he spotted Diana, he stood, twisting his hat in his hands, staring at her.

"You look beautiful, Diana," he said, not taking his eyes off of her. Behind him, her mother smiled proudly.

"Thank you," Diana said.

He drew in a breath and smiled. "All set?"

"I am." She grabbed her handbag and on the way out, she said to her mother, "Leave a light on, Ma."

Her mother nodded and waved them off.

Although the air was warm, Diana shivered, and Preston smiled at her. "Cold?"

"A little bit," she said. She was sorry she hadn't brought her coat.

"Here, let me warm you up a bit," he said, and he slung an arm around her shoulder.

They walked over to the community pavilion. Tonight's dance was a fundraiser for the Red Cross. Last week, they'd raised money for the Salvation Army. The Pavilion was at the far end of Pearl Street, overlooking the lake. It was a large octagonal-shaped building with a cupola that had been built at the turn of the century. All that white trim and glass gave it a romantic look, Diana thought. That evening, it was all lit up, looking like a jeweled star against the dark lake.

Preston held her hand as they went in and paid for their tickets.

The place was almost packed, and a quick glance showed that it was predominantly filled with women. There were some men in uniform and other men dressed in civilian clothing, many of whom, like Preston, were getting ready to ship out.

The energy was frenetic. The music was loud, and the dance floor was filled with couples dancing the jitterbug to the strains of Glenn Miller's "In the Mood." Diana began to tap her foot to the beat of the music, eager to get out there and join them.

Preston, with his arm around her waist, led her to a small table for two at the far corner. It was covered in a white linen tablecloth, and on top was a lit tealight candle in a frosted glass.

A cocktail waitress appeared. "What will you have to drink?"

Preston looked at her. "Diana? What'll you have?"

"A sloe gin fizz, please." She felt so grown up ordering an alcoholic beverage.

The waitress scribbled it down on her notepad and looked at Preston.

"I'll have a Genny," he said, referring to Genesee beer.

She nodded and wound her way to the next table.

A cigarette girl wearing a short dress and a tray of cigarettes held in place by a strap around her neck went around calling out, "Cigarettes! Cigarettes!"

Preston pulled out a pack of Camels and tapped out a cigarette. He held the pack out to Diana, but she shook her head. Once it was lit, he snapped the lighter shut and returned it to his pocket.

It wasn't long before their drinks appeared, and Diana sipped from her glass while Preston took a swig of beer from the bottle, not bothering with the glass.

He set his beer down and looked at Diana sitting next to him. "Are you ready to do some dancing?"

She nodded, holding her drink in one hand and the straw in the other and taking a sip. It had a nice tart taste.

Preston stubbed out his cigarette in the ashtray and stood and held out his hand to Diana. She jumped up and placed her hand in his.

The band, made up of middle-aged men, was fabulous, playing all the current hits from Glenn Miller, Tommy Dorsey, and Artie Shaw. Due to the shortage of men, some women danced together, and Diana suspected they'd be seeing a lot of that.

Preston was a wonderful dancer, his footwork impressive. He knew all the latest steps, and Diana couldn't remember when she'd last had so much fun. The air was energized around them. At the back of everyone's minds was the fact that there was a war going on, and it seemed to make them all determined to squeeze every bit of fun out of the evening.

One of the few times they sat down to drink and for Preston to smoke, Diana asked, "Where did you learn to dance like that?"

He laughed. "I've got three older sisters. Who do you think they practiced with?" He stubbed out his half-finished cigarette and stood again, hand out. Diana took a quick gulp of her now warm and watered-down drink.

As the evening wore on, she was perspiring heavily, but she was having such a good time she didn't mind. Preston was a lot of fun. By eleven, she declared it was time to go home. He wanted to stay later, but she begged off. She didn't want to worry her mother.

They spoke animatedly as he walked her home, and beneath the porch light, as Diana rifled through her purse looking for her keys, he threw an arm up against the wall.

"How about tomorrow night?" he asked. "Dancing?"

"Is there another dance?" she asked, snapping her purse shut, keys in hand.

"Yep, saw it on the board as we left the Pavilion. It's for the Ladies' Auxiliary. There are dances almost every night this week. And on the other nights, I thought we could go to the movies or something."

Diana smiled. She liked him taking charge and making plans for them. "I'd love to go dancing and to the movies."

"That's swell," he said. "You know, I've seen you around town before."

"You have? Where? When?" She was embarrassed to admit that she'd never noticed him.

"Yeah, you're such a knockout you're hard not to notice!"

Although she was secretly delighted, she blushed all the same.

"I couldn't believe my luck when I saw you walking down the street yesterday," he said with enthusiasm.

She smiled at him. He was excited when he spoke to her, and he seemed to really like her. The experience was heady.

"Can I kiss you goodnight?" he asked.

With a nod, she said, "You can."

With a broad smile, he whispered, "Come here, doll." He pulled her into his arms and began to kiss her in earnest. She got lost in it, and as he trailed kisses down the side of her face to her neck, she closed her eyes and let herself get swept up in the wonderful feelings.

Suddenly the porch light flicked on and off several times in a row, and Diana pulled away from Preston, breathless.

"Boy, you sure know how to kiss a girl," she said.

He grinned.

The porch light flicked on and off again, and Diana said, "That's my cue. I've got to go inside."

"I'll be here tomorrow night at seven."

"I'll be ready," she said.

He stepped back, holding on to her hand, until their arms were stretched out. "I had a great time, Diana."

"Me too."

He rushed her, kissed her again, and then hopped off the porch.

Inside, her mother stood by the front door, wearing a bathrobe over her nightgown and a hairnet covering her head full of pin curls.

"Ma, were you spying on us?" Diana asked.

"No, not at all," her mother said, appearing affronted. "I was getting a glass of water."

"All right," Diana said, not quite believing her.

"How was it?" Millie asked.

"It was a lot of fun. My feet are killing me from all the dancing. Anyway, we're going again tomorrow night. Can't wait."

They went out almost every night. The two nights where there were no dances scheduled, they went to the movies and saw *Reap the Wild Wind* with John Wayne and *Saboteur* with Robert Cummings and Priscilla Lane. In the darkened theater, they ate popcorn and Preston put his arm around her shoulders.

On his last night, he was unusually quiet as he walked her home. "Diana, will you write to me? While I'm away?"

She nodded. "Sure, but you'll have to write to me first so I know where to send my letters."

"I will, as soon as I get situated," he promised.

"Good. I'd like to hear from you."

"Thank you for a fabulous week. I can't tell you how much it meant to me."

"You're welcome," she said, leaning against the house.

"Now, Diana Quinn, I'm going to kiss you goodnight," he said. His voice was low in the shadowy darkness.

"I'd like that very much."

Chapter Twenty-Four

1943

Diana walked through the front door, kicked off her shoes, unpinned her hat, and threw it on the small side table.

Her mother appeared in the doorframe of the parlor. "Any luck?"

Diana grumbled and plopped down on her preferred part of the sofa, the squishy cushion whose spring was gone. She pulled up one foot and massaged it with her hands, noting the blister that had formed. The shoes, though pretty, were a bit too tight, especially in the summer heat.

She shook her head. "Nothing. No one is hiring. I even went to the grain and feed store, and he took one look at me and just about laughed me out of the place."

Millie gave her a sympathetic smile. Her daughter's tall and shapely form, her long honey-blond hair and her almond-shaped eyes were perhaps too glamorous for the feed store. "It would be hard to picture you there."

Diana supposed so. With a sigh, she said, "I don't miss Pennsylvania, but I can't help but think of all the jobs I could have secured back there."

With the end of the Depression and the US involvement in the war, the economy was picking up. That had yet to trickle down to the small town of Lavender Bay. But she was hopeful.

"I'll bring you a cup of tea," Millie said, disappearing to the kitchen.

Diana called out after her, "Ma, don't go to any trouble."

"No trouble at all," came the reply.

By the time her mother returned with a steaming cup of tea, Diana had just finished massaging her other foot. She winced from the stinging blister.

She held out her hand to accept the cup of tea from her mother.

"No letter today?" she asked. She and Preston had been writing back and forth regularly. He'd been home on leave for two weeks at Christmas, and they'd made the most of it, spending every day together. She'd even met his parents and his older sisters. But in January, he went back to somewhere in the Pacific.

Millie shook her head.

Diana frowned. His letters were the highlight of her day. But it had been more than a week since she'd received anything.

"Diana, he's out in the middle of the ocean. To be honest, I'm surprised his letters get here as fast as they do."

That was no comfort.

Millie sat near the front window in her chair of choice, an old armless oak rocker with a carved back that had come with the house.

Once her tea cooled, Diana sipped it and looked at her mother. "You don't seem too upset that I couldn't find a job." This puzzled Diana. Inheriting a house had been a blessing, but there were bills to be paid. There had been a little bit of money too, and the two of them hadn't a care in the world for the first few months after their arrival. But the source was dwindling, and it was determined that Diana should try and find some kind of job. They were eating a lot of broth and heels of old bread for their dinners. The curves on Diana's figure were beginning to disappear.

"I'm going to write to Cousin Herb," Millie said.

Diana couldn't imagine a man who talked so little writing a letter. Would it be worth a stamp for one or two lines? "Why?" she asked. As far as she was concerned, they'd left Pennsylvania and everything and everyone in it behind them.

"I'll ask him for a loan to tide us over."

Diana's mouth dropped open. "Don't."

"We need money."

"No, we are not asking Cousin Herb for money."

"I don't like it any better than you do, but what can we do?"

"I'll think of something. But hold off writing any letters to anyone," Diana instructed.

"All he can do is say yes or no."

Diana found this funny. "He should be able to handle that." Whether it was the fatigue or worry, she wasn't sure, but something made her break into peals of laughter, falling back against the sagging cushions of the sofa.

"What is so funny?" her mother asked sternly.

"We know your cousin is a man of few words. I'm picturing Herb's letter with one word on it: 'No'!" And she held her arms over her belly as she laughed harder.

"Honest to goodness, Diana, I don't understand your humor," Millie said, her mouth set in a grim line.

Diana sobered up. "That's okay, Ma, neither do I." A squeal of laughter threatened to emerge again, but she tamped it down, thinking she must be tired from all that walking around Lavender Bay in the heat looking for a job.

When she arrived home the following day after another unlucky day of job searching, her mother handed her three letters with military postmarks. Preston's familiar scrawl cheered her up to no end.

A month later, Diana burst through the front door. "Ma, I got a job!"

Her mother appeared from the kitchen, dish towel in her hand. "You did? Where?"

"Cheever Aviation."

"Is that over in Cheever?"

"I think it's in the name," Diana said.

Her mother pursed her lips. "Don't be smart. What will you be doing there? Secretarial work?"

"Not exactly."

"Then what?"

"They make C-46s."

Millie scowled. "What are those?"

"Planes for the military."

"It's a defense plant, then."

"Yes."

"What will you be doing there?"

"I don't know yet. I was only hired this morning. It'll be on the production line somewhere, but I haven't been assigned a job." Diana's excitement was hard to contain.

Her mother seemed unconvinced. "Isn't that a job for men?"

"Ma, all the men are gone. This morning, the place was packed with women of all ages applying for jobs."

"Really?" Millie found this hard to believe. Why would a woman want to work at a man's job?

"And here's the best part." Diana's eyes shone bright. "The pay is seventy cents an hour. Seventy cents! We won't know ourselves."

A slow smile emerged on her mother's face. "That comes to a lot of money."

"It sure does!"

"But how will you get to Cheever? We don't have a car," her mother said.

"I'm going to carpool with a woman named Joy Ruggiero. She passes right by Lavender Bay on her way to Cheever, and she said she'd pick me up. I'll help pay for the gas."

"But gasoline is rationed."

"We're war workers, so we're exempt," Diana said proudly.

"This is wonderful news, Diana."

"I thought so too."

"You should celebrate."

"That's my plan." Diana headed to her bedroom and called over her shoulder, "I'm going to the beach!"

Chapter Twenty-Five

The day was hot, and Diana walked down to the beach wearing a cover-up she'd made herself and a wide-brimmed hat she'd found in one of the closets. Under her arm, she carried an old bath towel.

She'd never lived near a beach before. It was a novel experience. In Pennsylvania, there were mountains, and she'd thought she'd never see anything as beautiful, especially in the fall when the leaves turned vibrant shades of red, orange, and yellow. But the lake possessed its own charm, and she especially loved those lavender-hued skies at nighttime. It was hard to beat. She'd been surprised when someone had told her that the shadowy mass across the lake was Canada. At first, she'd thought they were kidding, but it had turned out to be true. She'd never been to another country before, and she hadn't realized Canada was that close. She liked to look at it across the water, sitting there in a mysterious haze, and wonder what they were doing over there. Was someone on that side lying on a beach, looking across the water at the United States and wondering the same thing?

The beach was crowded.

She found an empty space on the sand to spread out her towel, not too far from the water. She didn't know how to swim, but she stepped into the lake up to her knees and splashed some water on herself. She was afraid to go any farther.

Once she cooled off, she returned to the old bath towel and sat down with her legs stretched out in front of her. She folded up her cover-up and created an impromptu pillow.

Trying not to be too obvious about it, she glanced around the packed beach. An elderly woman stood at the shore, holding hands with an elderly man, most likely her husband. With her free hand, the woman held up the skirt of her housedress and let the water rush over her feet, giggling like a schoolgirl. Blankets, towels, and old bedspreads were laid out all over the beach, bearing people of all ages. There was an obvious lack of young men; the few who were there must either be on leave or their health had kept them back from joining the military.

But there were girls Diana's age all over the place, mostly clustered in small groups of three, four, and five, laughing and talking loudly. Diana envied them. She hadn't made one good friend since she arrived. She saw some people regularly enough that they'd acknowledge her with a nod or sometimes even a wave if she was lucky. But the close friendships among these women had formed during their school years, and Diana had arrived too late. She thought of her friends back in Pennsylvania. Since the move, she'd lost touch. It was her own fault.

Hopefully, she would make some friends at her new job.

She settled on the bath towel and to take her mind off her loneliness, she pulled Preston's letters out of her bag. They were very romantic. She flipped over and lay on her stomach, feet in the air, and pulled the first letter out of its envelope and started reading.

Chapter Twenty-Six

Diana walked back from the canteen at the end of her lunch break, readying herself to sidestep Creepy Les, the assistant foreman. He was so named because of the way he treated the women at the plant. He opened his mouth to say something as she passed, but she picked up her pace. On the advice she'd received early on from some of the other women she worked with, she steered clear of him.

"Hey, Diana!"

Diana turned and caught sight of Sally, whose job it was to paint the American insignia on the planes, waving to her. She waited until Sally caught up.

"There's a dance Saturday night at the Lavender Bay Pavilion," Sally said. "Are you going?"

"You can bet on it," Diana said with a smile. She loved dancing. She loved jitterbugging. She went out every chance she got. And Saturday, she was on the day shift, so that would be perfect.

"Great! I'll meet you there."

With a smile and a wave, Diana trotted off to her post. The bell sounded, signaling lunch break was over and work was to commence.

She arrived at her buffer, breathless, and turned it on. As it started, she put her hand on her head, realizing she'd forgotten to put her headscarf back on. She pivoted to grab it off the workbench where she'd left it, her hair swinging behind her as she turned. That's when she felt it: the pull on her scalp as her hair wound into the buffer. She screamed, instinctively reaching out for something to hold on to, and then suddenly she was free. It all happened so fast. Her workmate saw it happening and lunged to turn the machine off, but it was too late.

Diana felt something wet draining down the side of her head and onto her shoulders. She put her hand up to her head, and it came away covered in blood. She turned slowly. Her workmate stood there with her hands covering her mouth, stifling a scream. Diana looked at the buffer. A section of her long hair—her beautiful, golden, honey-colored hair—was wrapped around the buffer with a large piece of pink flesh dangling from the end of it.

Her eyes rolled back into her head, and she hit the floor.

The next thing she was aware of was someone kneeling at her side, patting her hand.

"Diana! Diana!"

She swam back up to consciousness, out of the blackness and into the harsh lighting of the factory. For a moment, she wondered how she got on the floor. There was an incredible pain on the side of her head. She reached up to touch it.

"Don't touch it, honey," advised a woman she didn't know, someone who didn't work in her department.

"Ambulance is on its way," someone else said.

"You girls are told a million times to wear your headscarves." She recognized the voice of Creepy Les.

"Shut up, Les," said a female voice.

Things on the edge of her field of vision began to go from light to gray to black, and she could feel herself sinking back into unconsciousness. She almost welcomed it.

To the woman who was holding her hand, she said, "Can someone get my hair? It's on the machine."

The woman patted her hand and gave her a reassuring smile. "Don't worry about a thing, honey. We're going to get you to the hospital, right away."

The plant foreman, George Treadwell, arrived and looked down at her. His face paled and his expression was grim. Diana started to cry.

The crowd parted, and the woman holding her hand let go and stood up. Diana's good friends from her carpool, Laura and Joy, appeared, stopping short when they saw Diana. They were careful to keep their expressions neutral, but their eyes said it all. They rushed to kneel on either side of her.

"We're here, Diana," Joy said, giving her hand a gentle squeeze.

Diana looked at them through her tears. "Is it bad?" she wailed.

"It's going to be fine," Laura said, and she patted her hand.

"You'll be fine, honey," Joy said, "but we need to get you to the hospital."

A crowd had gathered around them, which meant that all work had come to a standstill in the plant. Diana closed her eyes.

Laura removed her own headscarf and laid it over the side of Diana's head. The pain was incredible. She fought to stay conscious. It might be a blessed relief to go under, but she was too afraid she might not wake up.

Two ambulance attendants arrived, pushing through the crowd with a stretcher. The incident was explained to them, and one pulled away the headscarf to assess the wound. His eyes met Diana's and all she saw in them was pity. She closed her eyes and cried as she was carted off, wishing she could turn back the clock and put that headscarf on.

Once she arrived at the hospital, things happened quickly. Apparently, they were waiting for her, having been notified ahead of time. Later, her recall of that time would be blurry, with only impressions.

Doctors and nurses surrounded her. She was grateful that she was the only patient in the room. One of the doctors leaned forward to examine her head wound.

"We've got a partial scalp avulsion," he said.

A nun stood at the foot of the bed, and Diana wondered how bad it was if they needed a religious figure present. At least it wasn't a priest.

"Diana? I'm Dr. Pellman," said the doctor. "We're going to get you into surgery to stop the bleeding and clean the wound up."

She nodded. She wanted the pain to go away.

Dr. Pellman addressed the nurse. "Prep her for immediate surgery." He looked back at Diana and said, "You're one lucky young woman. You could have been killed."

Of all the words out there, Diana would never have picked "lucky."

In the operating suite, the doctor explained that he was going to give her something to put her to sleep, and as things started going black, she'd never been so grateful.

When she opened her eyes, things were blurry for a bit and then came into focus. The ceiling above her had a water stain in the corner, the color of tea. Her eyelids felt heavy, and she fought to stay awake. Tentatively, she lifted her hand to the side of her head and felt around gingerly, but it was covered in bandages. Out of the corner of her eye, she saw her hair falling down over her right shoulder. But nothing fell over her left. The pain had lessened; they must have given her something. Her eyes continued to close, and she gave up, thinking that sleep might be better than being awake.

In fact, over the next few days, Diana wanted nothing other than to remain asleep. But the doctors and nurses encouraged her to stay awake. Her mother visited every day. Laura and Joy came regularly. The doctor said more than once how lucky she was, and she felt like punching him in the face.

She was in a ward with five other women, who were there for sundry things. She saw the pitying looks on their faces and heard the whispers to their visitors accompanied by not-so-subtle nods. She wanted to go home.

She'd just had her second skin graft. The first one had failed, and they took her back in, removed skin from the back of her other thigh, and were hopeful that this one would take. Dr. Pellman had explained to her that the skin graft was necessary to replace the lost skin and to help the wound heal faster. He'd made it sound like she couldn't do without it.

On the day they removed the bandages, Dr. Pellman came in with another doctor and a nurse. The nurse pulled the privacy screen around the bed.

"Let's take a look at the graft," Dr. Pellman said to Diana. He gently unwound the bandages, peeling them away, and smiled. "It's healing nicely. No sign of infection. If it continues on this course, you should be able to go home in a few days."

She couldn't wait.

"Will my hair grow back?" she asked.

The doctor hesitated before shaking his head. "I'm sorry. No."

She nodded, swallowing hard. "Can I see it?" she asked.

"Yes," he said. He nodded to the nurse, who disappeared behind the screen and returned almost immediately with a handheld mirror.

Diana drew in a deep breath and took the offered mirror. She closed her eyes and held it up in front of her face. When she opened her eyes, she came face to face with her new reality. On the left side of her head, the wound extended from the top of her ear to where her part used to be. There was no hair left on that side. The golden locks she'd been so proud of were gone forever. In their place was a large piece of skin sewn into place with big, black stitches.

It was beyond ugly. It was hideous.

She dropped the mirror in her lap and leaned over the side of the bed, vomiting all over the doctor's nice wingtip shoes.

Chapter Twenty-Seven

Diana removed her belongings from the bedside cabinet, packing them into the small suitcase her mother had brought for her. She was finally going home from the hospital. The neighbor had offered to give them a lift, but Diana had told her mother no. She wanted to go by taxi. She didn't want to see anyone she knew. Didn't want to have to make inane small talk.

"You'll feel so much better to be in your own bed," her mother said, emptying the top drawer of a few toiletries. There was a forced cheerfulness in her voice. A brightness Diana didn't think she'd ever feel again.

She finished packing—there wasn't much—and slammed the suitcase shut, anxious to get out of there.

"I'm ready, Ma. Let's go," she said, hoisting the suitcase off the bed. She was aware of the eyes of the other women in the ward on her. She'd not engaged with any of them, choosing instead to listen to their mundane conversations about husbands and children, knowing she'd never have those types of conversations. They'd tried to get her involved, but she'd only nod or shrug or, if it was a good day, give them a one-word answer.

As she made her way out of the ward with her mother at her side, they called out to her one after the other. "Good luck, Diana!"

There was that word again. Luck.

"Thank you," she said, her voice flat. Then she walked out of the ward and into the corridor, hoping she'd never have to come back to this hospital again.

Once home, she set the suitcase down in her bedroom behind the door, not at all interested in unpacking it. She undressed, pulled on her nightgown, climbed into bed, and turned toward the wall, her good side resting on her arm.

Her mother appeared in the doorway. "Diana, what are you doing?" Her laugh was nervous. "It's the middle of the day."

Diana shrugged. She had no energy to answer.

"Did you unpack your suitcase?" her mother asked.

"I'll do it later. I'm tired. I want to take a nap."

"All right. Will I close the door?" There was uncertainty in Millie's voice.

"Please."

Weeks later, Diana was hardly eating and had spent most of her time in her bed, despite her mother's best efforts. She couldn't see the point of getting up. For what reason? She'd lost her job and suffered a permanent disfigurement.

When Millie failed in her efforts to motivate her daughter, she enlisted the help of Laura and Joy, who visited regularly. Initially, Diana resisted their efforts. In the beginning, she lay on her side, blanket pulled up to her shoulders while they visited. Gradually, she sat up in her bed, pulling the covers up to her waist. This was progress. Other coworkers tried to visit, but Diana had her mother turn them all away, and eventually, they gave up. With nothing to do, Diana could outwait them all.

But Laura and Joy had their own ideas. And pretty soon, just to shut them up and get them off her back, she agreed to get out of bed and sit with them in the parlor.

Then a beautiful day came along, and they prodded her to sit out on the porch, her first time outside since she'd come home from the hospital.

She continued with these brief forays out onto the porch, only a few minutes at a time to get some fresh air. And if a neighbor passed by and waved, she returned the wave but stood and went inside to discourage anyone from approaching or trying to engage her in conversation.

Her new world was the interior of the house and the front porch, and she muddled along with the help of her mother and her two best friends. Every day was long and something to be got through. She took up smoking, hoping it would calm her nerves. It did, somewhat.

But then everything changed.

A letter arrived from Preston.

He was due home on leave, and he couldn't wait to see her.

Chapter Twenty-Eight

Despite all the encouragement from Laura and Joy, Diana dreaded the arrival of Preston. His letters were gushy and at one time, she'd found that endearing, but now it was off-putting. More than once, he mentioned her beautiful hair and how he wanted to run his fingers through it. Whenever it came to that part, she'd fold the letter back up and tuck it neatly into its envelope. In the past, she had always looked forward to Preston's letters, but today, she felt nothing but sadness. In the letter before the accident, he'd mentioned the subject of marriage and excitedly, she'd told some of her friends at work. How stupid could one person be? She had stopped rereading his letters. They were now in a box beneath her bed, gathering dust. There was no point.

Initially, she put off seeing him, making one excuse after another. But finally, he wouldn't take no for an answer and it was agreed that he would come over on the third night of his leave. Laura and Joy stopped by beforehand and helped Diana select a dress. She picked one that enhanced the color of her eyes. At least that's what Joy told her. There were no stockings to be had, so she was left with no choice but to go with bare legs. She had a great pair of legs, but they were no longer tan. It had been so long since she'd been down to the beach. The last thing she did was put on a headscarf, double-checking it to make sure it was secure.

When Preston arrived on her doorstep with a large bouquet of flowers, she was touched. What she had not expected was for him to pull her into his arms. It happened so fast that she felt her headscarf shift, and she quickly reached up and made sure it was still in place.

"Come here, beautiful," he said, kissing her on the lips.

Millie emerged from the back of the house. "Is that you, Preston?"

"Hello, Mrs. Quinn," he said. He'd draped an arm around Diana's shoulders, and Diana wished she could dislodge herself. It almost felt as if the walls were closing in on her.

Millie sensed Diana's distress. "What are your plans tonight?" she asked, the fingers of one hand splayed across her collarbone.

Preston looked at Diana, his arm still linked around her shoulders. "I don't know. I thought we'd go dancing."

That was the last thing Diana wanted to do.

Millie glanced at her daughter and said in an unnaturally high voice, "That sounds nice."

Diana gave a slight nod.

"I'll leave you two alone. Have a lovely evening," Millie said. "Not too late, Diana."

"No, Ma."

Millie disappeared down the hall and shut her bedroom door.

"Where would you like to go dancing?" Preston asked.

"I thought we could stay in," Diana said. She slipped out from under his arm and put some space between them, enough that she was out of his reach.

Preston frowned and put his hands in his pockets. "What's wrong? I thought you'd be happy to see me."

She didn't miss the hurt in his voice. "Of course I am, Preston. But I'm not the same person you knew before."

His grin was wide. "Don't be silly, Diana. You're the girl I remember. You're as beautiful as ever."

When she didn't say anything, he stepped forward, reaching for her hand. "Come on, I think we need to trip the light fantastic. You used to love dancing."

She pulled her hand out of his grasp. "I don't want to."

"Remember all the dancing we used to do? Remember, we swore we were going to have a whole bunch of little dancers ourselves."

Diana clasped her hands in front of her mouth to prevent a cry from escaping. With a shaky voice, she said, "I haven't been dancing in a long time."

Preston looked skeptical. "You? I don't believe it."

"Well, it's true," she said with more sharpness than she intended.

"We're going to have to do something about that," he whispered, sidling up next to her. In the past, that tone had always made her knees weak, but now it irritated her. Again, she stepped away from him.

He looked at her headscarf and said, "Did you want to get ready or something? Do your hair?"

Diana snorted; she couldn't help it. Why wasn't he listening to her? "Do my hair? Preston, didn't you get my letter about my accident?"

"Yeah, yeah, sure I did. You said you hurt your head at the plant."

Boy, she wished it were as simple as that. And now, she wished she'd told him the truth. The harsh reality of it. "It was a little more than me hurting my head."

He looked at her, saying nothing. Waiting.

"Preston," she said quietly, "I didn't tell you everything in my letter, and maybe I should have. I'm missing part of my scalp." She gestured to the left side of her head. "My hair is gone on this side of my head. The scarf is permanent. I will be wearing a head covering for the rest of my life."

Preston's Adam's apple bobbed up and down. "Sweetheart, it can't be that bad," he said, mustering a smile. He reached for her, touching her arm, but Diana flinched and stepped back. His smile faltered. "Come on, Diana, it's me, Preston."

"I'm trying to tell you that it *is* that bad."

"What about a wig?"

Diana shook her head. "They irritate my scalp." She had one tucked away in the closet in case of an emergency, but she'd never worn it, preferring the headscarves. The wig made her scalp sweat, which became uncomfortable.

"Let me take a look at it."

"It's not pretty," Diana warned.

"Why don't you show me and let me be the judge," he said gently.

Despite her refusals, he continued to pester her to see it, reassuring her that it would be all right. Finally, she gave in to his demands.

No one except her mother and Laura and Joy had seen the extent of her injury. She didn't think she trusted Preston as she did them. But she realized, sadly, they could not go forward until he'd seen it. They'd talked about getting married; she wouldn't be able to hide it from him forever.

As she untied her scarf at the nape of her neck, she had a sense of foreboding, of things ending. Her shoulders sagged a little. Slowly, she pulled off the scarf.

Preston took a step back, nearly stumbling. He blanched, his face going whiter than white, and his eyes widened. Diana hastily put the scarf back on, tying it tightly. She forced herself to look at him.

He was no longer simply pale. His color had taken on a greenish hue, and she wondered if he was going to throw up. She couldn't blame him. It was what she'd done when she'd first seen it in the mirror.

"So, you see why I can't go out," she said.

"Uh-huh." He shifted on his feet, swallowing hard, looking as if he might need a drink.

The silence stretched out between them. There was no more talk of going dancing, no more "sweetheart," only thundering silence. It was in the space of that silence that Diana made a decision.

"Look, Preston, we sure had a lot of fun."

He nodded.

"But you see," she said, "with you being away and everything, it's too hard for me. I want someone who's here."

"Uh-huh."

"And I know you spoke about marriage,"—Preston took in a sharp breath—"but I'm going to have to refuse."

"Huh?" he asked as if coming out of a stupor.

Diana raised her voice slightly and said again, "You spoke about marriage in your letters, but I'll have to decline." His emphasis on the subject had increased with every letter. Now she regretted not putting a stop to it at the time. It had been unfair to both of them.

If the relief that so visibly washed over him had been a wave, it would have knocked over the house.

"I appreciate the time we've spent together," she went on, "but it's time to go our separate ways."

Preston gave a slight nod. Diana met his gaze and clearly saw his discomfort. She lifted her chin. And even though she was shaking, she stood her ground.

He started to speak, but then stopped and cleared his throat and mumbled, "You're right, it's probably for the best."

There was a tiny part of Diana that had hoped he'd fight for her. But when no protests were forthcoming, when he didn't shout her down and tell her that he loved her no matter what, that little flame of hope was extinguished.

There was no point in prolonging this. She pivoted and walked toward the door to see him out.

Before he left, he surprised her by leaning in and kissing her cheek, and she forced herself to still the wave of emotion that rose up within her. He whispered, "Take care of yourself, Diana." And he slipped outside and was gone.

She closed the door behind him and sagged against it, swiping the tears that fell from her eyes.

That's that, then.

She headed toward her room and ran into her mother, who was emerging from hers.

"Where's Preston?" Millie asked.

"He's gone."

"Is he coming back?"

Diana shook her head. "No, he isn't."

"Where are you going?"

"To bed."

Bed was the safest place for her right now. She planned on crawling beneath the blankets and staying there. Because there was no reason at all to get up.

Chapter Twenty-Nine

1946

"You can do this," Laura encouraged Diana.

It was a bitter cold day in February, and Diana was wearing the hat her mother had knitted for her to keep her head warm.

Beside her, Joy nodded. "Honey, it's not like you need to let these people into your life."

Somehow, she'd let Laura and Joy convince her to take on a new venture: taking in sewing and mending. She'd managed to save a decent sum in the year she'd worked at the plant, but that wouldn't last forever, as she knew. The money from Aunt Lavinia was long gone.

Other than the ability to run a buffer, her skill with a sewing needle was the only one she possessed. Because of her accident, she'd never again work with industrial machinery. And that didn't matter anyway, as the war was over and the boys had come home and gone back to work.

Her first customer was due to arrive today, a woman who'd worked at the aviation plant in Cheever. On their last day at the plant, Laura and Joy had handed out index cards with Diana's information on it to their coworkers, telling them to contact her for mending, sewing, and alterations. The phone had started ringing.

After the war, Laura began searching for another job to help support her young family, and Joy went back to the role she relished most: wife and mother. Diana envied them their sure-footedness; each knew exactly what she wanted, whereas Diana wasn't sure what her life, post-accident, would look like or how she wanted it to be. It was similar to feeling around in the dark for the light switch, trying not to stub your toe.

Diana nodded, but her hands shook. She fingered the St. Anthony medal that hung around her neck. Joy had given it to her, and she found great comfort in it.

"You've only got one customer to deal with today," Laura reminded her. She'd opened the red leather diary she'd given Diana as a gift and tapped a varnished fingernail on the name written in pencil for that date. Diana stared at it and blinked. She was committed.

She knew her friends meant well, but she would have been content continuing on as she had been: not leaving the house and not seeing people.

As if reading her mind, Laura said, "I know you're nervous, but you've got to move on with your life."

Diana went to snap back at her, but Joy cut her off. "You know Laura is right. You can't hide out in the bedroom for the rest of your life. You're too young."

What good was it, she wanted to ask. It wasn't like she'd ever get married or have children. What was the point of leaving the house if only to be treated like something in a freak show?

The doorbell rang and Diana jumped, but she didn't get up.

"I'll get it," Laura said, and walked with purpose and expedience to the front door and opened it. "Hello, Phyllis."

Phyllis was someone Diana knew by sight. She'd worked in a different department. She was a tall, solid girl, almost six feet. And she was loud and blustery to boot. As soon as she crossed the threshold of the Quinn household, she said in a booming voice, "I see the gang's all here!" At her side, she carried a large brown paper bag.

Laura and Joy made small talk with Phyllis for a few moments, the three of them catching up on what they'd been doing since leaving Cheever Aviation.

Phyllis approached Diana. Tentatively, she reached out and touched Diana's arm. "How are you?"

"I'm okay," Diana said evenly. Before an awkward silence could set in, she nodded toward the bag in Phyllis's hand. "What do you need to have done?" She wasn't going to stand around all day and make small talk.

Phyllis opened the bag and pulled out a few long- and short-sleeved men's dress shirts, laying them over her arm. "These are my husband's. He has a habit of ripping open the buttons instead of just undoing them, so they need to be replaced." She handed the pile to Diana, who nodded. Then she reached back into the bag and handed Diana two pairs of dungarees. With a shake of her head, she said, "The knees are gone in these pants. The boys are as bad as their father with the way they beat up their clothes." She laughed, and Joy and Laura laughed with her. Diana managed a small smile.

"When can I pick them up?" Phyllis asked.

"How about the day after tomorrow?" Diana said.

"Perfect." She dug through her pocketbook. "Shall I pay you now?"

Diana shook her head. "No, wait until you come and pick them up."

On her way out, Phyllis said, "It was good to see all of you again."

As soon as she was gone, Diana let out a huge breath. She pulled her cigarette case from the pocket of her dress and with shaking hands, lit one. She took a long, satisfying drag.

"It wasn't that bad, now, was it?" Joy asked.

Diana shook her head. "No, I guess not."

"It'll get easier," Laura said. "You'll see."

"Now how about some tea?" Joy asked.

Diana nodded and headed to the kitchen, thinking she'd like something stronger, but tea would have to do.

Chapter Thirty

1947

"More tiramisu?" Sam asked Diana.

She shook her head. As much as she loved the dessert, she was stuffed. This happened every Sunday at Joy and Sam's house. Diana always ate too much. It was hard not to, the food was so delicious. It was a nice break from the steady diet of meat and potatoes she and her mother tended to eat at home. Today, stuffed shells had been on the menu.

"Are you sure?" he asked again from his seat at the head of the table. Joy sat to his right, and Diana sat to his left. Their three kids, along with Laura and her husband Edwin and their two girls, rounded out the rest of the table. For whatever reason, this place next to Sam had become her spot.

She laughed. You couldn't help but like Sam Ruggiero. He went out of his way to make people feel at home. "I can't, Sam."

"Well, if you won't, I will." He helped himself to a generous second portion. He looked briefly around the table and asked, "Anyone else? What about you, Edna? Edith? Put some meat on those bones."

"No!" Edna yelled, laughing.

"Oh, Sam!" Joy said. "He's put on twenty pounds since the war ended," she told her guests.

"But I lost twenty pounds while I was fighting the war," Sam was quick to point out, "so I'm right back where I started. Ain't I, hon?"

Joy gave up.

That's how it was in this house: loud and boisterous, and Diana enjoyed every minute of it. The weekly dinner was something she looked forward to in her long, dull week.

Still smiling, she stood along with Joy and Laura to begin cleaning up. As soon as they got up, the kids did also, and began running around the house, chasing each other. Neither Sam nor Edwin appeared to notice. Edwin moved to Diana's vacant seat and as she headed into the kitchen carrying a pile of plates, she heard their talk of Harry Truman.

Diana set her pile of plates on the counter. Joy was already filling the pan in the sink with water and dish soap. Laura began scraping what was left on the plates into the trash.

Diana made several trips to the dining room to clear the rest of the dishes. On her last round, Sam was leaned back, smoking a cigarette, while Edwin had both elbows on the table. The conversation had shifted from politics to baseball, specifically the Brooklyn Dodgers.

Smiling, she returned to the kitchen and scraped the last of the plates as Laura, dish towel in hand, had started to dry the dishes while Joy washed.

"Do you want me to put the rest of these shells in a smaller dish?" Diana asked, eyeing the roasting pan on the stove. The pan was too big for the small amount of shells that were left over.

"That'd be great." Joy nodded to a bottom cabinet next to her, adding, "You'll find a smaller roasting pan in there. You can cover it with tin foil."

Diana bent down and retrieved a more suitable pan for the leftovers. Using a large spoon, she transferred the remaining shells into the smaller pan, covering them with tin foil as instructed.

"How are things going at the answering service?" Diana asked Laura about her new job.

"Good, I like it," Laura said.

"You don't mind working overnight?" Joy asked, referring to the midnight-to-eight shift that Laura sometimes worked.

"Not too much. It's never more than two nights a week. Edwin isn't crazy about it, but it's work." Laura dried a plate and set it on the stack of plates on the table. With a laugh she added, "It is so much easier than the aviation plant."

"I bet," Joy said.

"And as it turns out, I like talking on the phone!"

They all laughed.

"Besides, I like the extra money. It will allow me to buy things I want for the house."

They knew of Laura's penchant for the newest appliance on the market, her most recent purchase being a brand-new washing machine. It had given Diana the idea to start squirreling her own money away to save up for something nice.

"I'll finish up here. Go on and sit down," Joy said when the last dish was washed. She wrung out the dish rag and began to wipe down the counters.

Diana followed Laura out of the kitchen. Laura took a seat next to Edwin at the table, but Diana kept walking, heading to the front porch. The air was humid, and the inside of the house was close. She pushed through the wooden screen door, holding on to it so it wouldn't slam shut. She sat on the wide porch railing and reached for an empty ashtray. She pulled out her cigarette case from the pocket of her skirt but realized she'd forgotten her matches. Not wanting to go back inside to get a light, she remained seated, holding on to her unlit cigarette, one thigh perched on the railing, the other leg extended, foot on the floor. She smoothed out her skirt, admiring the colorful pattern of orange, red, and yellow. She'd made a headscarf to match.

Joy and Sam lived one township over from Lavender Bay, further inland. There was no beach here, but there were plenty of vineyards. It was one thing she looked forward to on the ride out with Laura and Edwin: the sight of the seemingly endless rows of grapes growing on both sides of the highway. It was beautiful in its own right. Even Sam and Joy had a small vine of grapes growing out back, as Sam liked to make his own wine. Diana had tried it and had liked it very much.

She'd sit out here until Laura and Edwin were ready to leave, she decided. It wouldn't be long. Laura had mentioned something about the circus being in town, and she was going to take the girls as well as Sam and Joy's kids.

The screen door opened, and Sam appeared carrying a can of lighter fluid. He leaned over the railing and refilled his Zippo.

"I must be smoking too much, I seem to be refilling this more often," he said. When he was finished, he set the can down on the porch railing and nodded toward her cigarette.

"Can I light that for you?"

"Please and thank you," she said, holding it out for him.

He lit her cigarette and then his own before snapping his lighter shut and shoving it into his pocket. He took a long drag and stood there, looking into the distance.

"It's been a good summer," he declared.

"It has," Diana agreed. It had been perfect. Sunshine and heat during the day and little bits of rain, mostly overnight.

"Joy says you're doing well with the sewing and mending," he said.

"I am. The customers are starting to trickle in."

He nodded and took another hit off his cigarette. "That's how it starts. Once the word gets out, it isn't long before the trickle becomes a gush."

They were silent, but it wasn't awkward by any means. Sam was one of the few people Diana felt totally at ease with since the accident.

"I want to say something, and I don't want you to take it the wrong way," he blustered, adding, "Joy says I'm always sticking my big nose where it doesn't belong."

Diana couldn't help but laugh. But she didn't say anything, waiting for him to continue.

"I'm glad you've found something you enjoy doing. You know Joy and Laura were worried sick about you after the accident."

"I know," she said quietly. She didn't look at him, choosing to look at the house across the street with its rosebushes all lined up in front of it. She wondered if the scent carried over on the breeze.

"We're all glad that you come here every Sunday for dinner. Hell, you could come over seven nights a week if you wanted. And we're glad you've got your little business up and running."

Diana still said nothing, letting him continue.

He rubbed the back of his head. "What am I trying to say here?"

"I don't know, Sam." She couldn't keep the mirth out of her voice.

"Diana, the casualties of the war weren't only on the battlefields. It was everywhere: men and women who were injured working in defense plants, sweethearts and mothers and fathers who lost their loved ones . . ."

He stopped talking, took another drag of his cigarette, and then stubbed the butt out in the ashtray before lighting up another one.

"If there's one thing I learned from fighting in the war," he continued, "it's this: we've all been affected some way or another. Some worse than others."

"I know, Sam."

"I've seen enough death to last me a lifetime," he continued, and his eyes took on a faraway look. "We only have this moment right now. We don't know what's going to happen tomorrow."

"And?"

Now he looked at her, holding his cigarette between his thumb and forefinger, the ash on it lengthening. "Diana, you are a casualty of the war. Plain and simple. Just because you didn't pick up a gun doesn't mean that you aren't a casualty. Despite this, you need to create a life for yourself."

"What do you mean?"

He sighed, bringing up the cigarette and taking such a long drag that smoke drifted up into his eyes, causing him to squint. "You know me to be blunt, don't you, after all this time?"

"I do."

"What I mean to say is, you can't hide out for the rest of your life in your house. It ain't right." He shook his head as if for emphasis.

Diana protested. "But I feel safe there."

"I know you do," he said. "But you can't. You're too young to hide yourself away. You've got your whole life ahead of you."

She snorted. "Such as it is."

There was a brief flash of anger behind his eyes. It would be the only time in their lives she'd ever see that from him.

"There are many men who came home in a box that would gladly trade places with you," he said angrily.

Diana's cheeks reddened, and she swallowed hard. "I'm sorry, Sam."

He waved her apology away, the anger gone as quickly as it had appeared. "I'm not trying to make you feel bad, kid. But life is so precious. So, your life didn't turn out the way you thought it would." He shrugged. "Did I think I'd have to leave my wife and kids and go off to fight in a foreign land? Against the country of my parents' birth? Not in my wildest dreams." He paused and shook his head. "They were strange times."

She swallowed hard. Basically, he was telling her to stop feeling sorry for herself and get on with it. Maybe she'd been mollycoddled too long by her mother and

Laura and Joy. Maybe hiding out in her house was the path of least resistance.

"Look, Diana, I don't know anything. I dropped out of school in the ninth grade. But the way I see it, you should take your focus off yourself and your injuries and look for the good in life. Because life is for the living."

The screen door opened and Joy appeared, hands on her hips, still wearing her apron. "What's this? The Yalta Conference?"

Diana laughed. "No, Sam is just giving me some sound advice."

Laura and Edwin and all the kids had followed Joy out.

"Diana, are you ready?" Laura asked.

"I am." She stubbed out her cigarette in the ashtray.

"It'll be a tight squeeze with five kids, but we'll manage," Laura said.

Edna and Edith and the three Ruggiero kids jumped off the porch and headed to the car, opening doors, laughing and climbing in.

Laura stepped off the porch and called out, "Someone will have to sit up front!"

Diana stood and wiped off the back of her skirt, thanking Joy for the Sunday meal. She lingered for a moment. As she stepped off the porch, she turned and said, "Thanks, Sam."

He smiled at her, the warmth and genuineness that he was noted for, back. "Don't mention it, kid."

Chapter Thirty-One

Diana took Sam's words to heart. She lay awake at night, thinking about them. What was maddening was that she knew deep down that he was right. So many men had not returned from the war and here she was, getting a second chance. And what was she doing? Secluding herself in her house. Avoiding other people. Not engaging. But still she held back. Talk was easy. Doing was hard. But what was it FDR had said? "The only thing we have to fear is fear itself."

One Tuesday afternoon, after lunch, she said to her mother, "I think I'll go for a walk."

Her mother looked up at her, surprised. "You will?"

"Yes."

"That's a good idea. The fresh air will do you good."

Before she left the house, she checked her headscarf several times to make sure it was secure. The longer she delayed, the weaker the impulse to actually leave the house became. Finally, she muttered to herself, "Pull yourself together, Diana Quinn, and walk out that door." It was late September, and even though the sun was warm, the breeze was cool. Like the other seasons, fall had its own feel. Cooler air and weak, watery sunshine. Still, she tilted her head toward the sky as she walked, liking the feel of the sun on her face. She cut down their street, waving to Mr. McAlister as she passed, as he shoveled a pale of ash around the base of a fruit tree.

Her destination was the VFW, Veterans of Foreign Wars, on Primrose and Vine. She took the side streets over, avoiding Main, not quite ready to mingle with the throng of pedestrians. Children were back in school, so the streets were quiet. Some of the leaves on the trees were beginning to fade to yellow and orange. It was a pleasant walk.

The VFW was not a purpose-built building. It was a converted older redbrick home of Italianate architecture, with a low-pitched roof and tall, pedimented windows.

Taking a deep breath, she climbed the front steps and stood at the double front doors, suddenly unsure. Did she knock, or did she just walk in? There was a momentary sense of panic. A sign hung on the window reading *All welcome*. And that decided it.

Carefully, she tried the doorknob, and when it turned, she opened the door and stepped inside, finding herself in a long, narrow hall with reception rooms on either side. Pocket doors stood half open. A wide staircase with a decorative banister led up to the second and third floors. Sunshine slanted in through the beveled windows, casting distorted geometric patterns across the hardwood floor.

Coming from the back of the building was the deep sound of men's voices. Then some laughter.

Diana lifted her chin and straightened her posture. She walked down the hallway and called out, "Hello?" When no one answered, she cleared her throat and said louder, "Hello?"

When there was no answer—as it was quite possible they hadn't heard her—she followed the sound of the voices to the back of the house. Above her, there was movement upstairs, footsteps echoing across a floor.

She poked her head through the doorway of a large room that must once have been a library, as evidenced by the bookshelves on every wall.

The room was smoky, and the smell of nicotine gave her a craving for a cigarette.

Five or six men sat in club chairs, three of them arranged around a small square table with cards laid out on it. They all looked up at her and seemed to regard her with curiosity more than anything.

One man stood, an elderly gentleman with silver hair and a patrician nose, wearing a row of medals across the chest of his suit jacket.

"Can I help you?" His voice was gruff, but he didn't sound mean.

Aware of all their eyes on her and wishing she'd stayed at home minding her own business, she silently cursed Sam. She pulled out an index card from her purse.

"My name is Diana Quinn. I'm a seamstress. And, well," she stammered, all the words of the speech she'd prepared bunching up in her head and getting out of order, "I wanted to offer a discount on mending, sewing, laundry, and ironing for any veteran." She would do the sewing and mending, and her mother would do the rest.

She shifted on her feet, nervously holding her purse in front of her.

The older man said, "I'm Trevor Dann." He accepted the card she handed him and studied it. The other men watched him, silent. Diana felt as if she'd stepped into the lion's den. On the card was her phone number and a description of her sewing services.

When Trevor said nothing more, she said, "Anyway, I thought I'd drop it off in case anyone needs alterations or anything. Sewing. Mending . . ." Her voice trailed off.

Trevor narrowed his eyes at her and asked, "Are you a good seamstress?"

She stood a little straighter. Mustering some confidence, she said, "Yes, I am."

He broke into a smile. "That's good then." He pointed to a board on the opposite wall. "I'll put it up on the board over there. You said there's a discount for veterans?"

"That's right. It's there on the card," Diana said, pointing a red-lacquered nail to the index card.

"So it is." Trevor walked over to the board and pinned it up with a tack.

"Thank you," Diana said. She wondered if perhaps a female presence wasn't welcome in their lair. Trevor went to escort her out and she said, "I can show myself out, thank you." She paused in the doorway, half turned, and said, "Good day."

She stepped out into the fresh air and blinked as sunshine hit her in the face. There were still a few cards in her handbag, and she walked on and tacked them up in the post office and on the small corkboard in the grocery store. Finally, she walked into the offices of *The Lavender Bay Chronicles* and placed an ad for two weeks. As an afterthought, she added, *Discount for veterans.*

Chapter Thirty-Two

Based on the reactions of the men she'd encountered at the VFW, Diana did not expect a good response to her ad. She had a better chance of someone seeing her notice in *The Lavender Bay Chronicles*.

But a few phone calls did come from the veterans. And within the first few days.

And suddenly, she had a lot of anxiety about it. She wished she'd never asked them to tack up that card. Up until that point, all her clients had been women. And that had felt safe. There were so many unknowns. Strange men coming to the house. The increase in business. The new direction her life was taking.

"What is the matter with you?" Millie asked, unable to hide the exasperation in her voice.

Diana paced back and forth across the kitchen floor, smoking a cigarette. The day wasn't half over, and she'd already smoked her daily allotment.

Her mother looked at her, her expression both expectant and worried.

Diana kept walking, looking at the floor as she spoke. "A man is coming."

"I suppose with a name like Willard, it would have to be a man," her mother replied, not understanding.

Diana shook her head and took another drag off her cigarette. "I've never had a man for a client before. I don't know what to do."

"You'll treat him just like you treat all the ladies who come to the house," her mother said simply.

"I don't think I can do this."

"You can and you will," Millie said firmly.

Diana pointed to the headscarf covering her head. "What about this?"

"What about it? He's coming here for you to do some mending or sewing for him. Does your injury interfere with your ability to sew?"

"Of course not," Diana snapped. She stopped in the middle of the kitchen floor and folded her arm across her belly, as nausea had set in. "Look, when he gets here, turn him away."

"I will do no such thing." There was sharpness in her mother's voice. "Honestly, I think you're worrying for nothing."

It turned out that Millie Quinn was right. Diana had been worrying for nothing.

Willard Hefferle was young, barely into his twenties, skinny, and had served two years on a naval destroyer in the Pacific. He referred to Diana as "miss" and her mother as "ma'am." But he was also more nervous than Diana. And she soon forgot her own anxiety in an effort to calm him down.

She led him to the spare room where she did her work. As he walked in, he tripped over the carpet and went sailing into the bookcase, rattling it, everything on the shelves doing a slight dance before settling down. When he turned around, his face was puce. He fingered the brim of his fedora and stuttered, "I-I-I'm s-sorry about that."

Diana was quick to reassure him. "No harm done."

Perspiration broke out on his upper lip. She threw open the window. "Now, what can I do for you?"

"I've g-g-got two j-job interviews next w-w-week," he struggled to get out.

"Very good," Diana said. "Where at?"

"One's at Ch-Cheever Aviation, and the other is at G-G-Gibson's G-Grape Jelly factory."

"I used to work at the Cheever plant," Diana said.

"Did you?" he asked, genuinely surprised. His face had returned to a normal color.

"During the war. I worked with the buffers." She didn't go into her accident, deciding to keep that to herself. "Who is your interview with?"

"George Treadwell," he replied.

"He's a fair and decent man," she said honestly of the plant foreman. She nodded toward the brown paper bag at his feet. "What have you brought for me today?"

He pulled out a couple of shirts and a suit. All were crumpled. His face went red again. "I was h-h-hoping to get these l-laundered and pr-pressed for my interview." He reached into the bottom of the bag. "And here's my tie."

The tie was hideous, but Diana said nothing. It looked like an old man's tie. She took the suit in her hands and held it up, inspecting it. It was older. "When was the last time you wore it?"

"B-before the war. My mother's f-f-funeral."

"Have you tried it on to see if it fits?"

"No." A frown distorted his youthful features.

"Put it on, so I can make sure it's fitting properly."

His face went scarlet.

"I'll step out of the room. Holler when you have it on." Before he could respond, she left and closed the door.

It wasn't long before he popped his head out. "I'm r-r-ready."

The suit hung on him. He looked like a kid playing dress-up.

"It looks as though you've lost weight since the last time you wore it," she said.

"The war. But I'm working on getting my weight back up."

Diana got her box of straight pins. "I'm going to take it in for you so it fits properly. When you put the weight on, bring the suit back to me and I'll take it back out."

He frowned again. "W-w-will that be expensive?"

"No," she reassured him. "You'll get a discount for being a veteran."

His smile was the first genuine one since he arrived. "That's what they said at the VFW. That's swell."

She checked the waist of his trousers, tacking in pins where she'd take it in. The length was fine. Then she worked on the jacket.

When she finished, she asked, "When are your interviews?"

"Next M-M-Monday and Wednesday." And then, "Oh, and there's a b-b-button missing on one of the sh-shirts."

She nodded and penned some notes in her little notebook. "How about Saturday? Can you pick them up then?"

"That would be great, m-m-miss."

"Call me Diana."

She instructed him to remove the suit carefully so as not to dislodge the pins. He emerged from the sewing room, and she saw him out, telling him she'd see him Saturday.

When she closed the door behind him, her mother asked, "How did that go?"

"Fine, actually. He was more nervous than me," Diana admitted.

"See, I told you it would be all right."

Willard was back first thing Saturday morning. Millie had laundered and ironed his shirts and hung his suit out on the line to freshen it up. Diana had him try on the suit one more time to make sure she hadn't missed anything. She'd made him a tie, a simple navy one to go with his suit.

"Oh g-g-gee, is that extra?"

Diana shook her head. "No, that's on me."

"Th-thanks. That other one is my d-d-dad's tie."

She'd figured as much. She took a step back to get a better look at the cut of the suit, making a twirling motion with her hand. "Turn around slowly, Willard, so I can see how it fits." He did, and she had to admit she was pleased with the job she'd done.

She left him alone to change back into his clothes. While she waited in the kitchen, she did her sums with a pencil on a scratch pad and applied the discount.

She heard the door open, and he called for her. She took the suit from him and placed it carefully on the hanger so it wouldn't wrinkle. When she told him the total, he nodded, pulled out his wallet from his back pocket, and counted out the money into her hand.

"Thank you, Willard."

He smiled, proud to have a proper suit, pressed shirts, and a brand-new tie. "You know, m-m-miss—er, D-D-Diana, you remind me of my older sister."

"Does she live in Lavender Bay?"

He shook his head. "N-not anymore. When she married, she moved to West Virginia."

Diana hesitated before saying, "Can I tell you what your sister might say, if she were here?"

"Sure."

"Take some deep breaths before you go in for your interviews. To calm down. I have to do it myself at times."

"What c-c-could you be nervous about?" he asked, disbelief clouding his features.

If you only knew. She shook her head and said instead, "Remember, you served your country, so you can do this. Surely, a job interview wouldn't be as hard as fighting in the war."

"It's a different kind of hard."

"Well, you're not alone. Everyone is nervous at job interviews."

"They are?"

She nodded. She removed the shirts, neatly pressed and hanging on hangers, from the hook on the back of the door and handed them to him. As she walked him out, she said, "I wish you good luck with your interviews."

"Thanks, Diana!" He smiled and took his suit and shirts and headed out.

A week later, he called her to let her know he'd secured the job at Cheever Aviation. His phone call made Diana's day.

Chapter Thirty-Three

1950

That spring, as Diana's business was growing steadily, she and her mother got a new neighbor. The house next door, a two-story clapboard house, had been empty since the death of the previous owner. Through the grapevine, Millie had learned that it was a man moving in, a professor up at the college.

Millie couldn't hide her disappointment. "I was hoping for a young family or a woman my age." Despite only living in Lavender Bay for a few years, she had built up a nice network of friends. The elderly lady who'd previously lived next door had struck up a friendship with Millie over the small white picket fence that separated the two properties.

When Diana didn't comment, her mother said, "A college professor. A bachelor. He's probably one of those stuffy types. Smoking a pipe and talking over your head." This information and the presence of a new neighbor had no bearing on Diana's life, so she only half listened.

She was walking home one evening after dropping off some mending for a woman whose baby had arrived three weeks early and who was unable to come over and pick up her clothes. Although the air was cool, it was filled with the smell of wet earth and hope. Some of the trees had small, mossy green buds on them. Summer was coming.

It was almost dark by the time she arrived home. The light was on in the front parlor, casting a square of amber out onto the front porch. Diana opened the front door and announced as she walked in, "Ma, the baby is fine for coming early—"

But she pulled up short when she realized her mother was not alone. A man sat in the never-used wing chair by the fireplace. "Oh, I'm sorry, excuse me," she said. "I didn't know we had company." Immediately she realized this must be the new neighbor.

The man jumped to his feet and stepped forward, extending his hand. "Mark Sturges."

His hand was warm and firm as she shook it. Whatever she'd been expecting of the new neighbor, this wasn't it. He was older—he had to be close to forty—but he wasn't ancient, like she'd been expecting. There was a faint aroma of tobacco circling him that was not unpleasant. He wore a suit. He was half a foot taller than she and had a fine head of dark hair that he wore short and parted on one side.

Her mother stood from her rocker by the front window and held out her arm toward her. "This is my daughter, Diana, who I was telling you about."

What was there to tell?

"Ah, the name Diana, meaning heavenly or divine," he said with a smile.

Oh, dear Lord, she thought.

She waited for his gaze to travel to her headscarf, but it never did, his eyes remaining firmly locked on hers. His were as blue as sapphires.

"Sit down, Diana," her mother said as she and Mark returned to their chairs. "I invited Mark over for the evening. I might have pulled him away from something important."

Mark laughed. "Not really. The company is nice."

Diana sat down on the sofa and crossed her legs.

He pulled a pipe out of his pocket, held it up, and said, "Do you mind if I smoke?"

"Of course not," Diana said.

He retrieved a pouch from his other pocket, dipped his pipe into it, and shook off the excess. He lit it with a match and took a few satisfactory puffs. Soon the parlor was filled with the scent of cherry tobacco.

"Your mother tells me you're a seamstress," he said.

She shot her mother a glance, wondering what else she'd told him.

"Yes, I am."

"That's a handy skill to have."

"Mark teaches up at the university," Millie said. "And he's doing research on Jacques Aubert. Mark, what got you interested in our town founder?"

He appeared thoughtful and took a few puffs of his pipe before answering. "I liked his story. How he was blown off course and ended up here, naming the place for its beautiful lavender skies. It's almost like poetry."

Neither Diana nor her mother commented. Diana knew nothing about poetry, so she figured she should keep her mouth shut.

"Are you researching him for your job?" she asked.

He shook his head. "No. I've been fascinated by his story for a long time. I thought it might be fun to look into him."

Diana could think of other ways to have fun but said nothing.

"Good for you," Millie said.

Diana shot her mother a *tone it down* look.

"Where do you plan on doing your research?" Millie asked.

Diana almost snorted and was tempted to say, *Try the local cemetery*.

"That's the problem," Mark said. "He has been dead for a long time. The library will be a good start, and the historical society. And the cemetery. Although I gather there's no marker for his grave."

Diana shrugged. She knew nothing about Jacques Aubert or his grave, whereabouts known or unknown.

There was no more talk about the founding father of Lavender Bay. But they quickly got used to Mark's presence in their house. Diana could find no serious fault with him. She'd learned that he taught history over at the college. He kept his pipe and his pouch of cherry-flavored tobacco within reach at all times, the same way she always carried her cigarette case in a pocket of her dress. She thought the pipe made him look stodgy, but she also got the impression he didn't care what he looked like.

He walked over on the odd evening and as the weather got warmer, he sat out on the porch with them. Her mother kept a steady stream of pies and cakes going over to his house. On occasion, he joined them for dinner, always complimenting Millie on the meal.

But he had one habit Millie had to put a stop to. Every time she or Diana entered a room, he stood up. *Every time*. Finally, she told him, "Mark, you *must* stop getting up every time we enter the room. It's unsettling."

To which Diana had joked, "You're beginning to look like a jack-in-the-box."

In the beginning, she wondered why he didn't just stay in his own house; did he really need to be entertained all the time? But her mother was always more than happy to sit with him and chat. She liked to fuss over him. It was only when her mother explained to her that he had been married once and that his wife had died in childbirth along with their baby, a son, that Diana softened toward him. That was sad, and she felt sorry for him.

"Tell me, Diana, do you play chess?" Mark asked one evening as they sat out on the porch. Summer had ended, and they were already halfway through the month of September. The night air had turned chilly, and Diana had needed to go back inside for her cardigan and her mother's shawl. It would probably be one of the last times they'd be able to sit outside that year.

She tilted her head to one side and asked with a pointed look, "Do I look like a chess player?"

Her mother's expression was aghast. "Diana! Mark asked you a simple question."

Diana reddened. "Sorry."

But Mark was laughing. "You don't hold back, do you?"

"No, I suppose not."

"That's all right. Everyone will always know where they stand with you." He took a puff of his pipe.

Diana tried again. "Mark, I do not play chess," she said politely to appease her mother.

"I can teach you," he offered.

"We don't have a chess set here," she said, looking around as if one might magically appear. She looked over to her mother, who shook her head.

He said no more about it and after another half hour, he stood and left, bidding them both a good night. They watched as he walked along the sidewalk, taking everything in, pipe in hand.

"He's such a nice man," her mother said with a smile.

Diana couldn't argue with that.

Chapter Thirty-Four

The following evening, it poured rain, and Diana and her mother did not expect to see Mark. But he showed up carrying an umbrella in one hand and a wooden box in the other. He stood on the mat, wiping his feet, and when Diana opened the door, he handed her the wooden box, whose surface bore a pattern of alternating squares of light and dark woods in a checkerboard pattern. It was heavy enough that she had to use both hands to hold it. He set down his wet umbrella on the porch and followed her inside.

"Good evening to you both," he said.

"What brings you out on a night like this, Mark?" Millie asked.

"Wanted some company," was his answer. And looking at Diana, he said, "And I'd hoped you'd humor me with a game of chess."

"I don't know how to play," she reminded him.

"That's all right. I'll teach you."

"Okay." But she was unconvinced. She wished it was checkers instead.

"You can use that table," Millie suggested with a nod to a small table in the corner of the room.

Mark removed the potted plant from its surface and set it on the floor. then carried the table over to the armchair. "Let me get you a chair, Diana." He looked around the parlor, but Diana jumped up and said, "I'll bring one in from the kitchen."

"I'll get it," Mark said.

They both set off for the kitchen, shoulders bumping into each other. Diana laughed, and Mark looked amused.

"Mark, I'm capable of carrying in the kitchen chair."

"But I don't mind getting it for you," he said. They'd reached the kitchen by now.

"All right then," Diana said with a slight nod of her head.

He carried in the ladderback chair and set it on the other side of the small table. He went to sit in it, but Diana put her hand on the back of it and said, "No. I'll sit in this chair. You sit in the armchair."

With a laugh, he asked, "Are you always so bossy?"

"Mark, she's ghastly at times," Millie piped in from her corner of the room.

"Thanks, Ma."

Once they were seated, Mark opened the case to reveal a chessboard and pieces as beautiful as the box they came in. He laid the board out and set everything up. Like the box, they were made of two different types of wood: light and dark.

Diana was in awe of a possession such as this. If the house ever caught fire, she'd run out and leave everything behind, but she might go back for this.

"This is a beautiful set," she said.

Mark smiled. "It was handmade for my father for his fiftieth birthday." He laughed and said, "A long time ago. When he passed, it was given to me."

"I'm sorry for your loss," Diana said automatically.

Mark gave her a quick smile before it disappeared. "Don't be. He lived a long and happy life. He was a good man."

Sitting this close to him gave her the advantage of studying him more closely. Gray was just beginning to appear at his temples. His blue eyes were almost navy in color. The pipe hung from his mouth and when he took his two puffs, he clenched it between his teeth. His face was a study of concentration as he lined up the chess pieces: the lighter-colored set in front of her and the darker pieces for him. She couldn't make any sense of it.

"Do you play a lot of chess?" she asked.

"I used to, with another professor at the university, but he's since retired and moved on. We'd play every Wednesday night and sometimes the game would take weeks." He was animated when he spoke about it, and Diana thought he was a strange bird getting all excited about a game of chess.

"Wow, you're really wild and crazy," she said flatly.

He stared at her for a moment, and she wondered if she'd gone too far, but then he smiled and shook his head.

"Let's get started," he said, and he clapped his hands, causing Diana to give a little start.

Mark laughed. "I'm sorry, I get lost in my enthusiasm over this game."

"That's all right, although I can't guarantee I'll ever get to that level myself."

He nodded. "Fair enough," he said, and took another puff of his pipe.

Propping her chin on her hand, she watched as he picked up a small wooden token.

"How come you still wear your wedding band?" she blurted.

"Diana!" By her mother's tone, one she rarely used, Diana realized she'd crossed some invisible line.

Mark looked over at Millie. "It's all right, Mrs. Quinn." He held his hand out, the plain gold band sitting on his fourth finger. "I guess I'm not ready to be unmarried yet."

It was the saddest thing Diana had ever heard.

To dispel the awkwardness, she nodded toward the chess piece in his hand. "What's that?"

"Oh, this? This is a pawn." He set it on the board and demonstrated. "He can move one step at a time in any direction, but never backward. He's the weakest of them all."

He picked up another piece and held it aloft. It reminded Diana of a castle tower.

"This is the rook. It can be moved any number of squares forward or sideways, but in a straight line."

The next two pieces he held up were the knight and then the bishop, and it was here that Diana got lost. But she remained silent.

"What is the object of this game?" she asked.

"The object of the game is to capture the other player's king," he explained. He picked up the tallest chess piece. "This is the king."

"So, the king is the most powerful piece?"

Mark shook his head. "No. He's the most valuable piece. But it's the queen," he said as he picked up the second largest piece. "The queen is the most powerful piece on the board."

"Why?"

"Because the queen always protects the king."

Chapter Thirty-Five

It was not all smooth sailing with Diana's sewing business. There were some hiccups along the way.

"Oh no, Ma, not her," Diana groaned. "Anyone but her."

Vicky Vesta, one of their neighbors, needed a dress taken in. She was the same age as Diana and lived with her mother, Pearl, at the end of Peony Lane.

"She approached me at the butcher's. I could hardly say no," Millie said.

"She needs a dress taken in like I need a hole in my head," Diana griped. "She's only coming over here because she's nosy."

"I know that. But you can handle yourself."

When Diana and Millie had first moved to Lavender Bay, Vicky and her mother had brought over a welcoming basket with some baked goods. They were invited in, and once inside, their gazes swept around the room, noting the contents of the house. They'd been bold enough to ask for a tour. They touched things, picking up knickknacks and inspecting them. Diana thought they might as well have rifled through her underwear drawer. They had little to say about Millie's aunt, and Diana suspected they weren't frequent visitors. Maybe Great-Aunt Lavinia had figured them out.

Having realized that Vicky and her mother walked the neighborhood in search of news and gossip the way one would scour a strawberry field for the biggest, reddest, and juiciest berries, Millie never invited them in again. Millie and Diana would always wave to the Vestas to be polite, but that was as far as their neighborliness went.

Diana was anxious for this Vicky visit to be over with.

Vicky was right on time. She was an attractive woman, slightly taller than Diana, with a long trunk relative to her shorter legs. Her hair was sandy brown, and she wore it in the latest style, a chin-length bouffant.

"It's so good of you to fit me in," she said. Her eyes landed on Diana's headscarf and stayed. At her side, she carried a large bag that appeared full. Diana's heart sank.

"No problem," she said. She turned her back and said over her shoulder, "Follow me."

She led the way to her sewing room, aware of Vicky behind her, taking everything in.

"Oh, that wasn't here the last time I visited," Vicky said of a new picture on the wall. Diana was glad now that she'd closed the doors to the bedrooms and the bathroom.

Diana stood at the door of her sewing room and with a wave of her hand, indicated to Vicky that she should step inside.

"How can I help you?" she asked politely.

Vicky stared at her for a moment as if she didn't understand the question. But it wasn't that. She wasn't paying attention because her gaze was swinging around the room.

Diana nodded to the bag and held out her hand.

"Oh, yes, this." Vicky pulled a large pile of dresses out of the bag. There had to be six or seven. "I need all these taken in at the waist and the bust." With a deliberate smile, she said, "I'm getting married next month, and I've lost a lot of weight, but these dresses are too nice to throw out."

"Hmm," Diana said, inspecting the dresses. They weren't old but they weren't colors she would have chosen. Too garish. Again, she was aware of the other woman's gaze on her head.

She'd heard about the upcoming nuptials. The Vestas had made sure everyone knew that the reception was being held at the Lavender Bay Country Club, located on the second biggest hill in Lavender Bay, the first being occupied by the Gibson mansion.

"Slip the first dress on and I'll take your measurements."

"Oh, sure."

Diana stepped out of the room and closed the door while Vicky changed. She waited in the hall. When it seemed to be taking Vicky a long time to get the dress on. Diana gave a quick, short rap on the door and opened it. Vicky stood at the bookcase, examining the contents of the shelves.

Through gritted teeth, Diana said, "Shall we start with that dress?"

Hurriedly, Vicky shoved the book she was looking at back onto the shelf. "Yes."

"You don't want it hemmed, do you?" Diana asked.

Vicky shook her head. "No."

Diana moved the step stool from the corner to the middle of the room and turned to eyeball the dress. She waved for Vicky to step up onto the stool. Vicky had indeed lost a lot of weight; the fitted dress was shapeless on her. The bodice sagged around her smaller breasts with the extra material, and it could have been tighter in the waist.

"Lift up your arms, please," Diana said.

Vicky lifted her arms and Diana pulled the sides in, securing them with straight pins. Her neighbor never removed her gaze from Diana's head. It was unnerving.

"Ow!" Vicky said.

"Oh, I'm sorry, did I get you with the pin?" Diana asked innocently.

"Yes," Vicky said with a frown, rubbing her side.

Diana hurried through the rest of the dresses. When she was finished, she made notes in her book and laid the dresses over a chair. When she stood, she said to Vicky, whose gaze once again was fixed to the side of Diana's head, "You can pick these up next week. I'll call you."

Vicky seemed to hesitate and finally she asked, "Does it hurt?"

Pretending not to know what she was talking about, Diana said, "Does what hurt?"

"Your head."

"It depends." She put her hands to the scarf where it knotted at the top of her head. "Here, let me show you the scar. Maybe you'd like to touch it."

Vicky recoiled. "That's not necessary."

"Are you sure? You might be interested in the skin graft they applied after my scalp was ripped off. They had to take skin off my thigh for the first graft. When that didn't work, they did a second graft, taking skin off my other thigh. Did you want to see that too?"

Vicky reddened and said in a shaky voice, "Thanks, Diana. I'll wait for your call." And she rushed out of the room and the house, slamming the front door behind her.

"What was that all about?" Millie asked.

Diana laughed. "It turns out nosy Vicky actually doesn't want to see that side of my head."

"Oh, Diana, you're terrible."

"Maybe so." But this was Diana's business and for her to stick it out, it would have to be done on her terms.

Her rules. And she wasn't going to be the object of curiosity or ridicule. This wasn't a circus.

"Doesn't matter, we won't be seeing her again," Diana said with finality.

She finished Vicky's dresses a day earlier than promised. She folded them neatly, put them in a brown paper bag, walked down to the corner, and left them on the Vestas' front porch with a note attached that read "No charge."

Chapter Thirty-Six

As Mark became a more frequent visitor, he started bringing some of his records over with him. His preference was classical music by composers whose names Diana did not recognize and could not pronounce. Tchaikovsky. Rachmaninov. Some of it she liked, but she wouldn't want a steady diet of it. It added to her perception of him being stodgier than his age would dictate. She wondered if it was on purpose.

They continued to play chess a couple of evenings a week. By this time, Diana had begun to understand the game, but it was rare that she won a match. And when she did, she suspected that Mark had let her, although he'd never admit it.

One evening as they played, they listened to the radio and the endless chatter about Korea. North Korea had invaded South Korea, and America was going to war again. It was unbelievable. They'd barely recovered from the last one.

Mark moved his queen toward Diana's king and said, "Checkmate."

Diana leaned back in her chair in defeat, tired of all the talk about war and not in the mood for chess. She sighed. "I'm not smart enough for this game."

Mark's pipe almost fell out of his mouth. "Diana, please don't ever speak about yourself like that. Just because you're not book smart doesn't mean you're not intelligent. Your self-talk has a bearing on your life. Keep it positive."

She made a mental note of his advice and changed the subject.

"Can you believe we're going back to war?" she asked, helping him put the chess pieces back into their box. It was hard to imagine. The conflict was so far away it seemed as if it was something that had no bearing on them.

He pulled his tobacco pouch from the pocket of his suit jacket and refilled his pipe. "Yes, I can believe it. History has a tendency to repeat itself."

Reading between the lines, she asked, "Are you against this war or just war in general?"

He struck a match against the matchbook, the flame briefly illuminating his features, and lit his pipe, taking a few puffs to get it going. He waved his hand to extinguish the match and set it neatly in the ashtray with the rest of the discarded ones. "I'm against all war. I abhor any kind of senseless killing. War is nothing but barbarism, death, and deprivation."

"But you fought in the last war?"

He nodded. "I did."

"Why? If you abhor it?"

"I believed in the cause. And I couldn't stand by and let someone else go off and fight for me."

"What about Korea?"

"It was an act of aggression. And the Communist threat is real. But Americans have—I'm sorry—I should say *some* Americans have a romantic idea of war, of bravery and courage and defeating evil. It's not as simple as that."

"I suppose not," she said.

"People who go off to war, if they're not killed, they come back changed. It's something that can't be helped."

He sounded like he spoke from personal experience.

"My goodness, all this talk about war is depressing," Millie said with a forced smile, getting up from her rocker.

Mark stood up. "Apologies, Mrs. Quinn."

"I'll make us some tea," Millie said.

Diana unfolded her legs from beneath her and got off her chair. "Ma, sit down, I'll get it."

She made the tea and sliced up some cake, setting it on dessert plates. When she returned with the serving tray, Diana put a question to Mark. "Why can't women go off to war? Why is it always the men?" She tried to add gravity to her voice so her tone wouldn't imply that she felt her sex was missing out on all the fun.

Her mother spoke before Mark had a chance to answer. "War is no place for a woman."

Mark appeared thoughtful and added, "It's no place for a man either."

But Diana wouldn't be denied. "Isn't a woman just as capable as a man?"

Mark thought for a moment before answering. "Some would argue not, but I think it has more to do with historical chivalry. For as long as anyone can remember, women were always regarded as the fairer sex, in need of protection. In my own experience, I've met women who were braver than some of the men I knew." His gaze had turned inward.

This was one of the things Diana liked about their neighbor: the intelligent conversations. It was a pleasant change.

"Maybe we could talk about something more lighthearted?" Millie suggested. "Mark, why don't you play one of your records. Music always cheers people up."

"But not that one—that Requiem or whatever you call it by Mozart. Too sad," Diana said.

Mark grinned. "So you *have* been paying attention."

She smiled back. "Maybe a little bit."

CHAPTER THIRTY-SEVEN

1952

Diana didn't know why she let Laura and Joy talk her into going to the charity event at the Lavender Bay Country Club that evening. She must have been having a weak moment. Country clubs weren't really her style. Not that she'd ever been in one, but she had a general idea of the type of people who frequented such places: people not like her. Her friends approached it from the philanthropic angle, arguing that the event, hosted by Grace Gibson and her father, would benefit the local VFW. That brought to mind her one visit to the VFW and the number of veterans who visited her for alterations or mending or laundering or ironing. She felt compelled to go.

As she dressed, she grumbled, irritated. What more did her friends want? She was working full time as a seamstress out of her home, she went to Joy's every Sunday for dinner with Laura and Edwin, and she went to the beach with them and their kids. A couple of nights a week, she played chess with Mark. And as her mother had developed terrible arthritis, Diana did all the grocery shopping. From time to time, she went out to lunch with Laura and Joy, when Laura had a day off from her job.

But dinner and dancing? That was more of a couples' thing, and she'd be there alone, without a date, without a boyfriend. Without a *husband*. She would have preferred to stay at home. Who knew, maybe Mark would stop over. Though they'd seen less and less of him as of late. Diana was convinced he had a girlfriend, but her mother didn't think so.

She must have looked at her reflection a hundred times in the mirror. She was a long way from the young and pretty nineteen-year-old she'd once been. The years were piling on; she'd had her thirtieth birthday recently, and the idea of having children grew slimmer with each passing year.

The fashion of the 1950s dictated a fuller skirt on a dress and a cinched waist, usually with a thin belt. Poodle skirts were all the rage—she'd made a couple for Laura's girls—but she felt she was too old to pull off that particular look and besides, she wasn't that crazy about them. But that night, she wore a creation she'd made herself after seeing it in *Vogue* magazine. She'd ordered a similar pattern and bought enough red velvet material to make the dress and a matching headscarf.

Her mother's image appeared behind her in the mirror's reflection. Millie Quinn was the mature version of her. Diana could always guess what she'd look like in twenty years by simply looking at her mother.

"Diana, you look lovely."

"Do I?" she asked, her voice full of doubt. She felt once people's eyes landed on the headscarf, especially those who knew her backstory, they didn't notice anything else about her. She fingered the St. Anthony medal around her neck. Not that she was the praying type, but she thought, *Help me find some confidence and relief tonight.* Not for the first time, she wondered why she couldn't just be left alone to stay home. Home was safe.

Not to mention more entertaining now that they had a brand-new television.

Biting her lip, Diana said, "Maybe I'll stay in. I'll call Laura and tell her I have a headache."

"Oh no you don't," Millie said. "You're going out tonight. Besides, you used that excuse the last time."

Diana couldn't help but laugh. "I remember a time when you said I was going out *too* much."

"Yes, well," her mother stammered, "that was then, and this is now." She placed her hands on her daughter's waist and propelled her out of the room. "This will be good for you. I promise."

"The country club?"

"Never mind all that pomp and circumstance. It's for charity. A worthy cause."

Even Diana had to laugh. As soon as they reached the parlor, there was a knock at the front door.

It was Laura, who brought in with her the familiar scent of Shalimar. Edwin waited in the car idling at the curb.

Laura Wainwright Knickerbocker was now in her early forties and although she'd matured, she was still as pretty as ever with her blond hair and blue eyes.

She wore a fashionable dress of cornflower blue that matched her eyes. Diana thought she was lucky. Edwin worshipped the ground she walked on, and she had the freedom to spend her paycheck from Block Answering Service on things like dresses and furniture for her house.

"You look lovely, Diana. Did you make that dress?" Laura asked.

"I did. What do you think of the color?" Diana asked, holding out the sides of the skirt to give Laura the full effect.

"I love it. It's beautiful."

"We should go." Diana turned to her mother and said, "I won't be late, Ma."

"Stay as long as you want," her mother encouraged.

Boy, I must be a sad tale if my mother is telling me to stay out all night, Diana thought.

As they walked toward the car, the music floated out from the radio. The evening was comfortably warm, and the sky was bright pink with broad strokes of lavender. There was the sound of crickets and of a train going by in the distance.

"Is this the girls' first night without a babysitter?" Diana asked Laura. Her friend had mentioned that Edna and Edith thought they were too old for a sitter and wanted to stay home alone.

Laura rolled her eyes. "It is, although they were bickering over the boy next door when we left. Edwin hopes the house is still standing by the time we get home."

She pushed the front seat forward so Diana could climb into the back.

"Hiya, Diana," Edwin said as she settled in the back seat, smoothing her dress out beneath her so she wouldn't wrinkle it.

Laura looked over her shoulder and said, "Joy and Sam will meet us there."

Diana nodded, wishing she didn't have to go. Fingering the medal again, she determined she would have a good time. Or at least try.

Chapter Thirty-Eight

One after another, cars pulled up to the Lavender Bay Country Club, housed in a two-story redbrick Colonial with large white columns out front and black shutters flanking the windows. It looked like something out of a movie. The mansion was ablaze with lights inside and out, illuminating everything—the manicured, impossibly green lawn, the profusion of rosebushes of every color imaginable, and the well-tended box shrubs—in a white hue.

As Edwin steered the car up the long, winding drive to the top of the hill, Diana began to have serious doubts. From the back seat, she whispered, "I didn't think there were this many people in Lavender Bay."

Laura looked over her shoulder. "They're coming from all over. It's the biggest charity event of the year in this area."

Terrific.

When their car pulled up to the main entrance, two valets with short white jackets and crisp black pleated pants approached and opened the doors for them. Edwin handed the keys over, and the valet on the passenger side extended a gloved hand, helping first Laura and then Diana out of the vehicle.

She trailed in behind Laura and Edwin feeling like a third wheel, but as they crossed the threshold, she lifted her chin, determined to get through it, even if she had to grit her teeth to do so. In a few hours, she'd be safely home and in her bed in the comfort of her room.

The inside was packed. People milled about the grand and expansive front hall and winding staircase, which were done up in floral wallpaper and white woodwork. There were shouts and squeals as people recognized each other and hugged. Edwin pulled out their tickets and handed them in, and was given their table number. Diana pulled out her ticket from her purse and handed that in as well.

She stayed close behind Laura, not wanting to get swallowed up in the throng of smartly suited men and bejeweled and gowned women. She kept her head down, touching her headscarf every so often to make sure it was still there and in its proper place.

Men in uniforms similar to those of the valets moved elegantly around the place, carrying trays of champagne flutes. Edwin held up three fingers and was handed champagne from a white-gloved waiter. He handed a glass each to Laura and Diana. Both women immediately took a sip. Diana had never had champagne before; she liked it and took a second sip.

"Laura! Diana!" came the unmistakable voice of Joy.

Their friend wore her dark hair very short and curled around her face. She'd added bright red lipstick. She and Sam were coming up on their twentieth wedding anniversary, which they were planning to celebrate with a private party for their friends and family. Diana was looking forward to that.

Sam approached her, hands in his pockets, the flaps of his suit jacket hanging over his hands. "You clean up well, kid."

"Hi, Sam," she said with a smile.

"Ooh, your dress is lovely," Joy said with an appreciative glance.

"When do we eat? I'm starving," Sam said, looking around.

Joy rolled her eyes. "You just had a salami sandwich before we left."

"Yeah?" His tone was defensive, but there was no bite behind his bark. "That was my appetizer." He looked at Edwin and said, "You know how these places are, it's all about presentation. You'll get half a plate of food, and they'll give it some fancy name you never heard of. Never mind all that—pile the food high on my plate! Am I right?"

Edwin laughed. "As always, Sam."

"We're here to support a charity," Joy reminded him.

"And eat," Sam said with emphasis. He said to Edwin, with a nod toward his wife, "She's been married to me for almost twenty years, and my love of food always comes as a big surprise to her."

Diana couldn't help it that she snorted. Quickly, she looked around, hoping no one had heard that. She certainly didn't want to draw attention to herself.

Sensing an ally, Sam turned to Diana. "I'm right, aren't I, Diana? Surely you must have noticed it."

Joy looked beseechingly at her friend, but Diana was apologetic. "I'm sorry, Joy."

"Traitor," Joy said good-naturedly.

Sam handed Diana a quarter. "Here, thanks, kid."

Laughing, Diana swatted his hand away.

"Would you stop it?" Joy pleaded.

"You know how I feel about these places," Sam said. "They're stuffy. I don't like them."

Diana had a feeling that if she had a sudden urge to go home, Sam might be willing to take her. At least she had an out.

The five of them found their way to their table in the grand ballroom, and Diana found herself seated in the middle between the two couples, with Joy on her left and Laura on her right. Elbows on the table, she rested her chin on her clasped hands and looked around.

The room had high ceilings, and stately drapes hung along the walls and puddled on the parquet flooring. Along the western wall were French doors that led out to a terrace. The sun had almost set, and the sky was beautiful, with fading brushstrokes of pink and lavender. There were round tables seating twelve throughout the room. Adorning each table was a complicated candelabra centerpiece with tall, thin tapers and a garland of flowers wrapped around the base. Looking around, Diana guessed there to be hundreds of people there. She was glad she was seated; she could stay at the table for the rest of the night. On the north side of the ballroom, an orchestra began to play.

Laura was saying something to her, and she turned toward her and said, "Pardon?"

"Are you all right?" Laura asked, leaning toward her.

"Yes, why?" Diana asked.

"You've gone quiet."

"Have I?" She gave her friend a quick smile. "Just taking everything in. I've never been here before."

"Me neither. The country club wasn't here yet back when my dad was mayor."

The waiters interrupted them with the first course.

It was a soup that the menu called vichyssoise, which none of them knew how to pronounce. Sam tried it first, lifting his soup spoon to his mouth and tasting it, rolling it over his tongue before announcing, "We're good. It's potato."

Diana had never had it before and thought it was delicious. You could tell the war years and the Depression were truly over. When she was finished, she pushed her bowl forward. The soup was soon swapped out for small plates of julienne salad, of which Diana ate half. She didn't want to spoil her appetite. Wine was served all around the table. She still had half a glass of champagne.

There were three other couples at their table. Two were neighbors and friends of Laura and Edwin's and the third couple, who no one knew, had been assigned to their table. They were young, not more than twenty-two, Diana guessed, and were newly married. They hung on each other's every word and looked at each other adoringly. At one point, Joy leaned into Diana and whispered, "They'll get over all that lovey-dovey stuff soon. Once she's been picking up his dirty socks off the floor for a while, she won't think he's so wonderful."

Diana threw her hand to her nose to stop another snort from emerging. Not again. She was at her quota for the day. Even so, she couldn't help but watch them. It magnified her own loneliness. She would never know what it was like to be married, to have children of her own. To ward off an impending wave of despair, she picked up her wine glass and sipped from it.

Dinner was duck à l'orange with roasted potatoes and green beans. Dessert was chocolate mousse. When they were all finished, Sam said loudly to Joy, "Go in the kitchen and show them how it's done." There were giggles and twitters all around the table, and Joy elbowed him with a laugh.

"Gee, Sam, you must really like Joy's cooking," Diana teased.

"Like it? I live for it! I've told her, I have to go first. Because if she dies before me, I'll starve!"

Everyone burst out laughing.

When the last of the plates were cleared and the table linen brushed off with small brushes and dustpans, the lights were dimmed and the orchestra struck up. Immediately, Edwin took Laura by the hand and pulled her onto the dance floor with him, her laughing behind him. It made Diana smile. Joy coaxed Sam to dance, and for all the grumbling he did, he pulled her close once they stepped onto the dance floor and whispered to her the whole time he waltzed her around. Diana was happy for her friends, with their lovely husbands and nice families. Soon the table was empty except for her. She sat there alone under the dimmed lights of the chandelier, thinking of her home and her mother and wishing she was back on Peony Street. Absentmindedly, she fingered the medal that hung around her neck.

Laura and Edwin returned, their faces flushed and their eyes bright, both slightly breathless.

"I'm not as young as I used to be," Laura said, collapsing in the seat next to Diana.

"Excuse me, miss, do you care to dance?" asked a voice behind her.

Diana turned slightly in her chair. A tall, slender man with an enviable head of dark hair stood behind her. She was just about to decline politely when Laura butted in and said, "She'd love to!" With a shooing motion, she indicated that Diana should go. Reluctantly, Diana stood, smoothing out her dress, and turned toward the man.

He offered her his arm, and she linked hers through it. "I'm John Harmon," he said.

"Diana Quinn."

"Nice to meet you, Diana." He flashed a smile and even in the dimly lit room, she could see that his teeth were straight and white. *Moneyed* was the word that came to mind.

As he led her out onto the dance floor, Diana tried to remember the last time she'd gone dancing. Before the accident, it must have been. A lifetime ago. On the dance floor, he put his arm around her waist, and she slipped her hand into his other hand. The orchestra played "Stardust" as he led her around.

She'd forgotten what it felt like to be in the arms of a man. To feel that strength wrap around you with tenderness and care. Tears stung the back of her eyes.

He didn't talk too much; he seemed to be concentrating on his footwork. It was crowded on the dance floor and they bumped into another couple. "Sorry about that," John muttered.

She smiled up at him. "Not your fault."

"You know, I've been watching you all night," he said.

"You have?"

"I'm trying to figure out what a beautiful woman like you is doing here by yourself. Did you lock your husband in the closet at home?"

Diana laughed. "No, I'm single."

He looked down at her, gave her a high-wattage smile, and said, "Lucky me."

The orchestra began the second set, and he twirled her, causing Diana to bump into another couple behind her. As she moved away, she felt a tug on her scarf, and she realized the tail of it had gotten caught in the bracelet of the woman behind her. Panic engulfed her. Frantic, she freed her hands from her dance partner to brace her headscarf against her head. But it was too late; her scarf was pulled off, and she spun to retrieve it. Her breath came in short gasps. The woman dislodged the scarf from her bracelet and handed it back to Diana, but not before she got a glimpse of the side of Diana's head. Diana's hand was unable to completely cover her disfigurement. The other woman's mouth formed an "o," and Diana hurriedly refastened the scarf and turned around to face John, who stood there, eyes wide and mouth hanging open.

"Excuse me," she managed to get out. Turning on her heel and holding the scarf over her head with both hands, knowing it looked haphazard, she pushed her way roughly through the crowd, shaking. In the distance, she saw the French doors that led out to the terrace, and she shoved her way through the couples, head down, finally clearing the dance floor and running right into the front of a man, who held both her arms to steady her.

"Please let me go," she said, trying to release herself from his grip. But she couldn't use her hands because they anchored the scarf to her head. "Please, let me go."

There was something oddly familiar about the chest in front of her. The tie. The scent of cherry tobacco.

Mark.

Around them, the orchestra continued to play and the couples went on dancing. Diana felt removed from it all, as if all sound was being filtered through water.

He looked around and said, "Come on, let's get you out of here."

Chapter Thirty-Nine

Mark put his arm around Diana's waist and led her through the French doors to the terrace outside. The evening sky had gone from lavender and pink to navy. The air was warm but comfortable. Crickets chirped loudly. The land sloped away from the terrace, and you could no longer see the manicured greens of the golf course or the lake far off in the distance beyond it.

The flagstone terrace ran the length of the building and was bordered by a stone balustrade. Exterior lighting cast dim shadows across the terrace and the white cast-iron benches and small tables scattered throughout.

He led her to the far end, which was unoccupied.

In his eyes was the warmth and kindness she'd grown used to. There was comfort in his familiarity: the strong jawline, the prominent nose, and those eyes as blue as sapphires.

In the semi-darkness, he stood in front of her and asked, "Diana, are you all right?"

She nodded, unsure, but said, "I think so."

He reached up for her scarf, which she held against the left side of her head. "Let me help you with that."

But she was quicker than he was and stepped back, out of his reach. She knew she must look a sight with the skin graft on the left side of her head and the rest of her hair cut very short.

"Don't, Mark. I'll fix it myself."

"Of course. I didn't mean to upset you."

"Don't worry about it." She sighed. "Would you mind turning around for a moment so I can rearrange it?"

"Of course not," he said. He turned his back to her, leaving her hidden behind him. He reached in his pocket for his pipe, something she'd seen him do hundreds of times. The familiarity of it caused an ache in her heart.

Deftly, she removed the headscarf, shook it out, rearranged it, and placed it over her head, winding it into place. She felt around and once satisfied that it was secure, she said quietly, "You can turn around now."

With shaking hands, she went for her purse and realized she'd left it at the table.

"What's wrong?" he asked.

"I want a cigarette, but I left my purse inside."

"I'll be right back." He walked away, approaching a couple at the other end of the terrace and exchanging a few words with them. He returned with a cigarette in his hand, which he held out to her.

"Thank you," she said gratefully.

He pulled a matchbook from his pocket, tore off a match, struck it, and there was a sizzle and the bloom of a flame. He leaned into her to light her cigarette, then waved the match out and tossed it into a nearby bucket of sand placed on the terrace for that purpose. Diana took a satisfying lungful of smoke and blew it out the side of her mouth, the blue plume floating up along the side of her face.

They both leaned against the stone ledge topping the balustrade. Diana hopped up on it, and Mark parked half his bum on it.

"I didn't know you'd be here tonight," she said. What was unsaid and implied was that she hadn't seen him in a while.

"Some of my colleagues invited me," he explained.

He casually smoked his pipe, the air around them filling with the scent of cherry tobacco. Diana inhaled deeply, resisting the urge to close her eyes.

He waved his hand toward the cast-iron bistro tables. "Would you prefer a chair?"

She shook her head. "I'm fine, thanks." She took her time with the cigarette as it was the only one she had. She could easily go in and fetch her clutch, but she didn't want to leave him. And the evening was so pleasant.

"We haven't seen a lot of you lately," she said. "Ma misses your company." She did not take her gaze off him. But he didn't look at her.

"I've been busy."

"In the summer?" she countered.

He looked at her. "Do you miss me?"

Not understanding the question, she said smartly, "Of course. I was just starting to beat you in chess."

The laugh that erupted from him startled her. He was usually so reserved. "So you were."

She pushed him. "You didn't strike me as a sore loser."

He shook his head. "No, I'm not. But I figured it might be best if I didn't come around so much."

"Did we make you feel like you were wearing out the welcome mat?"

"No, not once."

"Is it me?" she asked. He looked up at her sharply. "I know I can be mouthy, and sometimes people don't get my humor."

"Those are some of your best qualities," he said softly.

Diana went quiet, trying to figure him out. He'd paid her a compliment, and she wasn't sure how to take it. A group of three tuxedoed men appeared and ended up at the opening of the terrace that led to stone steps. They were loud. She wished they would go away.

Soft strains of the orchestra floated out onto the terrace. The closed French doors muted the din of noise inside.

In the semi-darkness, she saw Mark swallow hard.

"I forced myself to stay away," he said.

Diana scowled. "Why?"

Mark pulled out his pouch and refilled his pipe, setting a match to it. He struggled to get the words out. "Because I've grown to care for you very much."

"We care about you too."

His ensuing sigh was one of sadness and lost hope. "No, Diana, that's not what I meant. I've developed feelings for you."

She blinked several times. There was something about being unburdened and enlightened; it was as if heavy chains had slid off you, freeing you.

With a shaky voice and choosing her words as carefully as one might navigate a minefield, she said, "What's wrong with that?"

"I'm too old for you."

"Says you."

"Yes," he said. "Says me. Diana, I was an old man at the age of twelve."

She burst out laughing. She nodded, adding, "Listening to classical music, playing chess, and smoking a pipe." She could so easily picture it.

The tension across his forehead disappeared and his posture relaxed. "Something like that."

"I'm thirty, Mark, not some nineteen-year-old ingenue."

"I know." He cleared his throat. "You could do a lot better." There was a missed beat, and he added, "Than me."

"I don't know if you noticed, but men aren't exactly beating a path to my front door," she said with a brittle laugh.

In all seriousness, he said, "Shame on them if they don't see what a gem you are."

Diana lifted one eyebrow and then frowned.

What was happening here?

"There you are!" came the voice of Laura as she rushed out onto the terrace. She came to an abrupt halt when she spotted Diana, her dress swishing around her legs as she did so. She looked over her shoulder. "She's out here!" Joy appeared as well, and smiled at Diana. They rushed over to her but pulled up short when they realized she wasn't alone.

"I'd like to introduce my neighbor," Diana started as they approached. "This is Mark Sturges, he lives next door. Mark, these are my good friends Laura Knickerbocker and Joy Ruggiero." Mark shook their hands, half amused and half wondering what her friends would make of all of this.

"Well, any friend of Diana's is a friend of mine," Joy said enthusiastically. Diana wanted to roll her eyes but refrained. She could practically see the images in Joy's head of her walking down the aisle to the strains of Mendelssohn's "Wedding March."

"The men are ready to leave," Laura told her, and she glanced at Mark. "Were you ready?"

Both she and Joy looked pointedly at Mark until he said, "I can give you a lift home, Diana."

"All right, if it's not too much trouble," she said.

He smiled. "Not at all. You live right next door."

"I need to get my purse," she said.

Joy threw her hand up. "Nope. I'll get it. Stay here."

Before Diana could protest, Joy and Laura disappeared, and within minutes, Joy returned with her clutch. She was smiling so hard at Mark that Diana wondered if her cheeks hurt.

With a wink, Joy said, "We'll talk to you tomorrow."

"Yes."

When she was gone, he said, "You have nice friends."

"They're wonderful." They were the reason she'd survived and created a life for herself. It was a debt that could never be repaid.

"Would you like to go inside," he asked, "or would you like to go home?"

It had been a long evening. She didn't have to think about it. "I'm ready to go."

Mark stuffed his pipe into his pocket and with his hand on the small of her back, he escorted her through the main room and out the front door, handing his ticket to the valet.

They drove in silence back to Peony Lane, Diana thinking about everything he'd said on the terrace. Had she read too much into it?

On Peony Lane, he pulled into his driveway. The porch light was on at her house. It wasn't late, a little after ten. Her mother would still be up.

They lingered. Took their time getting out of the car and stood for a few moments in the driveway, talking.

Diana looked around. The street was quiet. There were lights on in only a few of the houses. The stillness of the night relaxed her.

She voiced her thoughts. "It's a shame to go in on such a beautiful night."

She looked up at the sky. The moon was a pale yellow, and there was a sea of stars flung across the velvety sky.

"Would you like to sit on the porch? We could talk," Mark said.

"I would like that."

Mark had no chairs on his porch, so they sat next to each other on the steps.

"I suppose I should get some chairs. But I'm so used to sitting on your mother's porch, I never got around to buying any."

"There's really no need," she said.

"Maybe not."

He stretched. She hoped he wasn't in any hurry to go in. She was enjoying his company too much.

"I don't have any wine or anything like that," he said. "But I have a couple of bottles of Squirt in the icebox."

"That would be nice."

He stood and unlocked his front door and disappeared into the house. He soon returned with two bottles of Squirt, uncapped, handing her one before rejoining her on the step.

Diana took a sip from the bottle, unaware of how thirsty she was until the tart grapefruit soda hit her tongue.

It turned into a long conversation. Mark spoke about his late wife and the baby son he lost. He spoke about growing up with an older brother. Diana told him about the accident and how she hadn't wanted to live afterward. How her mother and her friends had supported her during her darkest hours.

Finally, dawn broke, and the sky grew gray along the horizon.

"Diana, I'm sorry, I've kept you out all night."

She stood. "Don't apologize." She wanted to tell him that it had been the best night of her life. As she grew older, whenever she heard crickets chirping or trains rumbling along in the middle of the night, she would always think of that night she spent on the porch steps with Mark, putting a name to the feelings she had for him.

He walked her home, although she told him it wasn't necessary.

When they reached her porch, he said, "Goodnight, Diana."

"Goodnight, Mark." Boldly, she lifted up onto her toes and kissed him on his cheek. His ensuing smile was beautiful.

As she laid her hand on the door, she turned to him and said, "And you're wrong, you know."

He frowned. "About what?"

"There is no one better for me."

And she left him there, staring after her, and slipped into the house.

Chapter Forty

Diana knelt on the floor of her sewing room, a smattering of straight pins hanging out of her mouth as she marked the hem on a pair of slacks Grace Gibson had purchased on a recent trip to New York City. Grace stood on the step stool, trying to stay still as Diana edged her way around her on her knees.

"So, did you enjoy yourself?" Grace asked.

Diana took the remaining pins out of her mouth. "I'm sorry?" She looked up at Grace.

"The benefit. At the country club. Two nights ago."

"Oh, that." Grace must not have heard about her disgrace on the dance floor, or she wouldn't be asking about it. Diana had done her best to banish the fiasco from her mind. Knowing that Grace was one of the organizers of the event, she focused her reply on the positive. "I did enjoy myself. The food was delicious, and the orchestra was divine." What she didn't say was that she enjoyed herself even more after the benefit. Sitting out on the porch steps with Mark until the light of dawn had awakened feelings in her that she had thought were long dead.

Grace smiled. "I'm glad to hear it."

Once she finished pinning the trousers, Grace jumped down from the stool. "That's a job done. When can I pick them up?"

"Next Tuesday?"

"Perfect."

After seeing Grace out, Diana was straightening up her sewing room, picking up errant straight pins from the carpet, when the doorbell rang. She jabbed the pins into the pincushion and headed toward the front door. When it rang a second time, she called out, "Coming." If it was her four o'clock appointment, the woman was early. Diana had been hoping to sneak in a quick cup of tea and a cigarette.

She opened the door to find Mark standing on the porch, holding a bouquet of flowers.

"Hello, Diana."

"Mark." Smiling, she stepped aside to allow him in. As he crossed the threshold, he looked around the parlor and smiled. "You've got new furniture."

"It was time."

"Um, these are for you." He handed her the bouquet of flowers: pink roses mixed in with some pink alstroemeria and white baby's breath. Diana had never received flowers before; even back when she was dating Preston, none had been forthcoming. It made her very happy. Her smile hurt her cheeks.

"Thank you," she said, touched by the gesture. "Let's find a vase for these." She went off to the kitchen, and Mark followed her.

"How's your mother?" he asked.

"She's well. She's at her bridge game today."

Diana pulled a glass vase from a cupboard, arranged the bouquet in it, and took a sniff. She filled the vase with tap water and set the arrangement in the middle of the table.

She invited him to sit down, but he said he couldn't stay. "I've got a faculty meeting in half an hour. Start of the new semester and all that."

She nodded.

A looming silence threatened to descend upon them. She thought of the other night, when they sat in the darkness and the conversation flowed around them.

"Thank you again for the beautiful flowers," she said.

His expression was pained, and for a moment she wondered if he was all right, if he was sick or something. Or worse, maybe he wanted to take back all those wonderful words he'd said to her the other night.

"Look, Diana, I don't know how to do this," he said.

"Do what?"

He waved his hand around, his face full of anguish. "This." He struggled to get it out. And because she didn't know what he was trying to say, she couldn't help him.

"Mark, you're going to need to be more specific," she said.

"I don't know what to do with you."

She laughed. "You don't have to do anything with me."

The frown on his face deepened. "I mean, how to court you. Is that even a word they use nowadays? I'm rusty, Diana."

His struggle, his worry, his pain, endeared him to her even more.

"We'll figure out what works best for us." she said. "I like being with you, Mark. And that's enough for me."

He nodded, the muscles of his face relaxing, the frown disappearing. "That's how I feel."

"But since we're being honest," she said, "I'd feel better if there was total transparency and you knew what you were getting into." She took a deep breath and slowly removed the scarf from her head, revealing the damaged side. She needed no mirror to know what it looked like. The large bald patch on the left side of her head, the thick ridges and discoloration of the skin graft that made up the landscape of her healed scalp avulsion.

He did not flinch. His eyes didn't widen, and his mouth didn't fall open. She saw no revulsion or horror in his features. He just was. Slowly, he moved closer to her as if approaching a terrified animal. Diana's eyes never left his face. He studied the side of her head, and she was afraid he was going to attempt to touch it. She hoped he wouldn't. But he didn't. He placed his hands on her upper arms, leaned in, and kissed her on the forehead.

"Still beautiful, Diana."

She sagged against him, inhaling the familiar scent of cherry tobacco. Tears pooled in her eyes. She stepped back and began putting the scarf back on her head.

"Let me try," he said in a whisper. He attempted to tie the scarf around the back, inspected his work, and announced, "I've made a right mess of it."

With a laugh, she whipped it off again and reapplied it, having done it a thousand times before.

"I suppose I shouldn't be so presumptuous," he said. He paused and took a step back. "May I call on you, Diana?"

"Yes, Mark, you may." And the smile she gave him could have lit up the entire town of Lavender Bay.

Chapter Forty-One

They were married the following spring. It was a small affair at the local church with a reception at her mother's house afterward, where they enjoyed finger sandwiches, champagne, and wedding cake. Diana wore a navy outfit with a corsage of pink roses pinned over her right breast and a white-and-navy floral silk scarf on her head. Mark wore a gray flannel suit. Laura and Joy served as her two matrons of honor, and a colleague of Mark's stood as best man.

It was a beautiful day. The sun was warm, and the sky was a soft blue. There was a gentle breeze. Laura took a photo of Diana and Mark beneath the blossoming cherry trees, and it ended up in a frame that Diana kept by her bedside for the rest of her life.

It made Diana very happy to live next door to her mother because she didn't want to be too far from her. She continued to work out of the spare bedroom in her mother's house, if only to see her every day and provide her with a bit of company.

They settled into wedded bliss, and Diana couldn't remember being happier.

They weren't married three months when Diana woke in the middle of the night to Mark screaming. Startled, she sat up and looked over at her husband. He tossed and turned on his side of the bed, twisted up in the bedsheet. His hairline was damp with perspiration, And he spoke loudly in his sleep. She placed a hand gently on his shoulder. "Mark," she whispered.

"Clear out, clear out!" he shouted. She reached for him; his pajamas were drenched in sweat. Again, she laid a hand on his shoulder and called his name softly. He came out swinging and caught her on the chin.

Stunned, she climbed out of bed and turned on the bedside light. The room felt warm, so she opened the window a few inches and a gentle breeze blew in, lifting the curtains from the sill. She walked around to his side of the bed and shook him again, calling his name, trying not to startle him and also trying to avoid another swinging arm.

When he emerged from the nightmare, it was suddenly, and he was fully awake. Looking at her standing over him, he frowned and asked, "What's wrong?"

"You were having a nightmare."

"Was I?" He seemed genuinely shocked at the revelation.

"Hold on, honey," she said. "Your pajamas are soaked." She went to his bureau and pulled out a clean pair. She sat them on the bed next to him and coaxed him to sit up. He seemed bewildered, looking around the room as if he'd never seen it before.

She reached over and began to undo the buttons on his pajama top. When she pulled it off, she tossed it by the door. She helped him into a fresh top and a pair of fresh bottoms and tucked him back into bed. She went to the bathroom and returned with a glass of water and a cool washcloth. As he drank the water, she mopped his forehead, brushing his hair aside. Once he was tucked in, she climbed back in on her own side, pulling the sheet and blankets up. She turned off the bedside lamp.

Into the darkness, she whispered, "You were having an awful nightmare."

"I was back in the war. It was so real," he said quietly.

"Have you ever had nightmares like this before?"

"Yes."

"What do you do about it?" she asked, worried about him and more than a little frightened herself.

"There's nothing that can be done."

"Oh," she said with a sigh.

"I'm so sorry to have woken you, Diana."

"Nonsense. That's what I'm here for."

"To change my pajamas in the middle of the night?" he asked.

She snorted and then said seriously, "I'm your wife. I'll do whatever I need to do."

He rolled onto his side to face her, and she did the same. She ran her fingers through his hair. This always relaxed him.

"Shh," she said softly.

There was no way she'd tell him he'd cuffed her good on the chin. He'd be mortified. Besides, it wasn't his fault.

The nightmares were sporadic and didn't seem to be triggered by any one thing in particular. But when Diana found herself to be pregnant, the nightmares increased. Diana might not have been a rocket scientist but given the fact that he'd lost his first wife and son in childbirth, it seemed plausible to her that increased stress might be to blame, which was understandable. She did all she could to reassure him that everything would be fine, but he remained doubtful. In the meantime, they were alone with it.

There was nowhere to go for help. It wasn't like you could share this sort of thing with other people or even with your doctor. You were expected to deal with it, get on with your life and somehow soldier on. She knew a thing or two about trauma and its aftermath, and one thing she did know was that you needed support. She didn't know how she would have got through those first years after the accident without the support of her mother and Laura and Joy. She habitually fingered the St. Anthony medal around her neck, whispering a silent prayer for her husband.

One morning, she was down in the kitchen when she heard Mark moving around upstairs. She'd turned off his alarm, as it was Saturday and he'd had a restless night. But when she heard him get up, she set about preparing his breakfast. Two eggs sunny-side up, two pieces of extra-crisp bacon, and two slices of toast, medium brown, lightly buttered. For herself, she prepared a whole grapefruit and two pieces of buttered toast. Sometimes, she cooked a piece of bacon for herself, but she'd lost her taste for meat since becoming pregnant.

Otherwise, she liked being pregnant. She still had two months to go. It was the best she'd felt since before the accident. Her appetite was good, and she'd made herself some smocks and maternity skirts in cheery fabrics.

Mark appeared in the doorway as she was setting his plate on the table. She filled his juice glass halfway and turned on the burner beneath the stovetop percolator. He hesitated, appearing sheepish. This was the norm after a night of nightmares. She wished he wouldn't be embarrassed. Not in front of *her*, of all people.

"Sit down, honey, your breakfast is getting cold."

He pulled out his chair and sat. He picked up his fork and knife, but they remained mid-air, hovering over his plate.

Diana sat next to him, sprinkling a teaspoon of sugar over the first half of her grapefruit and using her serrated spoon to dig out sections of the fruit.

"I want to apologize for last night," he said.

"Because you had a bad dream?" She shook her head and went on to the next section. "Don't ever apologize to me for that."

"I don't know why I keep having these dreams," he said. "The war's been over for almost ten years."

She shrugged. "I still have dreams of getting my hair caught in the machinery." Those dreams pushed her right back to the day of the accident and caused her to wake up in a cold sweat. But they were infrequent now. In the beginning, she had them all the time. She tried to think of the last time she had that dream. She paused, her spoon stuck in a section of grapefruit. Maybe six months ago? She thought back to what he'd said once: how war was no place for a man. She couldn't begin to imagine all the horror he'd witnessed. And she was pretty sure he wasn't alone. But it wasn't like you could go around and ask people.

Mark was saying something, but she hadn't heard him properly.

"I'm sorry?" she said.

"I said I wonder if sometimes I made a mistake in marrying you."

Her mouth fell open. "Haven't I been a good wife?"

He rushed to reassure her. "You've been a wonderful wife! I couldn't be happier. But it can't be much fun for you being married to me."

"I'm very happy," she said.

"You are?" he seemed surprised by this.

"Yes, silly," she said with a laugh. "Why would you think I wasn't?"

He sighed. "It's a lot to take on. The nightmares and stuff."

"No marriage is perfect or always smooth, is it?"

"No, I suppose not."

"I'd like to make a suggestion," she said.

He mopped up his egg yolk with a piece of toast, waiting for her to continue.

"You know there's a VFW over on Primrose and Vine," she said gently. She picked up the grapefruit and squeezed the last of the juice into her bowl.

He nodded. "Isn't that where they all get together and drink beer?"

"Not necessarily. Who says they don't serve scotch?" she quipped, referring to his drink of choice. She hadn't been there since that day all those years ago. But with all the women marching in and out of the house for mending and sewing, she'd picked up little bits of information about it. It sounded like an informal social club where veterans went to hang out. She wasn't too sure, but from what was said, it seemed to help some of the men to socialize with others who'd been through the same thing.

"I don't know," he said.

Diana scooped the juice out of her bowl until it was gone, and then she started on the second grapefruit half. The percolator hummed on the stove, the coffee bubbling up into the little glass knob on the lid. She stood and turned it down.

"It wouldn't hurt to give it a try," she said. "They're men who've served, like you. And you don't have to go in there and tell them about your nightmares, but it might be nice to be with other men who understand what you're going through."

He considered this.

"Why don't you take a walk down there today," she suggested. "It's Saturday. There's bound to be someone around. They might be able to give you more information."

"It sounds like you're trying to get rid of me," he said with an amused smile.

"Not at all. I only want to help you." She stood again, removed the percolator from the stove, and poured coffee into two mugs, handing one to Mark. She set hers down on the table and put her hand on Mark's shoulder. He patted it reassuringly.

He looked up at her and said, "I don't deserve you, you know."

"Oh yes you do," she said quickly. "Don't you remember what you told me a long time ago?"

The lines between his eyebrows deepened, and he shook his head and said, "No. You'll have to be more specific. I believe I said a lot of things."

"You told me that the queen always protects the king."

Chapter Forty-Two

1959

Diana pulled the wagon behind her, coming back from the beach. In it, Gail, four, and Louise, two, looked slightly dazed from an afternoon spent in the sun and splashing around in the water. Diana herself didn't know how to swim, but she was determined that the girls would learn. Laura's daughter, Edna, now almost twenty, was teaching Gail the basics. It was almost nap time, and Diana wanted to get the girls home before they fell asleep. Over her left shoulder, she carried a beach bag she'd designed and made herself. Joy and Sam had offered to give her a ride home, but she'd declined, saying she didn't mind the walk. It wasn't that far.

Images of a nice cool bath filled her head. She was hot and sweaty, and if the girls could stay asleep, she'd soak in the tub for a while. The heat and activity had made her tired as well.

As she approached home, she spotted Mark over on her mother's porch, the two of them sitting next to each other in the porch rockers. They stood as she came into view, Mark in his standard summer attire of light-colored pants and a short-sleeved shirt. She didn't know how he did it; she was overheating even in the light cotton shift she wore over her bathing suit.

He and Millie walked down the front steps to meet her. Mark went first and waited to make sure Millie got down all right.

"Gammie," said Gail, holding out her hands to Millie.

Smiling, Millie stooped to pick her up. "Did you have a good day at the beach?"

Drowsy, Gail nodded.

In the wagon, two-year-old Louise was fighting to stay awake.

"How was the beach?" Mark asked.

"Good, they love it there," Diana said.

Mark had never been. His excuse was that he didn't own a pair of shorts and didn't know how to swim. Louise lay back in the wagon, eyes closed.

"They're tired," Diana said, "and I'm going to put them down for a nap now."

She went to reach for Gail, who clung tight to Millie and wailed, "No!"

Millie laughed. "That's my girl. Diana, leave her with me. I'll put her down here."

"Are you sure?"

"Of course." And before Diana or Mark could say anything, Millie turned and went around the side of the house to go in the back door, carrying Gail and telling her what a good little girl she was.

Mark pulled the wagon to their house next door. With a glance at the sleeping baby, he said, "I'll carry her up."

"Thanks, hon. I'm going to soak in the tub for a while."

Diana dropped her beach bag on the floor as soon as she walked in. Mark followed her in carrying a sleeping Louise, and after closing the door behind him, Diana trailed him up the stairs and went into the bathroom as he laid Louise gently in her crib.

She filled the tub with tepid water and stripped down quickly, sinking into the coolness of it. She slid down until she was submerged, soaking her hair. She felt she might have sand in her scarred scalp, as it had irritated her since she got out of the water. Even though she never took off the bathing cap, it was inevitable that sand would get in. Sitting in the hot sun wearing a rubber bathing cap created a sweaty head. It was best to get it rinsed and washed.

The water was nice, and her body cooled down immediately. She stretched her arms out, noting the brown color of her limbs from spending a lot of time outdoors. It contrasted starkly with the milky-white color of the tops of her thighs, her belly, and her breasts.

Once her hair was washed and rinsed, she leaned back against the gentle slope of the tub, thinking she'd close her eyes just for a moment.

A knock on the door roused her, startling her.

"Diana?" Mark said on the other side. "Are you all right in there, or do I need to send in a search party?"

She laughed. "I'm fine. Be down in a minute." The bath and the short nap had revived her, and she pulled the plug. As the water drained out, she stood and climbed out of the tub.

Wrapping a towel around her, she darted to her bedroom to get dressed, choosing a red and white summer dress with straps that tied at her shoulders. She gave her hair a quick brush. What hair she had left, she wore short, just below her ear. One of the girls at the beauty salon came to the house to cut her hair in private, and they bartered: haircuts in exchange for mending. She fixed a matching scarf onto her head.

She gave a quick peek into the girls' bedroom, satisfied to see Louise on her back in her romper and sound asleep.

Holding the ruched bodice of the dress, she walked down the stairs barefoot, meeting Mark at the bottom.

"Can you tie these straps for me?" she asked.

"With pleasure, Mrs. Sturges," he said. Deftly, he tied the straps over her shoulders as he'd done a hundred times before. When he was finished, he laid a soft kiss on her tanned shoulder.

She and Mark made their way out onto the porch, and he carried two bottles of Coke from the fridge out with him, handing her one as they sat down on the steps.

As always, they clinked their bottles together and said at the same time, "Cheers."

"How's it going with the committee?" she asked.

Mark had come up with the idea the previous year that Lavender Bay should have a day to celebrate the town's founder. There had been plenty of local interest, and a committee had been formed. It looked as if the first annual Jacques Aubert Day would be celebrated the following year.

"Good. Everyone's in agreement that it should be celebrated on June fourth, as that's his birthday."

"That's great." The project had given Mark a specific focus. And between that, his job, his family, and teaching fellow veterans how to play chess at the VFW, he was kept busy. His nightmares had lessened since the girls were born.

"Did you have a good time at the beach?" he asked.

"Of course. The girls love it, and Gail is like a little fish with the swimming," she said with a smile.

"You know, I was thinking . . ." Mark started.

She smiled to herself. Mark did a lot of thinking. "Yes?" She took a refreshing gulp of the ice-cold drink.

"I think I'd like to go to the beach with you sometime. You and the girls."

"We'd love that."

"All right. Maybe next weekend if it's nice," he said.

"You know, you'll have to get a pair of shorts."

"Shorts?" He flinched. Of course, she'd seen her husband's legs, but she'd never seen him in a pair of shorts. "Can't I wear pants?"

"Honey, it's too hot at the beach for pants. You'll roast." She looked at him. "You must have worn shorts as a child."

"Only under penalty of death," he joked. "Mother used to say I was out of short pants and into long pants by the time I was three."

Diana laughed. "Don't worry about it, I'll make you a pair."

Chapter Forty-Three

The following weekend, Diana thought it would be best if the four of them went in the morning before the sun got too hot. She didn't want Mark to be totally uncomfortable for his first day spent at the beach.

The girls were ready, and Diana had the bag packed and parked by the front door. Earlier, she'd pulled out the wagon from the garage and wheeled it around to the front of the house. Mark appeared in the doorway as she put away the box of Raisin Bran and rinsed out the dish rag to wash off the Formica table.

Her husband stood there wearing a short-sleeved shirt tucked into a pair of tan shorts she'd made for him during the week. On his feet were a pair of dark socks and his good shoes. His legs, having never really seen the light of day, were whiter than white.

"Well, how do I look?"

Not wanting to discourage him, she said, "You look fine, honey."

Smiling, he said, "Great. Are you ready?"

"In a minute." She hadn't thought to get him a pair of sandals, so the shoes would have to do. She laid her finger on her lip and said, "Mark, why don't you put on an older pair of shoes?"

"What's wrong with these?"

"Those are your good shoes. They'll get destroyed at the beach."

"I see. Give me a minute." He disappeared, and she heard his footsteps on the staircase.

When he returned, Diana was waiting at the front door with Louise in her arms and Gail by her side. When she spotted her father, Gail jumped up and down. "Daddy! Daddy!"

Mark had put on an old pair of Oxfords he'd worn when they painted the downstairs. The tops were speckled with paint.

Diana bit her lip, trying not to laugh, and made a mental note to pick up a pair of sandals for him the next time she was in town.

The four of them walked to the beach. Gail walked along with them, and Louise sat in the wagon with the beach bag, a chair, and a beach umbrella.

"It's very hot out already, and it's not even nine o'clock," Mark noted, pulling a neatly folded handkerchief out of his pocket and wiping his brow.

This early, the beach was still empty. Diana set up the umbrella and a blanket as close to the shore as possible so they wouldn't have to trudge through hot sand to get to the water. She put a shoe in each corner to hold the blanket down. The wagon was parked at the edge of the umbrella, and Diana covered it with a towel to keep the metal from getting unbearably hot for the trip home.

"It's a beautiful day," Mark announced, staring out at the lake.

The lake was greenish gray in color and the sky an azure blue. The pale beige sand darkened as it got closer to the water, where it was flat and brown.

Diana put sun hats on the girls. Gail grabbed hold of hers and threw it off. Louise laughed and followed suit.

Diana knelt down on the blanket and said sternly as she put the hats back on them, "If you don't keep the hats on, we'll pack up and go home."

Gail was about to protest when Mark, now seated in a chair beneath the umbrella and smoking his pipe, said, "Girls, do as your mother says. Please." They both looked at their father. He so rarely scolded or disciplined them, preferring to leave that to Diana, that without further ado, they left the hats alone. Holding each girl by the hand, Diana walked them to the shore until the water washed over their feet. Both girls squealed. Behind her, she heard Mark laugh, and that made her smile.

She picked up Louise and swung her gently over the water, letting the waves tickle her feet and legs until the little girl was laughing uncontrollably. Next to her, Gail jumped up and down, splashing water everywhere and shouting, "Me, me, me!" Diana set Louise down in the surf near the shore so she could keep an eye on her. She picked up Gail and swung her out and back, her feet skimming across the water, and she yelled, "Wee!"

Under the umbrella, Mark sat with his legs stretched out, puffing on his pipe, a contented smile on his face. Diana kept the girls busy in the water for a while, and then they got out and knelt in the sand with the pail and shovels to build a sandcastle together.

"I don't know where you get all your energy from, Diana," Mark observed. "I'm tired watching you."

Diana smiled at him. "It's relaxing here, isn't it?"

"Surprisingly so. I had no idea," he said with a nod of his head.

Hopefully, he'd come again. She and the girls spent so much time at the beach. After a half hour of playing in the sand, Louise started to get fussy. Diana set them both on the blanket at their father's feet, scrounged through the bag, and pulled out something for them to eat. She handed Louise a bottle with juice in it, then used an opener to uncap the lid of a Coke bottle, pouring the dark liquid into two glasses and handing one to Gail. "Be careful," she said. Gail nodded and, holding the glass with both hands, she gulped from it.

Diana took the second glass, sipped from it, and handed it to Mark.

"Do you mind if I go into the water by myself? Can you keep an eye on the girls?" she asked.

"Go ahead."

She walked into the water. The girls were busy eating and drinking, and didn't notice their mother heading into the lake or they would have chased after her to join her.

The water was wonderful. She'd grown to love the lake, especially in the summer when it was as warm as bathwater. She went out up to her midsection, plugged her nose, closed her eyes, and disappeared beneath the surface, letting the water wash over her. When she emerged, she faced the shore and spotted Gail standing at her father's side as he poured more Coke into her glass. Louise sat on the blanket with her back to the water. Diana wanted to enjoy these few minutes to herself.

The beach was beginning to fill up as people decked out in swimsuits and sunglasses carried picnic baskets and other supplies across the sand. Blankets and chairs were laid out as people claimed their territories for an afternoon of sunbathing and swimming.

She dunked again, mindful of her cap. They wouldn't stay much longer. She wanted to be home by early afternoon to put the girls down for a nap and do some gardening.

There was a screech as Louise finally realized that her mother had gone into the lake without her, and she now stood at the shore, wailing and pointing at Diana. "Mama!" Mark was trying to entice her back to the blanket, but she only cried harder.

It was nice while it lasted, Diana thought. She held up her hand in a wave and called, "I'm coming!"

She stepped out of the lake, her brown skin glistening with water. Mark looked at her, a look that was familiar to her, causing her to smile, and said, "You look like Botticelli's *The Birth of Venus*."

It was his version of romance. She'd take it.

Louise clung to her legs, crying.

"Diana, where's your medal?" Mark asked.

"What?"

"Your St. Anthony medal. Didn't you have it on?"

Diana's hand flew to her chest, feeling around for the medal she'd worn for over ten years, the gift from her friend. She never took it off, not even when she went to bed. Panicking, her stomach roiling at the thought of the loss, she scanned the sand around her feet. She set Louise down, and she and Mark searched through everything, shaking out the blankets and the towels.

Mark knew how important the medal was to her. When they didn't find it, she turned and looked at the lake. "I must have lost it in the water. I have to go back in."

"Darling, you'll never find it."

"I have to try." She occupied Louise with some toys and filled Gail's glass with more Coke. Very slowly, she walked into the water, her gaze scanning the ground beneath her, left and right, looking for a glint of gold in the summer sunlight. The water was clear, and she could see the bottom with its little pebbles and tiny shells and the sand gliding back and forth with the rush of each wave, but she saw no medal. She walked slowly to the area where she'd been previously. The bottom of the lake was no longer visible here, the water too murky. She felt around with her feet, taking baby steps over the lakebed, but she had no luck. As she searched, she prayed. Over the years, she'd come to depend on this saint, the finder of lost things. The irony of praying to this particular saint to find his medal was not lost on her.

Back and forth, she covered a search area where she thought she might have lost it, but came up with nothing. She was so distraught that she didn't hear the girls crying and whining on the blanket. By the time she emerged from the lake, Mark looked harried, and the girls' faces were red, their noses snotty.

"Any luck?" he asked.

She shook her head. She felt sick inside. The medal had been a talisman of sorts.

"I'm sure it will turn up. We'll put an advertisement in the Lost and Found section of *The Lavender Bay Chronicles*," Mark said.

She nodded, saying nothing. She went around absentmindedly, gathering things and packing them away in the wagon. She rubbed both girls on their heads to get them to settle down. It was way past nap time. Mark pulled out the umbrella from the sand and folded it up and laid it in the wagon. He then lifted the girls one at a time and set them on the folded-up blanket next to the umbrella. Diana shoved everything else into her bag and they set off, with Diana carrying the chair and Mark pulling the wagon through the heavy sand.

At home, she wiped the girls' faces with a cool cloth, gave them their lunches, and laid them both down for a nap. Their room was on the northeast side of the house, which was the coolest. She headed back downstairs, where Mark had settled in at the dining room table to correct papers from his summer classes.

"I'm going to go back up to the beach and look some more," she said.

"Diana, you won't find it now," he said reasonably.

"I can at least look," she snapped.

He looked at her. Mark wasn't one to shout or yell or use harsh words. It wasn't in his nature.

She didn't apologize; she was too upset. "I won't be long. Please listen for the girls." And she turned on her heel and headed back to the beach.

She returned to the spot where they'd been earlier; another family had already staked out the space. The mother, a woman younger than Diana, looked friendly, and Diana approached her.

"Hi. I'm Diana Sturges. We were here earlier"—she waved her hand around the area where their blanket was spread out—"and I lost my necklace."

The woman made a sympathetic sound. "What does it look like?"

"It's a St. Anthony medal. Gold. On a gold chain."

"Do you think you lost it around here?"

Diana shrugged, helpless. "I'm not sure. I probably lost it in the lake."

"Oh," was all the woman said, her tone indicating defeat. "I'll keep my eyes open. And I'll tell my kids to look for it."

"There'll be a reward. I live on Peony Lane," she said, giving her the number, but knowing the chances of this woman showing up at her door with her medal were slim to none.

Kicking off her sandals, she repeated her earlier actions, doing a visual sweep of the shoreline and wading out to the area where she'd been enjoying the water. Or at least where she thought she'd been. She could no longer be sure. Without Mark and their belongings as her point of reference, she couldn't be sure if she'd gone too far north in the water or too far south. As she felt around with her feet and toes, tears threatened to spill over. Nearby, a group of young guys were throwing around a ball and dunking each other, laughing and shouting. She paid no attention to them until she got hit in the back with the ball. One of them, with a blond crewcut and the beginnings of a serious sunburn, came over, retrieved the ball, and asked, "You all right, lady?"

"I am. I've lost my necklace."

"Where?"

"I think here, in this area." She waved her hand around.

He whistled to his friends and waved them over. Both were dark-haired and freckled, which made Diana think they were brothers.

"She's lost her necklace," he told them. He turned to Diana. "We'll take a look for you."

"Oh, thank you. I can't swim."

"No problem. What does it look like?"

She explained it in detail and the three of them dove in, trying different areas as Diana waited, holding her breath. Every once in a while they came up for air before resuming their search. They began to get tired and weren't able to stay underwater for very long. Concerned about their safety and knowing a riptide could catch them off guard at any time, she told them to stop.

"We don't mind. We can look some more," said one of the dark-haired boys, spitting water out of his mouth.

Diana shook her head. "I really appreciate it, fellas, but that's enough. Hopefully, it will turn up."

They all looked at one another and shrugged. She walked out of the water, remembering she hadn't thought to bring her towel. She picked up her sandals. The young mother on the blanket asked, "Any luck?"

Diana shook her head. "No. None."

"It'll turn up. Have faith."

Diana nodded and walked off across the sand, carrying her shoes. Once she reached the pavement, she slipped her sandals on her feet, not caring that they were covered with sand. As she walked back home, she kept touching the top of her chest where the medal used to be, feeling naked without it. Feeling lost.

Now what would she do? How could she have been so careless as to wear it to the beach? Even though she'd done it a thousand times before, it seemed stupid in hindsight.

And now it was gone.

She walked home slowly, taking her time, looking around on the off chance that she'd lost it on the way down, although she was doubtful about that. Memories of Joy giving her the necklace, and where she'd been at that point in her life, barely leaving the house to sit out on the porch, came back to her. If she had a nickel for every time she'd fingered that medal, she'd be as rich as Grace Gibson.

When she rounded the corner onto Peony Lane, she spotted Mark sitting on the front steps with the girls. He still had on his shorts with the paint-splattered shoes. He held his pipe between his lips, and she could almost smell the cherry-scented tobacco. Gail and Louise sat on either side of him, looking up at him, rapt. Even though he spoke to them as if they were colleagues, they were entranced by him. It brought a smile to her face.

Mark caught sight of her and smiled, raising his hand in a wave. He spoke to the girls and pointed to her. Louise stood and screamed, "Mommy!"

Diana smiled. What she'd lost retreated to the back of her mind as she was reminded of all that she'd found.

Chapter Forty-Four

1994

Diana reached over and patted Mark on his knee to wake him. He sat up with a fright. "Huh? What? What?"

She laughed. "Mark, DeeDee is ready to start."

"Oh, oh, oh," he said, repositioning himself in his recliner. "I'm ready."

Angie ran into the room and came to Diana's side. Diana put an arm around the girl's waist and leaned into her. "Do you want to sit with Grammie and watch DeeDee's show?"

Ten-year-old Angie nodded and hopped up on her grandmother's recliner, nestling in on one side of her.

"Something smells good!" Mark declared.

Angie laughed. "I made brownies, Pop-Pop."

"I love brownies."

She wagged a finger at him. "You'll have to eat your dinner first."

"Will do." He pulled a handkerchief from the pocket of his cardigan and wiped his nose. The pipe was gone. A bout of oral cancer ten years previously had forced him to quit for good. Diana had also quit smoking, in solidarity. She missed the smell of his tobacco, but not to the point where she'd insist he strike up a match. He'd survived, although the chemo and radiation had nearly killed him. At the time, Mark wasn't able to be alone, so it was decided that while he was going through treatment, they would live with Louise, Martin, and the girls on Heather Lane. And once he regained his strength, they stayed, and had lived there ever since. Everyone seemed happy with the arrangement, though sometimes Diana wondered if Martin would like to have his home back. He never complained, but then he was easygoing, and it truly didn't seem to bother him. Every evening when Martin arrived home from work, Mark would announce, "Thank God you're here, Martin, I'm vastly outnumbered by females." She and Mark had matching recliners in the living room but with Louise's help, she'd created a small parlor upstairs for the two of them so Louise, Martin, and the girls could have the living room for themselves in the evenings.

As Louise and Martin both worked full time, Diana and Mark watched the girls. She would also tackle the laundry and have the dinner ready by the time they came home. She did that four nights a week. Friday night was pizza night, and Louise liked to cook on Saturdays and Sundays.

Other than trying not to get too involved in the girls' squabbles, everything seemed to work out.

"Ta-da!" Seven-year-old DeeDee burst into the room, sliding across the worn carpet and landing in front of them. She wore a costume Diana had made out of a pair of old curtains, using some discarded sheer scarves for the sleeves. Several rows of bright pink sequins adorned the cuffs, the hem, and the collar. DeeDee had been delighted when she'd seen it. For added effect, the little girl had put on her tap shoes, even though she'd been told several times by her mother that the tap shoes were for tap class and not for the inside of the house.

"What do we have here?" Mark said.

Diana had done her blond hair for her: masses of loose ringlets pulled back from her face with a headband, like one of the Irish dancers she had seen on television. DeeDee, always one for the theatrics, drama, and the extreme, had loved it.

It was only the four of them at home at present. Sixteen-year-old Maureen and fourteen-year-old Nadine were hanging out with their cousins, Esther and Suzanne. Already, they were pulling away. Diana could feel it, just like when Gail and Louise had pulled away from them at that age. She and Mark were getting farther and farther away from the newer generations. They were the generation that separated the rest of the family from mortality. She glanced over at Mark. At eighty-four, he was slowly beginning to fail. There was some difficulty with his memory and a new shuffling gait that had started in the last few months. She knew they couldn't live forever. As it was, they'd been married more than forty years. She'd love to make it to their fiftieth wedding anniversary, but there were no guarantees.

DeeDee launching into a song and dance distracted her from her thoughts. For a little girl, she had a booming voice and a large personality. If this one wasn't destined for Broadway, no one was. She did a little part of her tap routine, but it was difficult on the carpet. Diana thought they should get her a small square of plywood so she could dance in the living room. She usually practiced on the kitchen floor or outside on the driveway. Mark called her Happy Feet.

She twirled around and came to an abrupt stop, extending her arms and wearing a big smile. Diana clapped and gave a gentle nudge to Angie, who clapped along.

"Bravo! Bravo!" Mark said beside her, his voice feeble.

DeeDee bowed and said, "Now for my encore."

Angie groaned audibly, and DeeDee shot her the stink eye.

"Go on, honey," Diana encouraged.

DeeDee broke into song, something from some pop idol she and Angie listened to upstairs in their room on their CD player. Angie sang along.

DeeDee stopped in the middle of her song, gave a pointed look to her sister, and said firmly, "I don't need backup!"

"Fine!" Angie jumped off her grandmother's lap and ran upstairs.

DeeDee looked after her.

"Come on, Pop-Pop and I are waiting," Diana told her.

She finished her routine and soon took off.

It was late afternoon, the lull time before Diana had to get up and get the dinner ready. Mark had dozed off in the chair, and she turned on the television, lowering the volume. It was time for Oprah.

She glanced at her dozing husband. She still loved him; she couldn't help herself. They were as opposite as day was from night, but despite this, they'd managed to build a lifetime of love. She leaned back, listening to the opening credits and music of the Oprah show. She closed her eyes and let her mind drift back over all their memories.

PART THREE

ANGIE

Chapter Forty-Five

Angie headed out to her support group at the hospital sporting the Victory headscarf, the one her grandmother used to wear at the aviation plant before her accident. She felt it was appropriate. Arriving in the education room, she found a seat near Floyd and Nena, if only for the comic relief.

Nena nodded to the scarf on Angie's head and gave her a sympathetic smile. "Welcome to the club."

"Sadly, yes," Angie said.

"Don't be sad, little lady. There's a lot of perks," Floyd piped in.

She stared at him blankly.

He turned to Nena. "Tell her about the bonuses of being bald."

Nena held up her hand and ticked things off on her fingers. "First, you don't have to wash and style your hair anymore. Time saver. Second, no trips to the salon for expensive cuts and colors. Third, some people look better bald." She looked at Floyd and joked, "With you, we can't tell the difference."

Floyd laughed. "I never have to carry a comb with me anymore."

"And most of all," Nena said, "you never have to worry about a bad hair day again."

"Because every day is a no-hair day!" Floyd said, crossing his arms over his chest.

As Angie expected, she ended up smiling and laughing.

"What is that on your arm?" Nena asked Floyd.

Floyd lifted his arm to show a patch of duct tape on the elbow of his rust-colored cardigan. "I've got a hole."

Nena pursed her lips and scowled. "Throw that out."

"I can't. It's my favorite sweater, and it was a Christmas gift." He turned to Angie. "I think it brings out my eyes, what do you think?"

Angie shook her head and said, "I don't know what to think."

"A Christmas gift from what year?" Nena demanded.

Floyd looked up to the ceiling as if the answer might be written there. "1980?"

"What does your wife say?"

"Let's just say she picks her battles."

"Can't say I blame her," Nena said. "Angie, do you see what I've had to put up with for the last few months?"

Floyd chuckled. "Humor is the best medicine," he said, and he waggled his eyebrows.

"I'm not so sure," Nena said, but she was laughing.

Katharine proceeded to get the meeting going, and tonight's topic was dealing with well-meaning family and friends. She used air quotes around the term.

Nena got the ball rolling. "My sister-in-law, who's an airhead on the best of days, said to me, 'Well, at least you'll lose weight on the chemotherapy.' As you know, I'm never at a loss for words, but I was speechless."

"You, speechless?" Floyd interrupted. "I would have paid to see that."

Lisa, the young mother, spoke up next. "What's worse is when people don't acknowledge it. When they say nothing."

There was a chorus of agreement.

Lisa continued. "I think it's because I'm young and have little kids."

Nena gave her a sympathetic smile. "It's happened to me. I think people don't know what to say, so they say nothing. Or they're afraid they're going to put their foot in their mouth. And it turns your diagnosis into the elephant in the room."

"Angie, what about you?" Katharine asked.

"My biggest gripe is that although my family has been wonderful, they want me to 'rest' all the time. Sometimes, I feel okay, and I want to go to work. I love my job."

An elderly man across the circle nodded and added, "Same. Everyone wants me to nap. Or sit in the recliner. I was pretty active until my diagnosis, and I hardly ever sat down. Now they want to put me to bed."

"Let's discuss ways we can deal with these situations," Katharine said. She passed around a pile of worksheets.

By the end of the week, Angie had developed ulcers on the inside of her mouth, another side effect of chemotherapy. Christmas was bearing down on them, but she wasn't in the mood. At the back of her mind was the thought that she had another chemo treatment scheduled only days before Christmas, and she wondered what kind of condition she'd be in for the holiday. She'd informed everyone in her family that they'd be given gift cards, and they all told her that she didn't need to buy any gifts at all. But she'd ignored that.

Currently, she sat on her sofa with Debbie, who'd brought over some vanilla ice cream Angie was eating right out of the carton with a spoon. The mouth sores hurt so much she had to be careful, but the coldness of the ice cream helped.

They were waiting for Angie's mother and two of her sisters, who insisted on coming over to decorate for the holidays. Angie had almost protested, but decided to save her energy for more important things. While they waited, Debbie had retrieved Angie's dusty old box of Christmas decorations from the basement and assembled the brand-new artificial tree Maureen's husband had dropped off, which now stood in the front window. It had been many years since Angie had bothered with a tree. She was never home to enjoy it.

"Are you sure you don't want a spoon?" Angie asked Debbie, holding up the carton of ice cream.

"Nope."

"How's it going with Po?"

"Good news. I've managed to litter train him, and he no longer has to wear a diaper!"

"That is good news, indeed," Angie said, spooning ice cream into her mouth. A cat walking around wearing a diaper was something she'd never be able to unsee.

"Now to get his weight down," Debbie said with a sigh.

"Challenging?"

"He eats out of all the other cats' dishes and I hate to segregate him, but I might have to. He's only lost a pound since he's been with me."

"I'm sure you'll figure it out. It makes me wonder what you could do with my cat," Angie said.

"*Your* cat?"

"My stray. I'm thinking when I'm finished with chemo and radiation, I might bring him home to live with me."

Debbie practically jumped off the sofa. "Really? That's wonderful! When you're ready, let me know. I'll help you."

Angie smiled at her. She could always count on Debbie.

They were interrupted by the side door opening and Angie's family trailing in: Louise, Maureen, and Nadine, with Herman the dog bringing up the rear.

Angie hunkered down on the sofa, wrapped in a blanket, the ice cream put away, content to watch her mother, her sisters, and her friend do everything. After a walk-through of the house, Herman settled down at her feet.

"Are these all your ornaments?" Louise asked, holding open the flaps of the cardboard box and peering in.

"What more do I need? I'm hardly ever home," Angie explained. "Besides, I have a ton of decorations down at the café."

"But you don't live at the café," Nadine started and then backtracked. "Never mind, you do spend more time at the café than your home."

Maureen began draping colored lights around the tree. Louise and Debbie sorted through the box. "There won't be enough to cover the tree."

"Why don't you decorate the front part and leave the back of it bare," Angie suggested. It's what she used to do when she actually put up a tree.

The three of them stared at her, decided it wasn't worthy of comment, and returned to what they were doing. What little ornaments she had, they hung on the tree.

"I've got some things at home," Maureen said, fetching her purse and keys from the coffee table. "I'll be right back."

"Maureen, don't go to all that trouble," Angie pleaded. But it fell on deaf ears.

"It's no trouble at all," she said, and disappeared.

Angie wanted to ask, *Does it matter?* but figured that would not land well. Her mother and sisters took Christmas seriously, and there were no half measures.

Maureen soon returned with a box of decorations including a red and green tartan table runner that Angie took a liking to. Her sister laid it out over the coffee table and topped it off with a small centerpiece, a bayberry candle surrounded by a wreath.

Nadine turned the television on to a station that played Christmas music all day long.

After they left with the promise to return the next day with more decorations and ornaments, Angie settled back on her sofa, looking at all the holiday decor and listening to Celine Dion singing "So This Is Christmas."

So this was what people did on their days off during the month of December.

When Wednesday rolled around again, Angie headed over to the hospital for her support group. She made her way to the meeting room on the second floor, happy to see Nena and Floyd already there. She took the seat next to Floyd. She admired Nena's turquoise, purple, and fuchsia-colored headscarf and told her so.

"Hello, little lady," Floyd said to Angie.

"New cardigan?" she asked with a nod to his navy blue sweater.

He waved his thumb in Nena's direction. "Nena shamed me into buying a new one."

Beside him, Nena piped in, "Now you can wear this one for forty years."

Floyd laughed.

Grimacing, Angie said, "I've developed mouth sores."

Nena winced in sympathy. "They're very painful. But they do go away after treatment."

After treatment? Angie deflated.

Nena and Floyd bombarded her with suggestions.

"Use a straw," Floyd said.

"Popsicles, cold water, ice cream," Nena suggested.

"Avoid citrus. I learned that the hard way," Floyd said, his expression pained at the recollection of it.

"No hot drinks. No coffee and nothing rough like raw vegetables or granola. Nothing that could irritate."

"Jell-O's nice," Floyd said.

"Thanks, that helps," Angie said.

When Katherine called the meeting to order she announced, "I do have one piece of news before we start. Lisa has gone into the hospital. There's been a complication."

That sobered them up quickly. Even Floyd looked shaken at the news. It cast a pall over the rest of the meeting.

Chapter Forty-Six

Days before Christmas, Angie sat in her office, sipping a smoothie Tom had brought her—"to keep your strength up," he'd said—and going through the ballot box to name the cat. She had a chemo treatment the following day and she didn't know what shape she'd be in afterward to do this. So she'd cleared her desk and began to lay the ballots out, stacking those suggestions that were repeats, like "Coffee," "Mocha," "Coco," and a few others. It wasn't long before the top of her desk was covered with ballots.

In the end, it came down to two names she thought were cute, but she couldn't decide. She called Debbie, who picked up right away.

"Everything all right?" Debbie asked.

"Yes, I'm going through the ballot box, and I've narrowed it down to two names for the cat."

"What've you got?"

"Mr. Beans and Louie. I can't decide."

Without missing a beat, Debbie said, "Mr. Beans. He doesn't look like a Louie."

"Thanks, Deb. Talk to you later."

Angie stuck her head out the back door, spotted the cat, and said, "Your new name is Mr. Beans. Merry Christmas."

She closed the door against the icy air and called the phone number on the back of the ballot. No names were recorded on the ballots in the interest of no favoritism. Only cell phone numbers were provided. A woman's voice answered.

"Hi, it's Angie from Coffee Girl."

"Is this about the cat contest?" the woman said excitedly.

"It is. You've won. His new name is Mr. Beans."

"Wonderful." The woman identified herself as Kay Bright, director of the Lavender Bay Historical Society.

"Next time you come in, your twenty-five-dollar gift card will be waiting for you at the counter."

"Thanks!"

To celebrate, Melissa took a proper photo of Mr. Beans, who was looking well after putting some weight on. She had it printed and framed, and it hung on the wall in the café. A small engraved plaque was hung directly below it: *Employee of the Year.*

Christmas Day ended up being a bust. Angie was so sick after her chemo treatment that she spent the holiday at home in her nightgown and robe, beneath a crocheted blanket a customer had made for her, lying on the sofa while the rest of her family made their way over to Aunt Gail's house. Her phone had been ringing off the hook all morning with calls from her family and Tom, who all promised to stop over at different times of the day.

In the early afternoon, Debbie arrived with an armful of DVDs and a grocery bag.

"What are you doing here?" Angie asked, propping herself up on her elbows.

"And Merry Christmas to you too," Debbie said. "I thought I'd keep you company."

"Deb, that isn't necessary. What about your own family?"

Debbie rolled her eyes. "I stopped by my mother's to bring her her gift, and she was fighting with my brother. On Christmas Day! I don't need that. So, you're stuck with me."

"I think it's the other way around," Angie retorted and pointed to the bucket parked at her end of the sofa.

"No problem. I've brought ice cream: vanilla, strawberry, and chocolate mint. And Jell-O."

"Perfect." With a nod toward the DVDs, she asked, "What are our choices?"

Debbie went through the stack. "*Christmas Vacation*, *It's a Wonderful Life*, *A Christmas Story*, *Going My Way*, and *Die Hard*."

"Sounds good. Pick one and let's get started." She readjusted the blanket and got comfortable, happy to let Deb take care of everything.

The week after Christmas, Angie felt better enough that she went into work for half days. It was a bright, sunny day outside. The air was crisp, and the sky was blue. Two feet of snow covered the town of Lavender Bay.

She made her way around the café, wearing a mask as she was apt to when in public, on the advice of the nurse. She went from table to table, talking to customers and asking how their holidays had been. Everyone was in a good mood. The week between Christmas and New Year's was always a happy, relaxed time. She was still laughing at Java Joe's sandwich board. It read: *Coffee Girl, Bah Humbug!* To which she'd written on her own curbside board, *Java Joe, the Grinch of LB.*

Debbie had taken Mr. Beans to her house to litter-train him and would keep him there until Angie was finished with her chemotherapy. As Angie wound her way through the tables, proudly wearing one of Grammie's vintage Christmas scarves, she spotted Lisa, the young mother from her support group.

She broke into a wide smile. "Lisa! It's wonderful to see you." Similarly masked, Lisa stood and hugged Angie. She introduced her to her husband and her two daughters, who both strongly resembled their mother with their heart-shaped faces and bright green eyes.

Cups of coffee, hot chocolate, pastry hearts, and cinnamon rolls sat on the table in front of them.

"We were worried about you, we missed you at group," Angie said.

Lisa smiled. "Had a little setback. Got out of the hospital just before Christmas."

Angie looked at Lisa's daughters, glad their mother had made it home for Christmas. They were so young.

"How are you feeling now?" Angie asked.

"Much better."

"Will you come back to group?"

Lisa nodded. "Probably next week. I want to spend this week with my girls."

"The Floyd and Nena show is still in full swing," Angie told her.

Lisa burst out laughing. Angie noted how much better she looked since she'd last seen her. Not wanting to intrude on their family time, she wished Lisa well and told her she'd see her next week.

Chapter Forty-Seven

January 1st

It was a new year, and Angie was halfway through her chemotherapy schedule. Radiation was next. She was getting there.

Unlike other years, she'd allowed herself to sleep in rather than getting up early and rushing off to Coffee Girl. She'd get there eventually. Tom had said he was coming over that morning, and she excitedly looked forward to that. Over the last few months, something had definitely shifted in their relationship. She was hopeful and looking forward to seeing what unfolded. She washed down one of her nausea tablets with some milk.

There was a knock at the door and Angie answered it, a blast of cold air blowing in and causing her to shiver. She'd already put on her knit hat.

Tom stood there wearing a winter jacket, gloves, and a grin. At his side, he held an old-fashioned wooden sled with bright red metal runners.

"So, you do own a coat," she said.

"Of course," he said with a wink. "I'm not a total idiot."

She laughed, and he responded, "Get your coat and gloves, Evangeline."

"Okay, I'll be out in a minute."

She set her half-empty glass of milk down on the counter and quickly pulled on a coat over her sweater. She completed the outfit by wrapping a scarf around her neck. As she walked out the door, she pulled her winter gloves out of the pocket of her coat and pulled them on.

Tom stood in the driveway, looking up at the sky. "It's a nice day."

She looked up at the cloudless blue sky and the weak, watery sun. It was the type of crisp winter day that made you glad to be alive. As a kid, she'd loved days like this. She'd stay outside all day with DeeDee and Debbie, all bundled up in their snowsuits, building snowmen and igloos using old buckets.

"Ready?" he asked.

"I am."

They walked to the end of the driveway, where Tom stopped and set the sled on the snow-covered sidewalk. There was a small green-and-black tartan blanket, which he folded in half and used to cover the seat of the sled. "Hop on."

She hadn't been on a sled since she was a kid. Eagerly, she took Tom's outstretched hand and situated herself on the blanket, pulling her knees up and gripping the sides of the sled.

With apparent ease, Tom pulled the sled over the ankle-deep snow toward the best sledding hill in Lavender Bay, conversing as he went. At the top of the hill was the mansion that had been built by George Gibson, founder of Gibson's Grape Jelly. His daughter, Grace, resided there now, as she had her whole life. For as long as anyone could remember, the kids of Lavender Bay had flocked to that hill in the wintertime with their sleds, encouraged by old Mr. Gibson himself.

That morning, New Year's Day morning, the hill was crowded. The sunshine caught the colors of the various winter coats all over the hill: red, purple, yellow, blue, and green. It looked like a white cake covered in sprinkles.

"Hold on, Tom." Angie said.

He stopped and turned around.

"I'll walk from here." She stood up, folded the blanket, and tucked it beneath her arm.

"Ready for some sledding?" he asked.

"Definitely." She'd been looking forward to it.

She was breathless by the time she reached the top of the hill. The two of them arranged themselves on the sled, with Tom behind Angie. He held on tight to her.

"Hey, Mister," said a kid of about ten. "You're a little big for sledding."

"Says who?" Tom asked good-naturedly. Before the kid could respond, Tom pushed off, and their sled took off down the hill at a high rate of speed.

Eyes wide, Angie gripped the side rails, hanging on. She didn't remember the hill being that steep. Of course, it had been more than thirty years since she'd gone sledding.

Behind her, Tom shouted, "Woo-hoo!" and threw his fist in the air. His enthusiasm made Angie laugh.

They sledded for the next hour, until it became too much for Angie to climb back up the hill. Her nose was runny and her cheeks were cold, but she couldn't stop smiling.

As they left the hill, he offered to give her a lift on the sled, but she refused. Her breathing had returned to normal, and she was able to walk.

"I really enjoyed myself, Tom. Thanks."

"Living is found in the simple moments. Remember that."

With a grin, she mock-saluted him. He wrapped an arm around her and pulled her to him, kissing the side of her head. "Okay, smarty-pants."

She slid an arm around his waist and kept it there as they walked back to her house together.

Chapter Forty-Eight

The following week, Tom brought over some Chinese takeout for them to enjoy while watching the hockey game, which started at 7:05.

Her mouth sores were healing, but she didn't want to push her luck. Chicken wings were out, but she'd be able to manage noodles.

He stepped through the side door, kicking off his boots, which were packed with snow. He handed her a brown paper bag, which she set on the kitchen table and began to unpack.

"How are you?" he asked.

"Okay," she said truthfully. She didn't feel great, but she'd felt worse right after her most immediate treatment. She had good days and bad days. Some days she felt awful, usually immediately after treatment, and she'd noticed that with each treatment, the side effects intensified.

They were halfway through their meal when her phone rang. She glanced at the screen to determine whether she needed to answer it or not. She frowned when she saw Nena's name. "I have to take this."

Answering her phone, she said, "Hello, Nena," unable to imagine what she'd be calling her about. Probably to wish her a Happy New Year.

"Angie, I'm calling with bad news," Nena started, her tone serious.

"Yes?" she said, listening.

Floyd was dead. He'd taken a turn for the worse over New Year's week, had been hospitalized, and had died with his family at his side.

Angie hung up and gripped the table, shaking. How could Floyd be dead? She'd just seen him at the support group after Christmas and he'd looked so *well*.

Next to her, Tom's fork froze mid-air. "What's wrong?"

"Floyd's dead."

"Aw, man, really?" he asked in disbelief.

Although Tom had never met Nena or Floyd, he'd heard enough about them from Angie to realize they were important to her.

A rush of tears escaped. In a strangled voice, she said, "People die from this! Every week, I go to support group because they make me feel better, laughing it up with them, but the reality is, we've all got a dangerous disease." Her tears turned to sobs. She was afraid for Nena, Lisa, herself, and the rest of their group members.

She jumped out of her chair and began gesticulating wildly with her hands, her voice shaking as she spoke. "All this time, I'm not paying attention. I could die. I. Could. Die. I can't forget that. I need to wake up. I can't be so passive with my own life."

Tom stood and approached her, putting up his hands in a placating gesture. "Shh," he said.

"I don't want to die!" she wailed.

Tom still had his hands up and she rushed him, feeling this incredible need to be held, comforted, and reassured. He threw his arms around her and pulled her close, and she buried her head in his shoulder and sobbed. He rubbed her back and murmured softly, "Shh." When she was all cried out, she leaned back to look up at him. He cupped her face with his hands, using the pads of his thumbs to wipe away her tears.

"I'm afraid," she whispered.

"Understandable." He nodded. "I'll be with you every step of the way, Evangeline."

She blew out a sigh of relief. She slipped her arms around his waist and lay her head against his chest, hearing the reassuring sound of his heartbeat through his shirt. He rested his chin on the top of her head and held her tight. She closed her eyes and got lost in the embrace, wishing she could stay like this forever.

"I want to live," she whispered. "Really live."

She could feel him nodding. "I've got you."

Yes, he did have her.

Angie arrived at work the next day earlier than expected, having told her staff she wouldn't be in until noon. In the kitchen, Jordan and Caitlin, her two teenaged staff members who were off school for winter break, stood against the stainless-steel table, eating something. Melissa stood at the grill.

"Is anyone behind the counter?" Angie asked. Since the news of Floyd's death, she'd been in a sour mood.

"Joel and Iris are out there," Melissa said, using a spatula to flip a sandwich on the grill.

Angie put her hands on her hips. "What's going on here?"

"Melissa made us a grilled peanut butter and jelly sandwich," Jordan answered, wolfing down the remainder of his.

"Really?"

"Really," Caitlin intoned. "It's the bomb."

"Is it?"

"Want to try one?" Melissa asked from the grill. "I was experimenting."

Angie's stomach was feeling all right, but she didn't want to push it. "Sure, I'll try a bite."

"I'll eat the other half," Jordan said, and then reddened and looked at Angie. "If you don't mind."

Angie had doubts about this. A grilled PBJ? Melissa handed her a plate with half a sandwich on it. It was lightly grilled, with smooth peanut butter and Gibson's Grape Jelly. She took a bite and lifted her eyebrows. It was delicious. Rich but yummy.

Iris walked in and spotted Angie eating the sandwich. "Those are delicious, aren't they?"

"They are."

"I suppose if Elvis could eat fried peanut butter-and-banana sandwiches, we can eat grilled PBJs," Iris said.

Angie kept busy that morning, but before the lunch rush, she retreated to her office to think about Floyd and be sad for a little bit. If she'd learned anything, she'd learned that grief denied was only grief delayed.

As she sat in her chair, crying, thinking of her loss, an undercurrent of fear coursed through her. If someone like Floyd, who was so funny and full of life despite his serious illness, could suddenly take a turn for the worse, what hope did she have?

Tom arrived, interrupting her descent into despair. She was glad to see him. He parked in the chair on the other side of her desk. "Just checking in to see how you're doing."

She was going to say "I'm fine," but decided to go for honest. "I'm struggling this morning."

"Talk to me."

She leaned back in her chair, clasping her hands over her belly. The tail of her headscarf hung over her shoulder. She gathered her thoughts and voiced her concerns to Tom.

"It's natural to feel that way. Of course you're upset. Of course you're scared," he said.

"But what do I do?"

"You have to deal with the emotions and feelings as they come up. Talking about it helps."

"It does," she said. It made her feel less alone. "You know, I feel so tired I wish I could go home and take a nap," she admitted.

Tom shrugged. "Why can't you? Listen to your body. You can't do everything, Evangeline. And no one expects you to."

"Maybe I will."

"Go home and lie down for an hour."

Her shoulders slumped. She hated the thought of abandoning her staff when the lunch hour was almost upon them.

"Come on, I'll give you a lift home." He stood.

"No, Tom, I appreciate that, but I can drive myself."

He nodded and stood at the door to let her walk past. As she did, he placed his hands on her shoulders and gave her a gentle massage. She stopped and closed her eyes. "That feels good."

"Good. Now go home. I'll talk to you later."

Melissa and Iris exchanged a look when Angie told them she was going home for a little while.

"I'm sorry to abandon you at the start of the lunch hour."

Both were quick to reassure her.

"Don't worry about a thing," Iris said.

Melissa smiled. "Everything is under control."

"Thanks."

She went home and once there, she turned the thermostat up, changed into her pajamas, and crawled into bed, sleepy. She pulled off her headscarf and tossed it on the nightstand.

When she awoke, it was nearing four o'clock. She would have jumped out of bed, but she was too sleepy. She was angry at herself for not setting an alarm. When she turned on her phone, she saw several missed messages, mostly from her staff, wondering if she was all right, and one from Debbie, asking how she was doing.

She typed off a quick text to Melissa, telling her she'd be there soon.

Later that night when she should have been asleep, she was wide awake, on her back, staring up at the ceiling. She kept glancing at the clock. It was after midnight. With a heavy sigh, she thought she might get out of bed. It was too late to call anyone. But she picked up her phone anyway and rang Tom.

"Evangeline?"

"Did I wake you?"

"Nope. Just watching the sports recap on ESPN."

"Do you ever sleep?"

"Sure." He paused and asked, "Everything all right?"

"I can't sleep."

"Okay. What would you like to talk about?"

"Let me think . . . I know, tell me where you were and what you were doing twenty years ago."

He chuckled. "Do you really want to know?"

"I do."

"Twenty years ago, I was just finishing my last year in the Army."

And Angie had just filed for divorce.

"Tell me about the Army," she said.

"Really? It's boring."

"I'm interested."

He launched into his time in the military, and before long, Angie began to yawn.

"Was that a yawn? See, I told you it was boring."

She laughed, her eyes getting heavy. "No, it isn't. It's interesting." There was satisfaction in knowing a little bit more about him.

"Go to bed, beautiful. My work here is done."

"Good night, Tom."

"Goodnight, Evangeline. I'm glad you called me."

"Me too."

Chapter Forty-Nine

It had been a terrible mistake on Angie's part to go into work the day after the fourth infusion. She should have taken Esther's advice—her cousin had picked her up after the infusion—and stayed home. What had she been thinking? Experience told her that her symptoms intensified with each treatment. Hadn't the nurse warned her? Why couldn't she listen? Currently, she was at her desk with the door closed, vomiting into a bucket. There was no window in the room, and soon the sour smell would permeate everything. The smell alone induced another round of retching. She was also freezing and wore her winter coat and her knit hat. If chemo made you feel this awful, how could it help? She couldn't have this in her café. Somehow, she had to get home.

There was a knock on the office door.

Not now, she thought, but said, "Yes?"

Melissa popped her head in. "Quick question—" She scrunched up her nose. "Oh, jeez, Angie, you're sick?"

"Yes. But I'll be fine."

"You should go home."

"Yes," Angie agreed. As much as it pained her to admit it, she didn't belong at the café today.

"I'll give you a ride home."

"No, that's okay. You stay here and look after things. I'm going to call my mother."

"Okay. I'll be right back." And before Angie could say anything else, Melissa closed the door behind her and was gone.

Angie dialed her mother's number.

"Angie? Are you all right?" Louise asked as soon as she answered the phone.

"I'm at work, but I need to go home. I'm sick," she said. Her stomach revolted again, and she leaned over the bucket, but there was nothing more to come up except bile.

"I'll be right there, honey," Louise said, and hung up.

Angie sat back in her chair, relieved. She rested her elbow on the arm of the chair and closed her eyes and covered them with her hand, waiting for the violent wave of nausea to subside, wishing it away. She felt shaky and clammy.

There was another knock, and Melissa popped in without waiting for an answer, closing the door quickly behind her. She carried a bucket in one hand and a can of air freshener in the other.

Mortified, Angie said, "Melissa, you don't have to do that. I'll clean up."

"Stop it, Ang. Let me help you."

Angie sighed, not having the energy for a fight.

Melissa set the clean bucket next to Angie's feet. At the bottom of it was about an inch of water mixed with some disinfectant. Without a word, she removed the offending bucket and sprayed the air freshener around liberally before slipping out of the room.

She returned a moment later and poked her head in. "Did you get a hold of your mom?"

"I did, she's on her way. I'll go out the back door."

"Okay, I'll head back."

She closed her eyes and opened them again quickly. "Look, Melissa, if you think you need to hire another person, if only for the four a.m. starts, go for it. I'll leave it up to you."

"Okay, will do."

They were interrupted by the arrival of Angie's mother. "Okay, Angie, honey, come on, let's get you home."

What was it about other people being so kind when you were at the lowest of your lows that made your chin quiver and tears well up? Hurriedly, Angie swiped at her eyes.

Louise came around to her side of the desk. "Come on, let's go."

Angie stood but her legs were shaky. Gosh, she felt wretched! Louise got an arm under her. "Lean on me," she said.

"Okay, Mom."

"Let me help," Melissa said.

Louise didn't refuse. "My car is right out the back door."

Between the two of them, they managed to help Angie into Louise's car. Once inside, Louise reached over and pulled the seatbelt over Angie and buckled her in.

"I'm sorry, Melissa," Angie said.

"Would you stop?" Melissa said. "Go home and rest."

Angie could only nod, and when the door was closed, she leaned her head against it and shut her eyes, wishing she could go to sleep and wake up feeling better.

She'd expected her mother to drive her home but instead, it looked as though they were heading toward Louise's house on Heather Lane.

"Mom?"

"Honey, I'd like you to come home with me so I can look after you."

Although she would have preferred to sink into the silence of her own space, Angie hadn't the energy needed to protest, so she went along with her mother's suggestion, slightly unwilling.

Her mother helped her up the steps to the front door. Once they crossed the threshold, Angie managed to make it to the sofa and collapsed in the corner of it. It amazed her how weak she felt. She hardly had the strength to move herself. It scared her, but she tried not to think about it too much.

Her mother had disappeared upstairs and returned with a heavy quilt. "Here, why don't you put your feet up."

"Is that Grammie's quilt?" Angie said, fingering it. It brought a smile to her face because she hadn't seen it in a long time, and she remembered when her grandmother had sewn it together. Angie had been young, in elementary school.

"It is. Look at it, it's in great shape considering its age." Louise beamed proudly. "Mom had so much talent when it came to sewing, and yet neither Gail nor I can sew on a button."

"Didn't Grammie teach you?"

"She tried, but the two of us were hopeless," Louise said with a laugh.

Angie eyed her mother and lifted an eyebrow. "Probably too much goofing off."

Her mother agreed with a nod. "For sure."

Angie stretched out on the sofa, adjusting a throw pillow behind her head until she was comfortable, and spread the quilt out over her. Yawning, she pulled it up to her chin.

"Let me get you a bucket," Louise said.

"And maybe a glass of water. I want to take one of those nausea pills."

"Good idea."

Louise returned with both items, setting the bucket on the floor next to the sofa and handing the glass of water to Angie, who sat up. She set the pill on her tongue and followed it with a small sip of water. She set the glass on the coffee table and made herself comfortable again.

"Do you want me to put the television on?" her mother asked.

Angie shook her head. "No, I'm good. Unless The Price is Right is on." That's what they'd always watched when they were home from school with Grammie and Pop-Pop.

"No, that's off the air."

"Wow, that was around a long time."

"I remember Grammie watching it when it first came on television over fifty years ago," Louise mused.

Angie yawned.

"Honey, I'll be in the kitchen if you need me." As Louise stepped away, she turned and said, "I'll try not to make too much noise."

"Do what you'd normally do, Mom. Even if I don't sleep, I can rest. Hopefully, the vomiting will stop."

"Hopefully," her mother repeated softly. The worry lines on her forehead had deepened.

As Angie lay curled up beneath that wonderful old quilt, she listened as her mother puttered around the kitchen, her radio on low, tuned to some oldies station playing all the hits from the 1960s and 1970s. The sounds of the radio, the dishwasher, and whatever her mother was doing began to lull her, and her eyelids became heavy and soon she drifted off.

When she woke, snow was falling heavily outside. She disentangled herself from the quilt and sat up, brushing her hair back, looking around and remembering where she was and how she got there. The radio was still on low in the kitchen. On the coffee table, next to her glass of water, was a tumbler of what Angie suspected was 7UP. Her mouth felt like it was full of cotton, so she reached for the glass and took a sip. 7UP. Flat. She smiled. That, too, had been a staple of childhood sick days. Feeling groggy, she forced herself to stay upright, resisting the temptation to curl up beneath the blanket. She reached for the remote and powered on the television.

Her mother popped her head in from the kitchen. "You're awake," she said.

"I am. I was tired."

"That's to be expected. How about some lunch?"

Angie scrunched up her nose. "I'm afraid to eat anything." She rubbed her hand across her belly. "I don't think I can handle anything."

"What about toast?"

Angie thought for a moment. "I'll give that a try."

"Good."

It took her three tries to stand up from her mother's low sofa. Shaky and lightheaded, she surfed along the edge of the furniture to get to the bathroom and then on toward the kitchen.

She met her mother halfway.

Louise held a plate of toast in her hand. "What are you doing getting up?"

"I wanted to stretch my legs, and I had to use the bathroom," Angie said.

"All right, but sit down at the table," her mother advised, following Angie back into the kitchen, the plate of toast in one hand and her other hand set gently on her daughter's back.

Angie slumped into the chair. Her limbs felt shaky and weak. For treatments five and six, which she expected to be worse, she wouldn't leave her home. And going to café was definitely out.

Louise set the plate of toast down in front of Angie. "How about a cup of tea?"

"I'll try it," Angie said. She took a small bite of toast, chewing slowly, hoping it would stay down.

As her mother went about making tea, she cast side glances at Angie, keeping an eye on her. She handed her a steaming mug. "No milk. But I did add some sugar."

"Thanks."

Louise sat in the chair at the top of the table, kitty corner to Angie. She leaned forward. "I know you feel lousy. But you've got only two treatments left. You're almost there, honey."

"I know, Mom," Angie said weakly. But then after that, she had radiation and at that moment, it didn't bear thinking about.

Chapter Fifty

Melissa continued to bake, and when nausea sidelined Angie from taste testing, she left it up to the rest of the staff. As promised, the café showcased Melissa's creations as a weekly special, and customers were asked to rate their preferences. Melissa's mini fruit tarts were by far the favorite. A small pastry shell filled with blackberries, raspberries, and a little bit of kiwi and strawberry, with a glaze to die for, was so popular that Angie insisted it be added to their regular list of items. It didn't go unnoticed that Melissa had a spring in her step these days. And she became even more inventive in the kitchen, creating delicacies like macaroons flecked with gold leaf, and chocolate-glazed poached pears that were almost too beautiful to eat. As delicious as these creations were, they were too high-end to be added to the existing pastry case lineup. Angie mulled this over. She certainly didn't want to discourage Melissa, as it appeared she was going through a very creative phase, and if anything, that needed to be encouraged. She wondered how she could utilize her assistant's talents better.

At the end of the month, Angie received a certified letter stating she'd been granted a license to operate a food truck starting in the summer. She gave a couple of whoops and a yelp, causing some of her employees to come running to make sure she was all right.

She held the letter aloft, waving it in the air. "We did it! We're going to run a food truck at the beach starting in the summer." Everyone clapped.

The new venture gave Angie a sense of purpose. Something to look forward to. More than ever, she was anxious to be done with treatment and move on with her life.

With the letter in hand, she crossed the street to see Tom. His café was full, and there was a line at the counter. Smiling to herself, she realized it had been stupid on her part to be jealous of Java Joe's. There was more than enough room in Lavender Bay for two cafés.

As she walked by the counter, she asked, "Hi Everett, is Tom around?"

"He's in the kitchen, hold on," he said. She was about to protest and say, "Don't bother him," but her nephew disappeared. Tom appeared, wearing an apron and holding a towel.

"Evangeline! Come on back," he said.

She went through the door marked "employees only."

"What's up?" he asked, leading her back to his office.

"Did you hear from the town about the food truck license?"

Tom was gruff. "I did. No go."

"What? You didn't get it?" she slumped against the office door. Disappointment washed over her on his behalf. It took the joy out of her own news.

"Nope. Hey, it's okay. Wasn't meant to be." He studied her for a moment. "I take it you were granted a license." When she nodded, he broke into a huge grin. "That's awesome, Evangeline. Congratulations!" He pulled her into a hug and kissed her.

If the shoe were on the other foot, she would have been sour about it. But not Tom.

"I don't know," she said. "I don't want to do it if you won't be there."

"Don't be ridiculous," he said firmly. "This is a golden opportunity."

She'd had daydreams of their food trucks parked next to each other on the beach. What fun would it be if he wasn't going to be there? "You're right, it's a great opportunity. I just hope I'm up to the task of getting it up and running." Thoughts overwhelmed her. Maybe it was too much. "I don't know. It's going to be a lot of work between the café and the food truck." She bit her lip.

"You know, this might be a blessing in disguise. Since I don't have to get my own food truck set up, I can help you with yours."

Angie frowned. "You'd do that?"

Tom shook his head and stared up at the ceiling before looking at her. "What am I going to do with you? You're so intelligent, but sometimes you're clueless."

Confused, she stared at him.

"Don't you know there isn't anything I wouldn't do for you?" His eyes searched hers.

She smiled and whispered, "I know now."

CHAPTER FIFTY-ONE

After chemotherapy finished, there was a month break before Angie started radiation treatments. Although she still wasn't one hundred percent, the fact that the chemo was completed gave her a definite boost. The first radiation session had taken the longest as they'd tattooed her with markers on her breast and underarm to mark the area to be irradiated.

With Tom's help, she'd sourced a truck for her summer venture. She left it up to the staff to come up with a menu. She and Tom spent evenings together knocking ideas back and forth. Melissa's year at culinary school had served her well. She continued to run the café efficiently and to create delectable baked goods, which allowed Angie to rest and take care of herself.

Radiation treatments were Monday through Friday for six weeks, starting at the end of March. They didn't take as long as the chemo infusions, and she was usually in and out. Her mother's ride roster was running full throttle, and her rides reliably appeared to take her where she needed to go.

She stood at the kitchen table and ate a banana quickly, something to settle her stomach. As she threw the peel into the bin, there was the *toot-toot* of a car horn from her driveway. She glanced at the clock; Edna was right on time.

Quickly, she pulled on her winter hat and a coat with a hood as it was misting out. As she walked out the door and locked it behind her, she double-checked her pockets for her gloves.

Edna's boxy light blue 1984 Chevy Impala sat idling at the end of the driveway.

When Angie tried the passenger-side door, it was locked. The elderly woman, with some difficulty, undid her seat belt and leaned over to unlock it. Angie opened it and got in as Edna buckled herself back in.

"Good morning, Angie."

"Hiya, Mrs. Knickerbocker."

"How are you feeling, dear?" Edna asked.

"Okay."

Hands on the steering wheel in the ten-and-two position, Edna looked in her rearview mirror as she slowly reversed out of the driveway, the back end of her car hitting the pavement as she did so.

She never drove over thirty-five miles an hour, even when she got out to the highway. It was as if she were on a leisurely Sunday drive out in the country. She spoke the entire time, but never took her eyes off the road. There was a slight mist, and the slow, hypnotic movement of the windshield wipers made Angie drowsy.

"I'm delighted your mother called me to give you a ride for your treatment," Edna said. "I do want to help. You know I've been coming into Coffee Girl since it opened."

The truth was, every time Louise ran into Edna, the latter pestered her to include her on the roster. To appease her, Louise added her name, but not before running it by Angie first.

"I heard through the grapevine that you're seeing a lot more of Java Joe," Edna said.

And there it was. It was true, of course. The previous night, she and Tom had gone to the movies, Angie's first time going to the theater in years. Despite Edna's obvious nosiness, Angie was amused. She might have to make him a sandwich board to wear around his neck saying "My real name is Tom."

"We've become . . . good friends," Angie said, not wanting to reveal too much.

"Ha! I knew it," Mrs. Knickerbocker said triumphantly. "That's how these things start, you know. Friendship. You just had to catch up with him."

"What do you mean?"

"You can tell by the way he looks at you that he's quite smitten."

"You can?"

"Since day one."

"I never noticed," Angie said.

Edna snorted. "How could you? You're too busy giving him a hard time."

"Am I?" Although she knew it was true. Had she known on a subconscious level that he found her attractive and was interested in her? Is that why she'd been rough on him? To discourage him because she had a failed marriage in her past and had no time for romance?

"You know he's a wonderful man," Edna said.

Angie was discovering that, but decided to keep it to herself. "He's been very nice to me while I've been sick," she admitted. But she wasn't about to start picturing herself marching down the aisle with Tom waiting at the other end.

"Be kind to him," Edna said softly. "That kind of man only comes around once in a lifetime."

As Angie tucked this piece of advice away, she couldn't help but wonder if the elderly woman was speaking from experience.

Chapter Fifty-Two

The side effects of the radiation weren't as bad as the chemotherapy, but Angie did suffer from fatigue and some discomfort in her armpit. By spring, she was getting tired of not feeling like herself. The finish line was in sight—she was marking the days off on her calendar with a thick black Sharpie—and the closer she got to it, the more irritable she became.

But there were a few positives. She and Tom still bantered back and forth with the sandwich boards. Some nights she lay awake thinking of what to write: a witty comeback or something smart and sassy. What did it say about her that she actually dedicated time to this? To her, it said she was able to think about something other than her café.

One afternoon after treatment, she stopped by the café and asked Melissa to join her in her office. They sat on opposite sides of Angie's desk.

Angie started with, "I could not have gone through treatment without you. You are an invaluable member of my team here. You really stepped up to the plate, and I appreciate it."

Melissa smiled and nodded.

"Let's talk about your baked goods. We've added the fruit tarts and the mini chocolate tarts to the permanent collection." The latter was a favorite of Angie's, a hazelnut-and-chocolate mixture with crushed pistachios sprinkled over the top of it. Sometimes, Melissa adorned them with edible wildflowers.

Melissa smiled proudly.

Angie chose her words carefully. "But the high-end desserts like the poached pears, the raspberry mousse, and some of the others, are not the right fit for the café."

Melissa's smile disappeared and she shifted in her chair. "I—"

Angie held up her hand. "But I've had a lot of time to think about things. And those are fabulous desserts you've created. Honestly, this place isn't good enough for those types of desserts."

"I wouldn't say that," Melissa said.

"I would, and I own the place." Angie tapped her pen against her desk. "We're going to be busy this summer with the food truck. And Jordan and Caitlin have expressed an interest in working there during the summer months. So that's perfect."

Melissa stared at her.

Probably wondering where I'm going with all of this, Angie thought. *Come on, Ang, land the plane.* "But I had another idea. I was thinking of opening a catering business. High-end desserts. You know, for weddings and bridal and baby showers and, well, for any event."

Melissa sat up straighter in her chair.

"And I thought you'd like to be in charge of that," Angie continued. "I'd make you a full partner in the catering business, and you could create those high-end desserts to your heart's content. We'll consult our lawyers and draw up an agreement that's satisfactory to both of us. I mean, if you're interested."

She hardly had the words out of her mouth when Melissa jumped in and said, "I'm definitely interested. But what about my work here at the café?"

"Initially, the catering business won't be full time, so you can work your shifts here around that. We'll have to hire new people for the food truck and the café. Plus, think about a name for the catering business."

"And what about you?"

"Now that my treatment is almost finished, I'll be back running things here as much as my health allows. But maybe not eighty hours a week." The truth was, she had plans for her life. She intended to step back a bit, to focus a little more on her personal life, and that included Tom.

"I don't know what to say," Melissa said.

"Think about everything I've said. Sleep on it and let me know."

They both stood up, the meeting coming to a close.

Melissa spoke. "I've already thought about it, and my answer is yes."

As Angie came around the side of her desk, Melissa surprised her by throwing her arms around her. "Thank you so much!"

When they pulled apart, Angie looked at her and said, "No, thank *you*."

As they walked out of the office, Angie said, "I'm heading home. I've got company coming."

"Okay. I'll see you tomorrow."

"Yep." Angie pulled on her coat and walked out the back door. Her café was in good hands.

Debbie was already parked in Angie's driveway, waiting for her. They both got out of their cars, and Angie hugged her friend hello. Debbie could not hide her surprise. Angie wasn't a touchy-feely sort of person, but maybe that needed to change as well. Maybe you had to show the people you loved how you felt about them.

Debbie opened the back door of her car and pulled out the cat carrier. "He's all set. He's litter-trained and ready for his new home."

Angie peeked in the carrier. "Hello, Mr. Beans. Welcome home." She took the carrier from Debbie and went inside. Debbie followed with a bag in each hand.

Angie set the carrier down on the kitchen floor and opened the gate at the one end. The cat did not budge.

"Give him time, he'll come out," Debbie said. She set the bags on the table, one cat food and the other kitty litter. "I've brought some things to get you started, kind of like a housewarming gift."

"Aw, thanks." In anticipation of her new roommate, Angie had gone to the pet store and purchased two small dishes, some cat food, treats, a litter tray, and a few toys. She'd also picked up a cat bed and found a place for it in the living room.

"Come on, I'll make coffee," she said.

"Great." Debbie removed her coat and hung it on the back of the chair.

As they sat at the table and drank coffee, Mr. Beans tentatively stepped out of the carrier and looked around. He was hesitant but looked at Angie and meowed. She leaned forward and held out her hand, which he approached, allowing her to pet him.

"Welcome home, Mr. Beans."

Chapter Fifty-Three

Jacques Aubert Day

June fourth rolled around, and with it, the inaugural day of Lavender Bay's food trucks. It was a pleasant, sunny, sixty-five degrees that morning, and the lake was still and glassy-looking. The beach was empty except for walkers. It seemed as if nearly everyone in Lavender Bay was standing in the parking lot at the end of Pearl Street, waiting for the ten a.m. unveiling.

Angie was there early to make sure everything was set up. Jordan and Caitlin, out of college for the summer, arrived early to help her. They wore their Coffee Girl uniforms as Angie still needed to order T-shirts for the food truck. It was on her list to do later that day.

The town had assigned spaces at the back of the parking lot to each of the trucks. Angie's was right in the middle. She wasn't sure how that would affect business; she'd have to wait and see.

She double-checked the sandwich board. She'd had Iris write it up last night. *Special of the day: Melissa's Grilled PBJ.* Gibson's Grape Jelly had gotten wind of the fact that their grape jelly was being used in one of their sandwiches and bought advertising space, and their logo had been painted along the side of the truck.

The disappointment over Tom being denied a food truck license lingered, but there were so many good things going on that Angie remained upbeat and positive. First, she was finally finished with her treatment. Second, her hair was beginning to grow back. Currently, the minimal fuzz on her head made her think she resembled a tennis ball. Third, Mr. Beans had settled in nicely at his new home, and she loved his companionship. He was more than a stray cat; he was family.

It was also Jacques Aubert Day, and that held special importance as it was her grandfather who'd gotten that ball rolling. Sporting one of Grammie's headscarves, she felt the presence of both of them that day. The schools in Lavender Bay were closed to celebrate the founding father's birthday, and children of all ages hung around with their families in the parking lot. Balloons were being given away for free, and the town had all sorts of activities planned for the day: a parade, live music in the park later, and a carnival located up near the highway.

She couldn't fault the town hall for their food truck selections. They'd picked quite a variety. Her truck served coffee, iced coffee, and pastries in addition to the grilled PBJs. She was sandwiched between a salad truck called Leaves and an ice cream truck she suspected would give them all a run for their money. She could have used an ice cream truck when she had her mouth sores, she thought wryly. Another vendor served hot dogs and hamburgers, and the final one was a taco truck.

She went over a few last-minute things with Jordan and Caitlin. She felt a little shaky, but it was due to nerves. As ten o'clock approached, more and more people began to arrive until the entire parking lot was filled.

Angie's family approached. Her mother, Aunt Gail, her sisters and cousins and their families all swarmed her, congratulating her. Yesterday, she'd received flowers from DeeDee, wishing her luck. Debbie also showed up and hugged her excitedly. She then situated herself on the perimeter of the crowd.

"Are you ready?" Louise asked.

"As ready as I can be," Angie said, drawing in a deep breath.

"It looks like everyone and their brother are here," Allan remarked.

"I hope so."

Tom arrived next. He hugged her and kissed her hello. "Best of luck."

"Thanks."

He slid an arm around her waist.

She recognized a lot of her customers, who made a point of wishing her well on her new venture. Edna Knickerbocker and her sister, Edith Bermingham, were there, on opposite sides of the crowd, of course, to keep the peace.

The mayor arrived to cut the ribbon and pull down the drapes that covered the signage over the trucks for a bit of drama for the official opening. A photographer from *The Lavender Bay Chronicles* double-checked his camera equipment.

Before the grand opening was to start, she spotted Nena with her family. She waved her over and when she arrived, she hugged her. She'd finished her treatment months ago and her hair was beginning to grow back. Nena had her grandkids by the hand.

She introduced Nena to Tom and her family. Nena reached behind her and pulled a tall, good-looking man forward. "And this is my husband, Alfred. The man's a saint for putting up with me." Her husband smiled at her.

"You can say that again," he cracked.

A podium had been set up front and center, and when the mayor stepped up to it, he waved his hands to get the crowd to settle down. The mayor, who was known to be long-winded, proved no different today. Halfway through his speech, Angie stopped listening. When he pulled out the scissors to cut the ribbon that had been stretched in front of all five food trucks, Nena quipped behind her, "Finally! I was going to go up there and cut that ribbon myself."

The mayor posed, scissors mid-air, so the photographer could get a photo for the paper. After the ribbon was cut, aides jumped forward and removed it and the posts it had been attached to.

Starting with the first truck and moving left to right, the mayor pulled the drapery cord over each. When he arrived at Angie's, she glanced quickly at Tom. She covered her mouth with her hands, unable to contain her excitement.

The curtains opened, revealing the sign above her food truck.

Tom and Angie's Coffee Club.

Tom stared at it and then broke into a wide grin. "Well, I'll be . . ." Laughing, he picked her up until her feet lifted off the ground and kissed her hard. Setting her down, he said to her, "You know, this means we're partners."

"Yeah, we are."

Her mother leaned in and said, "That was a nice touch."

Chapter Fifty-Four

Summer

Angie waited outside of Coffee Girl. The cafés weren't even open yet. The sun was just coming up over the horizon, and already the day was heavy with heat. She wore a light-colored scarf and held a wide-brimmed hat in her hand. Her hair continued to grow, and she currently compared it to a Chia Pet. She was in a great mood. The first set of scans she'd had since she completed treatment had come back all clear. She wasn't yet fully recovered from treatment but every day she felt more like herself. Tom suggested they take the day off together to celebrate, and she suggested they go fishing as she knew it was his favorite pastime. She didn't really care what they did, as long as she could be with him.

Tom pulled up and parked his pickup against the curb. He jumped out and greeted her with a kiss. "Ready?"

She nodded. "I am."

He opened the back of his truck. "I've got something for you." He pulled out an army green fishing vest identical to the one he wore, and handed it to her.

"Ooh, his-and-hers fishing vests," she teased.

Tom laughed. "Okay, smarty."

She gave him her best smile.

"Let's go," Tom said.

She hopped into the passenger side of the truck and buckled up. They were going out on the lake, but the boat dock was located past Lavender Bay. Angie'd been out twice already with Tom and knew his favorite spot. As he pulled away from the curb, she looked back at the sandwich board in front of Coffee Girl.

Before his arrival, she'd chalked *Angie + Tom* and drawn a big heart around it. Smiling, she turned to face forward.

They took Tom's boat, a twenty-foot center console, out to his favorite spot on the lake. In the distance was the town of Lavender Bay. She could almost make out Nadine's house, which backed onto the lake.

Tom whistled as he set up his gear for the day, and mused aloud about what they'd possibly catch. Angie got comfortable and put on her hat and sunglasses.

Tom cast his line over the side of the boat and settled in. He had the patience of a saint. She supposed he'd need patience to put up with the likes of her.

The sun climbing in the eastern sky was strong and hot, and within minutes of getting situated, Tom pulled off his T-shirt. This was probably Angie's favorite part of fishing. The rumors about the tattoo on his back were true, but they did not do it justice. The American flag looked as if it was flapping in the breeze, the colors of red, white, and blue vibrant and strong. The eagle in front of the flag was large and stared straight at you.

She settled back against the cushions. "Tom, I'm thinking about getting a tattoo." In the past, she'd been ambivalent about them, thinking *to each his own*. But she had since changed her mind.

"Okay," he said.

"Do you think your brother would do the ink?"

"Yes."

"I want to cover that dent in my breast," she told him.

"Understood."

"Maybe flowers and a butterfly or a hummingbird." She could so easily picture it.

"Angie, stop talking, you're scaring the fish away."

Laughing, she said, "Okay."

She leaned back, letting the warm sun wash over her. The water lapped gently against the boat, rocking it slightly.

It felt as if she had a new lease on life.

A second chance.

Epilogue

Angie and her sisters were all gathered in their mother's backyard. As it was so warm, they were having Sunday brunch outside. Gail and Esther and Suzanne were absent, having rented a cottage in the Finger Lakes for the week.

They'd turned the calendar page to August, and it wouldn't be long before summer was over. Angie pushed that thought from her mind, deciding to enjoy the beautiful day.

They all took turns carrying brunch items outside. The sound of a neighbor's mower filled the air. Birds chirped along the back fence, flitting from one birdhouse or feeder to another.

For the first time in a long time, she felt like herself. She had the energy levels of the old Angie. That didn't mean she spent more hours at her café; it meant she had more time and energy to enjoy life.

She'd made a batch of her cinnamon rolls with the cream cheese frosting and was in the process of tackling one with a fork. She and her mother and sisters were lined up on lawn chairs, watching all the birds at the feeder and the bumblebees flying lazily from one flower to the next.

Louise kicked off the conversation. "Has anyone spoken to DeeDee recently?"

No one spoke up at first.

"Gosh, it's been a couple of weeks," Maureen said. "It was a text, though."

"Same here," Nadine said.

Angie thought back. "I called her two weeks ago, but it went to voicemail. She texted me the next day and said she was super busy with rehearsals and would call me when she got a chance."

"That's what I mean," Louise said. But they weren't sure what she was getting at.

"What's wrong, Mom?" Nadine asked, sipping her coffee.

A robin flitted around in the grass, chirping and picking up seed that had spilled from the feeder.

"Well, I always talk to DeeDee three times a week. But lately, she has one excuse after another. She's going off to rehearsal, she has a date, or she's going away. But I don't know. Something doesn't feel right."

"What do you mean?"

"For instance, she told me the name of the play she's in, but then when I spoke to her again, she gave me a totally different name."

"Do you think she's not working at the moment?" Maureen asked.

"That's exactly what I think." Louise said.

"What about the boyfriend?" Nadine asked.

With DeeDee, there'd never been any shortage of boyfriends. Vivacious and pretty, she was never alone for long.

"She never mentions him anymore. And when I ask about him, she always says something vague like 'he's fine.'"

"You think they broke up?" Angie asked.

"Yes. I think she's possibly unemployed and hurting after a recent breakup."

"Plus, she's gone off the grid with us," Maureen said.

Louise looked worriedly at her daughters. "Something's not right. I can feel it in my waters. I was thinking of flying down there, but she's so thin-skinned."

DeeDee had always been high-strung and sensitive, ever since she was a child. Angie didn't know if it was her personality or if it was from being the youngest of four girls. She couldn't say either way.

"No, Mom, you don't have to go, I'll go," Maureen said.

Nadine piped in. "I'll go too."

"Me too," Angie added.

"Do we want to fly or drive?" Nadine asked.

Florida was about a twenty-hour drive.

Angie raised her hand. "A road trip might be fun."

"I think so too," Maureen said.

It was agreed then that the three of them would clear their schedules and drive off as soon as possible to see what was going on with their youngest sister.

Acknowledgements

I could not have written this book without help. Many thanks to Rachel Matte and Paula Verdetto who were gracious enough to share their personal stories dealing with cancer. God Bless You. Also a shout out to Kristen Robillard, M.D., who patiently answered all my questions (and there were a lot). Thanks to Roswell Park Cancer Institute for providing information about breast cancer and various treatments. Thanks to some gracious people over at the Chemotherapy Support Group on FB who also answered my questions. The one thing I learned is that everyone's breast cancer journey is different. There are so many factors that come into play in regards to treatment. Any mistakes are mine.

Note

To stay up to date with new releases and receive exclusive bonus material, sign up for my newsletter at www.michelebrouder.com

ALSO BY MICHELE BROUDER

The Lavender Bay Chronicles
The Inn at Lavender Bay
Lost and Found in Lavender Bay
Second Chances in Lavender Bay
New Beginnings in Lavender Bay (coming in January 2025)

Hideaway Bay
Coming Home to Hideaway Bay
Meet Me at Sunrise
Moonlight and Promises
When We Were Young
One Last Thing Before I Go
The Chocolatier of Hideaway Bay
Now and Forever

Escape to Ireland
A Match Made in Ireland
Her Fake Irish Husband
Her Irish Inheritance
A Match for the Matchmaker
Home, Sweet Irish Home
An Irish Christmas

The Happy Holidays
A Whyte Christmas
This Christmas
A Wish for Christmas
One Kiss for Christmas
A Wedding for Christmas

Audiobooks
Coming Home to Hideaway Bay

All books available in ebook, paperback, and large print paperback. Audiobooks coming soon.

Printed in Great Britain
by Amazon